The
SKELETON
IN MY CLOSET
Wears a

Wedding
DRESS

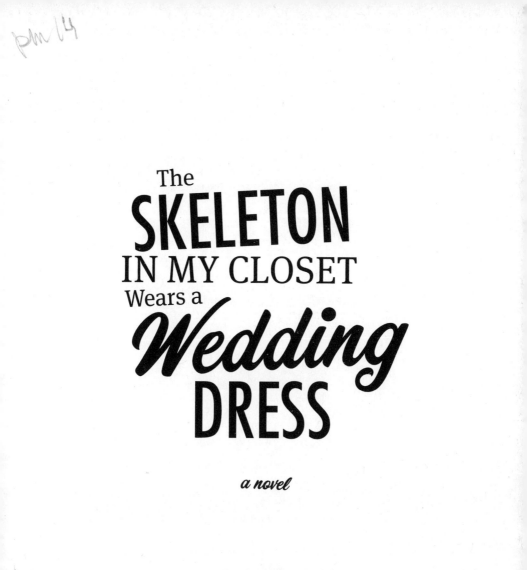

The
SKELETON
IN MY CLOSET
Wears a
Wedding
DRESS

a novel

Sally
Johnson

Covenant Communications, Inc.

Cover image: *Pink Sport Shoes* © Lucop courtesy of istockphoto.com

Cover design copyright © 2014 by Covenant Communications, Inc.

Published by Covenant Communications, Inc.
American Fork, Utah

Printed in the United States of America
First Printing: May 2014

20 19 18 17 16 15 14   10 9 8 7 6 5 4 3 2 1

ISBN: 978-1-62108-397-9

To Steve
for encouragement and taking the kids so I could write and Emmett,
Audrey, Esther, and Eve for being as proud of me as I am of them.

Acknowledgments

THERE ARE SO MANY WHO deserve to be mentioned for the help they've given me. Though I hate to name names because I might forget someone, there have been some who have gone above and beyond and deserve a huge thank you.

First of all, thank you to my husband, Steve. You are more than supportive and encouraging. I love that you let me indulge in my passion—and that you didn't mind that I painted the laundry room door Tiffany blue because it was "for the book."

Thank you to my editor, Samantha Millburn. I appreciate your taking care of my "baby" when you had just had your own baby. Thank you for answering all my questions and being patient with me through this whole process.

Trisha Luong, thanks for being the other half of my brain and for loving my book and my imaginary friends as much as I do. I appreciate how much you read for me even though you hate to read.

Michael Evon, you probably didn't know what you were getting yourself into when you offered to read my book, but your suggestions have been some of the best.

My brother Carl, thanks for giving me the male perspective and being my consultant on divorce. Becca Wilhite, thank you for all of your help. Every fledgling writer needs a Becca.

Deanne Blackhurst, I'm so glad we sat by each other at LDStorymakers Conference. Thank you for your help and advice.

Janna MacKay and Katrina Brush, thank you for all of your help.

Virginia and Carolyn Johnson, thank you. Virginia you were one of the first willing readers, and without the two of you, my knowledge about and description of BYU would have been very outdated.

Summer Johnson, Tamara Seiter, Tamara Passey, and Karen Prueitt, I appreciate your being willing readers too. Thank you, thank you!

Audrey, thank you for the encouragement by way of notes, and Esther for the constant flow of creative ideas.

And finally, Mom and Dad, thank you for everything.

Chapter One
You Never Get a Second Chance to Make a First Impression

THIS WAS A MISTAKE.

I mean, why would I be trying to meet guys? I was barely divorced, and I wasn't even completely recovered from it yet. And what if Travis changed his mind?

But here I was at my BYU singles ward opening social two weeks after school started feeling *anything* but social. I'd been feeling this way since last April when my husband unexpectedly left me. As for being here tonight, my overly energetic roommate Rhonda insisted that I accompany her and our other two roommates to the activity.

"This is your first chance to make a good impression," Rhonda said.

The only impression I wanted to make was the one my head made on my pillow every night.

I could have helped plan this evening, having been offered a calling to serve on the Relief Society committee that was in charge of this activity. But I turned it down, much to Rhonda's horror.

"What is your calling?" She pounced as soon as I returned from meeting with the bishop on Tuesday night.

"Aren't you supposed to wait until Sunday, after it's announced?"

"Sure, if it was something important, like Relief Society president. But she's already been called, so it's not that."

"My calling wouldn't be important?" I suggested.

Rhonda backpedaled. "No, no, that's not what I meant. I mean, every calling is important—"

"I didn't get one," I interrupted, letting her off the hook.

"What do you mean? They're bringing in, like, the whole ward tonight to issue callings." Rhonda was truly taken aback.

"Nope. No calling. Dodged that one."

"I don't get it. Everyone gets a calling. Unless . . ." She was thoughtful for a moment. "Oh, okay." Rhonda looked as though understanding had just dawned on her. "Ohhhh."

"Oh, what?" I demanded, annoyed by the insinuation.

"You can't *have* a calling."

I nearly choked in disbelief. She was way off. "It's not that I can't *have* one; it's that I don't *want* one. I declined."

"You declined?" She stared at me. "Are you kidding? You're not supposed to turn down a calling. There's a reason you're called to a calling."

I knew the reason. It was to encourage me to be social. But she didn't need to know that. "I'm not picking and choosing callings." I exhaled, trying to be patient. "I didn't want a calling. Any calling."

"But you're not supposed to do that, Sophia. You're not supposed to . . ."

I didn't wait for her to finish. "But I did," I said quietly.

There were a lot of things I wasn't supposed to do. Like get married at eighteen and four months later get divorced. I had lived the freshman fantasy of meeting and marrying my eternal companion my first semester at BYU. Infatuation over Travis Duckk helped me escape another freshman blight: the typical "Freshman Fifteen" weight gain.

Travis's last name was Duckk, which, at the time, seemed to be his only flaw. I never liked the name, but I'd thought I was being petty. And it was petty, but I hated going from Sophia Davis to Sophia Duckk. At one point, I suggested keeping my own name, but he was offended. So in the end, I made peace with the fact that I would be Sophia Duckk. But name or no name, I'd thought I was one lucky duck.

So here I was, a year later, back in the same position I was last year: suddenly single. The only difference was the baggage I now carried. Having the opportunity to attend another round of opening socials, family home evening groups, and ward activities sounded dreadful. And tonight's theme, "speed dating," did not thrill me. Dating was not high on my priority list, but neither was getting out of bed, getting dressed, or going to class.

Since the surprise breakup of my marriage, I'd become just a little bit bitter. My brand-new therapist at the counseling center told me it was a natural reaction as I dealt with my recent trauma. Trauma, drama, it was all the same to me: I wished I *didn't* have to deal with it.

Not only did I not want to deal with it, but I also didn't want to tell anyone about it either. I was worried what the reaction would be. Divorced Mormon girls at the ripe old age of nineteen were probably pretty rare at

BYU. I figured it would just make people uncomfortable. Why would I want to put myself out for rejection again?

As for this evening, I seemed to be in the minority with my lack of enthusiasm. People were practically buzzing as they took their seats at the tables set up along the perimeter of the room reserved in the Wilkinson Center, or the Wilk for short. The idea was the girls were seated by apartments on one side of the tables, the guys were grouped likewise by apartments on the opposite side of the tables, and we had two minutes to visit with the person sitting across from us. When the buzzer rang, the guys would move down one seat at a time until they had visited with every girl in the room.

Offering minimal information was my remedy for handling this evening's activity. The first set of willing and able young men sat across from us with two minutes on the clock.

"Hi, I'm Taylor."

"Sophia."

"It's nice to meet you."

"You too." I could at least be cordial in my disinterest.

"Where are you from?"

"I'm from Vegas. And you?"

"Cedar City. What year are you?"

"I'm a freshman." I could have and should have been a sophomore. But I'd put my education on hold to work full-time supporting Travis, who was starting his second semester of prelaw. The only things I gleaned from helping him study were some eye strain, a little bit of legal jargon, and hours of reading boring, useless stuff, since he divorced me soon after. "And you?"

"Sophomore. I just got back from my mission."

"Where'd you go?" A returned missionary usually liked to talk about his mission.

"New Zealand Auckland Mission."

My roommate from last year was currently in New Zealand serving a mission. "Did you know a Gretchen Clark?"

"Sister Clark?" He looked thoughtful. "Doesn't ring a bell."

I didn't know what to ask next, so I said, "Brothers? Sisters?"

"Three brothers, two sisters, and I'm number two. How about you?"

"I have an older brother. He lives with my parents and has a computer software job."

The timer rang, announcing our time was up. "Nice talking to you," I called out politely as he moved with his roommates to the next table.

Here we go again, I thought. I wasn't sure I could make small talk over and over again through fifteen male apartments.

"I'm Jordan," the next one said as he introduced himself. "I'm from Southern California." He looked the part: tan, slightly shaggy blond hair, good-looking, muscular, ultrawhite teeth. "You're, like, going to make the perfect Mormon trophy wife."

I pictured a trophy with the metal topper slightly crooked, as if it had been dropped one too many times and then donated to Deseret Industries. "Oh no, no, no." I managed a small laugh, trying to hide my surprise at his assuming words. "Don't be deceived. I am far from trophy material."

"Well, you look pretty perfect to me." He smiled confidently.

"Nobody is perfect," I said softly, resulting in an awkward pause. "So what about you? What's your major?"

"I'm a Spanish major."

"Spanish, huh? Did you serve a Spanish-speaking mission?"

His face lit up. "Yes, Argentina Cordoba Mission. How about you? Any mission?"

"Nope, no mission."

"How about a major?"

"Nope, no major."

"How about a minor?"

"Nope. Can't say I have that either. I do have a goal to have a major someday, but that means I would have to commit to something." I paused and gave a little laugh. "And I may or may not have commitment issues."

"Does that go for relationships too?"

"Right now, yes." There was another awkward pause. I think it was safe to assume that was not the answer he was looking for.

The timer saved me. *Next*! I felt like shouting as another guy sat down.

"Hi. I'm Bradley." He was about six feet tall, wiry, hair almost shaved. Being five ten, I had a rule when I was dating to only go out with guys who were taller than me. His deep tan made his eyes look very blue. I wondered if he was a lifeguard.

"I'm Sophia."

He grinned. "Didn't I see you riding a bike up to campus a couple of days ago?"

"I'm pretty sure it wasn't me." In fact, I *knew* it wasn't me.

"Really? I could swear it was you."

I twisted my mouth. "I, uh, don't know how to ride a bike," I confessed.

"You're kidding. You can't ride a bike?"

"Only if it's stationary, like the exercise kind."

"Why?"

"It's kind of a long, embarrassing story." I didn't want to get into my childhood stories.

He looked at his watch. "I've got one minute and five seconds," he encouraged me, then waited.

"Okay." I cleared my throat. "I was learning to ride without training wheels, and I went down a hill, got out of control, crashed into a block wall, and knocked out both of my front teeth. I was so traumatized I refused to ever try riding a bike again."

He smiled. "You're making that up."

I think he thought I was flirting with him, but I wasn't. If I was making up a story to be more attractive to him, it would be something way less embarrassing.

"Do you think you'll ever learn to ride a bike? I could teach you."

I shrugged. "It's not on the top of my to-do list." I had things of higher priority, like recover from my divorce, get over Travis, and get on with my life.

He nodded his head slowly as if processing my response. Before he could suggest anything else, the buzzer rang, signaling it was time to move on.

The evening continued with the same get-to-know-you questions— What's your name? Where are you from? What's your major? Did you serve a mission?—until finally we were at the last round of rotations.

I rested my head in my hand. Reluctant socializing was exhausting.

"You look ready to be done," the next guy said, taking a seat.

"I am." I looked up to see who I was talking with. Out of all the guys this evening, he had the best opening line. Or maybe the most accurate.

"I'm Luke. I'm your apartment's home teacher." His voice was warm and creamy, like a cup of hot chocolate. The rest of him was okay too, I supposed. Not that I was interested. He was tall and had brown hair, hazel eyes, straight teeth (always a plus) that were not blindingly white, a nice jawline, and a great smile. He was nice enough looking (again, not that I was looking), but not the stop-your-heart gorgeous, Abercrombie and Fitch model–type Travis was.

"Nice to meet you," I said politely.

"Any luck tonight?" he asked.

His question caught me off guard. It was the same sort of question I would have asked. "What do you mean by luck?"

"You know, did you meet anyone interesting? Someone of eternal significance? Isn't that the whole point of this activity?" He raised an eyebrow.

I laughed. "Honestly, I wasn't *interested* in meeting anyone *interesting* tonight. My roommate Rhonda"—I pointed my finger at her—"insisted my eternal salvation was at stake if I didn't come."

"And?" He looked amused.

"And I haven't had any huge revelations since I came."

"Yeah, me neither." He rolled his eyes and laughed. "Thank goodness, huh? That could be scary."

"It's been known to happen at BYU." I should know.

"Yes, it has. In fact, our roommates look like they're hitting it off." He nodded at Rhonda, pointing out what seemed to be an intense conversation.

"I'll have to get the scoop after." I was glad it was her and not me. She probably was too.

The buzzer rang. "Well, it was nice to meet you, but I didn't get your name."

"Sophia."

"Sophia. I'm sure I'll see you later." He smiled again before getting up from the table.

"Yeah, see you around." That is, if I happened to get out of bed someday.

The activity ended but not without the same, if not more, excitement. Then it was time for treats. Time to pursue some of the more interesting encounters of the evening. Time to cozy up to that cute guy or girl to see how far one could get with flirting. Time for the wallflowers and sweet spirits to at least enjoy a brownie . . . or two.

* * *

Rhonda's main priority upon reaching home was to analyze the evening.

"Oh my gosh. There are definitely some super cute guys in this ward. That was so fun."

She jumped onto the couch and patted the cushion next to her. "Come on, girls. Sit. We need to discuss."

Sarah, our RM roommate hailing from Denver, Colorado, obediently sat.

Claire, our other roommate, the accounting major, dismissed herself. "I thought the whole thing was kind of lame."

From what I had gathered, which was quite a lot since I was home most of the time, Claire didn't do much other than study.

"Well, come on, Sophia. You, if anyone, should have plenty to talk about." Rhonda scooted over to make room for me.

"What?" I was confused. I didn't feel like anything had happened worth gushing about. I was just happy I'd survived.

"Guys were definitely checking you out tonight."

Sarah nodded in agreement.

"Oh," I said dully. "I hadn't noticed." I truly hadn't.

"How could you *not* notice?" Sarah asked, her eyes wide.

"Quite easily, actually." I said almost to myself.

"Gosh, Bradley Benson practically asked you out right there at the table," Rhonda said.

"Bradley the bike guy?"

"Yeah," Sarah chirped.

Rhonda filled me in. "Bradley-one-of-the-most-sought-after-bachelors-in-the-ward Bradley. He's totally athletic, outdoorsy. He is a river guide down near Moab for whitewater rafting trips, and he rock climbs."

I could see myself on *America's Funniest Home Videos* falling backward off the raft and being left behind. I was so *not* an outdoorsy kind of girl.

"Good thing I'm not seeking." I laughed weakly, trying to downplay their detailed analysis of his possible interest.

"He's a hot commodity," Rhonda said, and they giggled. Had I been like that last year?

I was relieved when the attention turned to a TV show Rhonda wanted to see.

Claire declined watching it, and I fell asleep on the couch. So much for roommate bonding.

Chapter Two
The Shopping Guide

THE ARRIVAL OF THE WARD directory brought life as we knew it to a temporary standstill.

The directory was delivered on Sunday, immediately after church. Rhonda snatched it out of the guy's hand so fast it gave him a paper cut. I think if she hadn't been so excited to get it, she would have apologized.

"We got the shopping guide, girls. It's here." She hurried to the couch, sat down, and did this clapping in succession thing I noticed she does when she's excited.

"You're kidding me," I muttered as she leafed through it. It was quite an impressive compilation. This ward did not skimp on quality. Instead of apartment group pictures, there were individual photos of each member on glossy, full-color pages. It was in yearbook form and supplied everyone's phone number, major, hometown, and favorite scripture. When I filled out the information sheet given to me at church, I'd thought it was for reference purposes for the bishop. I didn't think it'd be published in the ward directory. If I had known, I wouldn't have put down my favorite scripture as Jacob 3:1: "But behold, I, Jacob would speak unto you that are pure in heart. Look unto God with firmness of mind, and pray unto him with exceeding faith, and he will console you in your afflictions, and he will plead your cause, and send down justice upon those who seek your destruction."

I was sure people would wonder why I chose that one. I couldn't deny I'd had Travis in mind when I wrote it down.

"How did our ward pay for these? They look expensive. Are we going to have to do fund-raising to cover the cost?" I said as I flipped through the pages.

"Bishop Shaw owns a printing business," Rhonda said. She would know; she was like a fountain of knowledge ready and willing to share.

I think the real purpose for the individual pictures was to allow closer examination of each ward member/candidate for dating and/or marriage. But maybe that was just my take on it. Unfortunately, the only information not included was one's dating status. But we had Rhonda.

Rhonda produced a black Sharpie out of nowhere and boldly wrote at the bottom of some pictures an *A*, *D*, or *E* for "Available," "Dating," or "Engaged."

We continued studying—I not as fervently as Rhonda and Sarah. It was hard to be interested when I was still semi in love with my ex-husband, who was not at all in love with me anymore. Whoa, did I just admit that?

Then we arrived at the page dedicated to our apartment.

The first picture was of Claire. She was a pretty girl and looked almost exotic, mostly because of her pouty bottom lip. But she was always so serious that she never smiled, and it detracted from her looks. I thought about taking Rhonda's black Sharpie and drawing thick eyeliner on Claire's picture. With her black hair cut straight across at the bangs and shoulders, if I added the eyeliner, she would look like Cleopatra.

"I don't like my picture," Sarah said.

"You look good," Rhonda volunteered.

"Look how blue your eyes are." I tried making her feel better as I stole a glance at the picture. I thought it was good. Her thick blonde hair was cut in a bob slightly above her jawline, and her smile lit up her face.

Rhonda's picture was screaming at me to draw an apron on it. She was a combination of Martha Stewart's ideals and Rachael Ray's personality.

"Oh. Let me see my picture." Rhonda pushed her face close to the glossy page. She let out a huff. "I can't decide if I should cut my hair or perm it."

Perm it? Did anyone perm their hair anymore? Her dark brown hair came down to the middle of her back and was slightly frizzy. A good flat iron and some layers would do her hair wonders, but I wasn't in the mood right now to help others with makeovers.

And then there was me.

I was not looking directly at the camera but off to the right, having just turned my head when the picture was taken. Out of the corner of my eye, I'd thought I had seen Travis. But thankfully, that would have been impossible since last I knew he was transferring to the University of Utah. Photographer boy had offered to retake it, but I didn't bother.

I looked forlorn.

Rhonda interrupted my analysis. "I know who you look like," she said. "Barbie. You know, as in a Barbie doll?"

It was true. I had heard it all my life. I had the long blonde hair, the green, almond-shaped eyes, the cute, tiny nose, and the full lips. I used to care what I looked like. I'm a little bit ashamed to admit I was vain about my looks. I liked how Travis constantly told me how beautiful I was. Somewhere along the line, vanity ceased to matter. Maybe it was when Travis still divorced me despite my being, in his words, "breathtaking."

"Yes. You do," Sarah excitedly agreed.

"We have *got* to find you a Ken," Rhonda said, searching through the directory.

"No. No, you don't." I put my hand over the booklet to stop her. "You know what happens to Barbie dolls, right? They end up with ratty hair, a missing arm, and a chewed-off foot. It's not pretty, and I don't need a man to add to my fate."

Sarah looked at me strangely. Rhonda stopped midpage.

Rhonda was quiet. "Just having a little fun, Sophia."

"I know." They were still staring at me. It wasn't their fault they didn't know about my divorce, and I wasn't ready to share yet. Instead, I cleared my throat. "It's just I don't find Ken all that attractive, and I'm definitely *not* looking for a husband." I tried to lighten the situation.

"Who said anything about husbands? Sometimes it's just fun to date." Rhonda went back to studying our page, then added as an afterthought, "But if I met my future husband, I wouldn't complain." With her black sharpie, she wrote "Available" across the bottom of each of our pictures.

Across mine, I would have written "Single," or more appropriately, "Suddenly single."

* * *

Sunday evenings were the designated time for the weekly check-in phone call to my mother. She would've liked more frequent calls, but I found myself resisting.

These calls were meant to be a reassurance that I was, in fact, surviving and thriving in Happy Valley. But they were more for her than for me. Sometimes I couldn't handle my mom. She was the poster child of positive mental attitude (I nicknamed it PMA). She always looked on the bright side of things to find the silver lining.

Having her daughter pitched into a deep, dark depression was beyond her comprehension. She did not understand why I couldn't pull myself up by the bootstraps and not wallow in bed all day. She told me I needed to move forward. And although she listened to me and cried with me, there was always a pep talk waiting on the other end of a crying jag.

Returning to school had not been my idea but was the brainchild of my mother and older brother, Dan. When I made the mistake of getting out of bed more than one day in a row around the beginning of July, Mom took it as a sign that I was ready to move ahead. Full speed ahead.

She convinced me I needed to come back to the Y. She convinced me that I needed to get out of the house and be around other people. If I had some structure to my life and purpose to my day, I'd be back to normal in no time.

Normal. I didn't know what normal was anymore. The person I was pre-Travis was no longer the person I was post-Travis. I'd lost touch with my friends. I'd lost touch with myself. I'd lost my sense of purpose. I'd lost my trust in the world. I'd lost my rose-colored glasses and didn't like what I saw without them. And I was teetering on the edge of losing my faith.

Travis had been such an all-consuming presence in my life, swooping in, sweeping me off my feet, and then just dropping me. He was a black hole, sucking the meaning out of my life and then throwing me away.

I wasn't prepared for that. The courtship had been so fast and furious I'd thought it would continue from there like a hurricane picking up force as it moved along in its path.

But instead, here I was divorced—at a complete standstill.

But I had a plan upon returning to school.

I would pretend to be a normal nineteen-year-old girl attending college. I had explanations. I had stories. I had outright lies if necessary. I even had Visine. And I would fool them. I would fool my parents. I would fool my roommates.

I just couldn't fool myself.

I had an explanation, if need be, for why I had been through the temple, and it was mostly true. Or as true as I could deal with having someone know about. I would say I was going to get married, and in the very end, it hadn't worked out. I would just leave out the part that I *did* get married. But for the time being, I would rely on modesty, layering my clothes, and doing my laundry when no one else was around. Hopefully, the subject of receiving my endowment would never come up.

Chapter Three

Sometimes You Have to Fake It to Make It

MONDAY MORNING I WOKE UP to voices. Luckily, they were not in my head. It was just Claire talking on her phone. Because if she was talking to herself, I wouldn't be the only one with some unresolved issues.

I carefully opened my eyes to find it was still dark. I could make out Claire sitting on the end of her bed, facing away from me. It sounded pretty heated, so I didn't want to interrupt by getting up. But I didn't want to be nosy either. I wasn't sure what to do.

"Yeah, but, Mom, he says a lot of things. Like he's going to actually get a job. Or that he's going to help with school expenses. He hasn't done either. I don't think he's made any effort."

There was a pause.

Claire shook her head. "I don't agree. Mom, if you keep making excuses for him, he's going to keep doing nothing. I can't believe he hasn't even come to see you in the hospital."

Okay. I didn't know how much more I wanted to hear. Claire had made no mention, that I knew of, that her mom was in the hospital. And there were some bigger issues going on with whoever "he" was. So I rolled over in bed and then rolled back, hopefully signaling her that I was waking up.

She took the hint. "Hey, I need to go. I'll try to get up to the hospital tonight. When are you being released? Okay."

Another pause.

"Okay. Feel better, and I'll see you tonight." As she stood, I sat up, yawning.

"Is someone sick, or was I dreaming that?" I asked, hoping she wouldn't accuse me of eavesdropping.

"My mom." Claire gathered her book bag and planner.

"Is she okay?"

"She will be." Claire slung her bag over her shoulder and went into the kitchen.

I wondered if Rhonda knew anything about Claire's mother. Claire was usually out the door by 7:00 most mornings, so I climbed out of bed and waited for Rhonda in the kitchen, eating my usual Pop Tart and Diet Coke for breakfast while Claire packed her lunch, which consisted of a sandwich, an apple, and crackers. But what was really bizarre was she counted the crackers before she put them into a baggy. I counted seven.

"Why do you count out your crackers?" I asked her, wondering why only seven.

She scowled at me, then replied, obviously annoyed, "Portion control." She made some instant oatmeal in a mug to take with her. While she was waiting for the microwave to finish, she eyed my can of soda and said, "I think my mom uses that to take oil stains off the driveway."

I was tempted to tell her my opinion about oatmeal but decided against it.

"Oatmeal would be healthier." She grabbed her steaming mug, stirred it, and left for campus.

Rhonda rushed into the kitchen a few minutes later. She seemed a bit stressed as she searched through her food cupboards. This was not her usual behavior. Usually, she read her scriptures at the kitchen table while eating a bowl of cereal. Then she turned on her computer to check her e-mail and her social network accounts and sometimes to peruse Mormon dating sites.

"What are you doing?" I asked her.

"I'm looking for my cookbook."

"To cook breakfast?" Too much effort this early in the morning.

"No. I want to make cinnamon rolls for family home evening tonight since I'm the cochair of our group. I need to be sure I have everything before I go to campus."

Family home evening was another activity I wasn't as enthusiastic about as Rhonda. "What about buying some Pillsbury ones?"

"*That* would be cheating," she said.

I didn't think it was cheating. It was easy and convenient, which I thought was the way to go.

Rhonda was still searching when she asked, "What time do you have classes this morning?"

"I don't," I said, opening the fridge for another Diet Coke.

"Do you even go to school?" Rhonda stopped and looked at me.

"What?"

"Do you? Go to school?"

"Yeah. Why?" I gave her a look like she was crazy. But her wondering if I went to school wasn't all that crazy of a question considering I didn't go that much.

"You're always here. You're here when I leave; you're here when I get back. I don't ever see you studying, and you're always reading or watching TV."

Very astute observation. "Well . . . I'm taking a light load this semester." As in nine credits.

"How light? Like one class?"

"No, just most of my classes are Tuesday/Thursday classes. I only have one Monday/Wednesday/Friday class."

I chose classes I thought wouldn't require much effort. My parents would absolutely kill me if I completely failed this semester, since they were footing the entire bill of tuition and living expenses. But they didn't understand how hard it was for me to get out of bed, never mind get up to campus.

Rhonda was still suspicious. "Really?"

"Oh, please, Rhonda." I managed a jovial, dismissive laugh. "I do. It's not like I'm leading some secret life you don't know about." No, that was last year's life.

Eventually, Rhonda left, but not before putting a huge message on the white board by the front door: "FHE tonight. 7:00 p.m., here. Don't be late." I could tell Rhonda's calling as family home evening cochair would not let me wallow in the pity party she did not know about.

I wandered into Sarah's room, where she was making her bed. I had forgotten to ask Rhonda about Claire's mom, but maybe Sarah knew something.

"Hey," she said, pulling up her homemade quilt and arranging a couple of stuffed animals near her pillow.

I leaned in the doorway. "Did you know Claire's mom is in the hospital?"

"She is?" Sarah's response told me I was not the only one who didn't know. I sometimes worried that I was so wrapped up in my own life that I somehow missed what was going on around me.

"Yeah, I guess so. She didn't say what for though."

Sarah checked her backpack, then zipped it up. "Does Rhonda know?"

"I forgot to ask her before she left."

"Well, let me know if you find anything out." Sarah glanced at the clock, then said good-bye and headed to campus.

Once again, I had the apartment to myself.

Recovering from a divorce was sort of like being on a roller coaster: it was a constant ride of emotional ups and downs. Mondays were always kind of hard. I didn't know if it was that I was coming off of the weekend or just that everyone seemed to be going on with their lives. Or maybe it was that having roommates around on Sunday provided a nice distraction.

Last night during my weekly call to my mom, her advice was, "Sometimes you've got to fake it to make it. It's like when you go to a service project but you don't really want to be there. Then you get into it, and in the end, you are glad you went. If you make the effort to feel better, you will start feeling better."

And I did try. Some days I got up and convinced myself that day *could* be a good day. But then there were other days when I didn't have the energy to convince myself and I went back to bed. Today seemed like one of those days I wouldn't be able to find the energy to fool myself. But instead of climbing into bed, I wandered around the apartment deciding what to do with myself until my afternoon class.

Sometimes I surfed the Internet, usually checking to see if Travis had posted anything on Facebook. So far nothing had been updated since he'd changed his status back to single. I thought "divorced" was a more appropriate description, but maybe he was like me, unwilling to admit it. Or maybe, like me, he wasn't sure that leaving me was a good decision.

After I checked on him, I occasionally looked up my roommates or other people I used to know, but that list was pretty short.

Other times, I wandered around the apartment in search of a distraction. I would check out my roommates' framed pictures, read the quotes on their walls and bulletin boards, leaf through their magazines—basically, I was finding ways to distract myself from my sad state of being suddenly single.

Claire and I shared a room. Claire was a minimalist, having next to nothing for belongings. Her bed was made, clothes neatly put away, closet doors shut. She was barely there. Physically and socially.

My side of the room wasn't quite as stark but didn't have much more in the way of personal possessions. There was a lone book about being happy that I had never read—a gift from my mother—my scriptures, and a small plant precariously on the edge of succumbing to death. My mother had placed all of these "accessories" there when she'd helped me unpack. My clothes were in a heap in my closet, since I'd stopped caring about my appearance. I only cared that I was able to shut my closet doors and keep my dirty laundry safely behind them. Other than the obvious possessions, I had a few things stashed that no one knew about. I kept my mementos from Travis shoved between my box spring and mattress and a small framed picture hidden in the back of my closet. My wedding ring hid in the velvet box it came in in the very corner of my pillowcase. Sometimes I put it back on my finger, held out my hand, and had a good cry.

If it wasn't for my messy bed, with its billowing down comforter and my struggling plant, there would be no signs of my existence.

The bedroom Rhonda and Sarah shared was the complete opposite of our room. It was a home away from home. Between the two beds was a framed cross-stitched sign proclaiming "Families Are Forever."

Rhonda's bed was covered in a patchwork quilt (probably hand quilted), and there was a picture of the Salt Lake Temple hanging on the wall above it. A set of scriptures, a journal, several cookbooks, and a selection of *Martha Stewart Living* and *Every Day with Rachael Ray* magazines took up her shelves. A set of R2-D2 bookends held together Rhonda's Disney DVD collection. And last but not least, she had a seventy-two-hour kit in a box under her bed. The front of the box read, "If ye are prepared, ye shall not fear."

Sarah's bed was always neatly made. Her walls were covered with pictures of her family, nieces and nephews, and pets, along with a picture of the Denver Temple, a picture of Jesus, and various quotes. Her shelves were lined with books by Jane Austen, the Little House on the Prairie series, and all of Anne of Green Gables.

I sat down on Sarah's bed and looked around their cheerful room, a simple reminder that life could be happy. I was trying to work up the energy to fake it in an attempt to make it.

Chapter Four
FHE

I WAS HIDING IN MY BEDROOM, still planning on skipping FHE, when it started. It had been a taxing day of dwelling on photos of Travis and crying into his old T-shirt I kept hidden under my pillow. I went to my one class and then overexerted myself by going to the Wilk to meet with my counselor at the counseling center. I left with more encouragement similar to my mother's: you gotta want it. Meaning, if I wanted to feel better, I needed to at least make some sort of effort. I thought I *had* been making an effort—I had made it to the center, hadn't I? I decided counseling sessions needed to be scheduled for Friday afternoons because they were so emotionally draining.

When I got home, I recovered by taking a short nap. By the time Sarah came home from school just after three, I was sitting on the couch pretending to be absorbed in *Les Misérables*, the unabridged version. Later, I was drawn into the kitchen by curiosity as Rhonda meticulously piped frosting onto her cinnamon rolls. It was exhausting just watching her. By 7:00 p.m., I was in my room, ready to listen to my iPod, pull the covers over my head, and hope for a better day tomorrow.

"Hey, Sophia." Rhonda popped her head around the doorframe. "Family home evening is starting."

"I'm pretty tired," I said, excusing myself.

"You have to come. You sustained me in my calling, and that means you need to support me."

I'd sustained her? I guess I had. A week ago at church the bishopric did a mass calling and pretty much asked the whole auditorium (excluding me) to stand and be sustained.

"Besides," she continued, "you get to meet our FHE family. It'll be fun."

Socializing wasn't that fun anymore. "Mmmm. I'm just gonna stay here."

"Sophia, if you don't come out, I will have everyone come here, and we'll have it in your bedroom."

I hadn't seen this much spine from her before. But with such conviction for attending social events, should I have been surprised? Was she going to march up to campus next and drag Claire home from the library so that she too could attend FHE?

I frowned. "You're kidding, right?"

"No. I am not going to have anyone left out."

"I don't feel left out," I protested. "I'm choosing not to come."

"Not on my watch. Now up and out, or I'm bringing them in."

"Did you grow up in the military? You're a drill sergeant," I mumbled.

Rhonda disappeared for a second. "Hey, guys," she yelled loudly. "Why don't you come back here, and we'll get started."

"Okay. Okay." I flung the covers off dramatically. "I'm up. And by the way, having boys in bedrooms is against BYU off-campus housing rules." I felt like I was living with my mother. Was I going to have to deal with her the whole year? I could only hope she would find a man quickly, have a short engagement, and plan a Thanksgiving wedding to get her off my back. Kind of like what I did.

"This is our roommate Sophia." Rhonda walked me into the crammed living room and led me to a tight space on the couch. Was she under the impression we could both fit there? I sat on the floor instead.

"Since this is the first time, we're going to play an introduction game. Along with introducing yourself, tell us one lie and one truth about yourself, and we have to guess which is which."

Ha. Easy, I thought. I would just tell two lies since I was trying to avoid sharing too much personal information about myself.

Rhonda continued. "I'll go first. My name is Rhonda Jesop, no relation to the polygamist. I'm from Salt Lake City. I am a junior majoring in elementary education. I like baking and scrapbooking. My truth and lie: I won first place in a recipe contest, or I blew up my mother's microwave."

My first thought was the microwave story was the lie. Rhonda was in the kitchen too much to make a mistake like that. But then again, you never knew with her. Sometimes she did unexplained things, like forget food in the microwave overnight or leave her gallon of milk on the counter for hours.

After several guesses, she confessed. The microwave story was the lie. But she did let us know that she almost blew it up by putting metal in it, but she shut it off just in time. Oh, Rhonda. Was she going to accidentally leave the gas burner on one night and kill us all?

Sarah was next. "I'm Sarah Sellers. I'm from Denver, Colorado. I served my mission in Rochester, New York. I'm a junior majoring in nursing. Let's see, one truth and one lie. Hmmm. Oh, okay. On my mission, I did or did not follow the mission rules?"

My guess was she followed them. Sarah was very straight-laced. She even told me (nicely) she was concerned about my Diet Coke consumption. She thought I drank too much of it and might endanger my Word of Wisdom worthiness. I told her (nicely) it was currently my only vice, so please let me enjoy it in peace. She hadn't said anything since. But occasionally, I noticed a worried expression when she saw me drinking it.

I was right. Then the game continued around the room. Oh my gosh. There were four apartments in our group, a total of sixteen people, and this was going to take forever.

"I served my mission in Brazil. I'm a Spanish major . . ."

"I'm getting married December 28 . . ."

"I'm graduating this semester. I'm twenty-five, so I guess according to Brigham Young, I'm a menace to society. I'm hoping I'll meet someone soon . . ."

Next was our home teacher/elders quorum president, Luke, the guy with the creamy voice. I thought of him as EQP, since it was a lot easier than saying elders quorum president. "My name is Luke James. I'm studying architecture. I served my mission in London, England."

Someone, who I think was one of his roommates, yelled out, "So did you or did you not follow the mission rules?"

His eyes narrowed for a brief moment, then he laughed. "Any mission rules I may or may not have broken I have repented of, and the Lord remembers them no more."

Most of the room laughed. He continued. "I was a counselor at Especially For Youth the last two summers. That's it."

"Where are you from?" someone asked.

"Oh yeah. I'm from Southern California."

I wouldn't have taken him for a SoCal boy. He didn't look the part of the good-looking surfer dude.

"What is your truth and lie?"

"I have to think about it. How about Sophia goes, then we come back to me?"

I was surprised he remembered my name. Then all eyes were on me. Had we already made it around the room? I hadn't decided yet what to tell about myself.

"I'm Sophia Du . . . Davis." Great. Not that I cared what impression I made, but I didn't want to sound like I stuttered. "I'm a freshman. I don't have a major. I'm from Las Vegas—"

"Vegas, baby," a guy across the room yelled.

I wasn't surprised by his outburst. It was a standard response when I said where I was from. Along with, "Do people really live there?" and "Do you live in a casino?" Aside from the obvious evils of gambling, drinking, and general immorality abounding on the Las Vegas Strip, there were nice residential communities and lots of strong Church members there.

I didn't continue. There wasn't anything else I cared to add.

"She likes to read," Rhonda said.

"What's your favorite book?" the "Vegas Baby" guy asked.

"Um, how about the *The Art of Homemaking* by Daryl Hoole?" I said brightly, figuring he would be able to tell I was not serious. "What's yours?"

"The Book of Mormon, of course."

"Of course," I said. I should have seen that answer coming.

I thought he was done, but he continued. "What's your ideal date, and will you go on it with me?"

His boldness caught me off guard. Why would he ask me out in front of everyone? "I'm sorry, I can't," I blurted out. "I'm allergic to testosterone." Oh. My. Gosh. Did I just say that out loud? I didn't mean to.

There were a couple of laughs before Rhonda broke in. "Hey, we're not playing the dating game. That's next week. Let's say a closing prayer, bless the food, and then there are homemade cinnamon rolls for everyone."

Saved by the prayer. I didn't even have to make up my two lies.

"Wait, wait," Sarah interrupted. "Sophia didn't get her turn."

I shot her a look of death, which she deflected with a smile.

"I went on stage at a rock concert, or I spent a night in jail," I said without even thinking. I wasn't doing too well with the "think before I speak" approach tonight.

I considered for a split second saying I had CTR tattooed on the small of my back. But then people might want to see proof.

"That's a tough one," Rhonda said nicely, but her expression was screaming *really?*

After an awkward silence, I laughed. "I'm kidding; neither one is true."

There were a couple sighs of relief. "I'm not that interesting." Which was true. But it also could have been a lie if they knew the truth about me.

"Let's go eat *homemade* cinnamon rolls," I said loudly, with staged excitement. Anything to take the attention off of me.

Chapter Five
If It's Worth Doing, It's Worth Overdoing

THE WARD SHOULD HAVE OFFERED Rhonda a calling as a one-woman social committee because she would have been the right woman for the job. Her motto was "if it's worth doing, it's worth *over*doing." Her passion for socializing, baking, and life in general definitely followed this motto.

Friday nights quickly became a standing get-together at our apartment. Rhonda didn't just hang out with a couple of friends; she made it an *event*. She took charge by making treats, inviting people over, and planning the activity. Sometimes they watched movies or played games, board or video. The first time she hosted one, Bradley (the bike guy) showed up. When Rhonda mentioned he was coming, I decided I suddenly had laundry to do and snuck down to the laundry room. I know, real mature of me. The problem was, I knew Bradley was interested. And I was not. I didn't believe the cure for a broken heart was to throw myself back into the deep end of the dating pool. I preferred to be invisible.

However, he caught me coming back in, and I felt it would be rude of me to just excuse myself and go into my room. I decided from now on I needed to stay and wait for my laundry.

"Hey," Bradley called to me as soon as I shut the front door. He followed me into the kitchen, leaving what looked like a rousing game of Battle of the Sexes. "You should come play."

I hesitated. I knew it was one of those fake-it-to-make-it moments, where maybe if I joined in I would eventually have a good time. But I just didn't want to. "Not tonight." I hoped he would leave it at that.

"At least have a cookie with me." He looked over at the refreshments.

"I guess one cookie wouldn't hurt."

He grabbed the cookies from the counter and set them on the table. "Hey, do you have any milk?"

"Nope. Diet Coke?" I grabbed a can from the fridge and held it out to him.

He shook his head. "Nah, I never drink carbonation. It robs your muscles of oxygen."

I gave him a weird look. "Where did that come from?" I kept the can for myself and popped it open.

"I teach rock climbing. I have to make sure people properly hydrate themselves."

"Good thing I will never try rock climbing, then." I took a long sip.

"Never say never." He smiled. Maybe he thought he was tempting me with something fun. But I knew I wouldn't. When I hiked the Y last year, I ended up with a sprained ankle, and the time I went skiing with Travis and his parents, I avalanched down the slope. Rock climbing could possibly be the death of me.

"I didn't know you were so athletic," I said, although Rhonda had already told me.

"Speed dating night didn't give us much time to talk."

"Two minutes isn't long," I agreed.

"I looked for you after, but you disappeared."

"Oh, I was there. I rushed over to grab a brownie before they were all eaten."

There was an outburst of laughter from the other room.

"Now, what did you say your major was?"

I hadn't. "I'm still undecided. How about you?"

"Construction management."

"Great," I said. I searched for something more to say. "We always need houses built."

Bradley became animated. "I want to do so much more than that though. I want to get involved with rebuilding New Orleans."

"Why New Orleans?"

"I served my mission there. I saw the devastation caused to both the city and the people because of Hurricane Katrina, and it changed my life."

My divorce changed my life, but I wasn't about to volunteer that. "I bet. So how do you get involved? Is that what you want to do for a job when you graduate?" I thought Rhonda had mentioned he was close to graduating.

"First I'm going to volunteer for Habitat for Humanity. Have you ever done that? It's awesome."

I silently shook my head no. His enthusiasm was sort of taking over the conversation.

"I'm going to Mexico in November for three weeks to do it."

"In the middle of the semester?" I was surprised. "How can you do that?"

"I only have three credits left to graduate."

I cocked my head, trying to understand. "You're only taking one class? Didn't they have it in the spring or summer?" I wouldn't want to do another whole semester for just one class.

"I couldn't miss the whitewater rafting."

Huh. That was something I'd be okay with missing.

"Besides, they didn't offer it then."

"Oh. So you can still pass the class even if you're gone for three weeks?"

"I've already arranged it with my teacher. And doing something like that will look great on my résumé."

I realized he was at a completely different point in his life. He was thinking about résumés and careers and means of support. My life was consumed with convincing myself to get out of bed each morning and reminding myself I *could* move on with my life.

More laughter came from the other room.

"How do you know it's a serpentine belt?" a guy asked.

"I know about cars." Sarah laughed. "My dad owns a garage; I've worked on cars before."

"You didn't tell us that at FHE," Rhonda said.

"I can't tell you all my secrets," Sarah said.

When the laughter died down, I looked at my watch. "I'm gonna go get my laundry and do a couple of things. Maybe I'll see you around?" I was hoping he realized I was saying good night.

"We still on for that bike riding lesson?" Bradley looked hopeful.

"It's okay if I never learn to ride a bike," I said gently.

"You don't know if you haven't tried."

I had tried. It didn't work out so well the first time.

Chapter Six
Fast and Testimony

FAST AND TESTIMONY MEETING IS usually uplifting, but today it was more a case of "did that person really just say that?" I was not mocking testimonies by any means; in fact, I desperately wanted to hear something that would give me a bit of hope to cling to, if only for a short while.

The first person up, Simon something, compared life to riding his moped. He explained how easy it was to be focused on where he was going. But one day, he noticed a girl on the side of the road who needed help. Normally, he would have driven on by, but he stopped. (I'm guessing she was pretty.) He helped her and felt good about serving her. He compared that to missed opportunities to serve others because we might be "too busy mopedding through life." He made a good comparison but didn't say anything that resonated with me.

Next up was a girl named Brittany. I didn't know her since I hadn't made any attempts to make friends. But I still hoped she would have some pearls of wisdom.

Unfortunately, no. When she stood up, her hair was seriously two times bigger than her head. I reminded myself not to be judgmental; she could have a good message to share. Then she opened her mouth.

"My manicure/pedicure turned out so good this week I just had to get up and share my testimony. Because when you feel good about yourself, ya know, you have a glow about you. People notice that. It's like when we have the Spirit, we feel good. So we should all try to feel good about ourselves, like go to the spa, and others will want to have the Spirit like we have."

Did she seriously share her testimony about going to the spa? Really? I looked around the auditorium, and others seemed to have the same reaction I had. But that was what was in her heart, so she assumed it was worth sharing. She did bring up the point that people notice when we feel good about ourselves. Or in my case, don't feel good about ourselves.

After Brittany, Claire distracted me. She was reading her scriptures and very elaborately marking verses. She had a full set of "scripture marker" colored pencils and was meticulously lining the verses on the pages. Some verses were multicolored, with certain words in certain colors. Go figure Claire would have her scriptures color coded.

I leaned over and whispered, "What do the colors represent?" When I marked my scriptures, I usually used whatever color I could find at the time.

Claire looked surprised, maybe that I didn't get it, but also put out. "Each color stands for something."

"Well, yeah, I get that. But what do they stand for?" Okay, so maybe I didn't need to carry on this conversation during the middle of sacrament meeting, but I was genuinely curious.

The best way to describe her reaction was petulance. She seemed annoyed that I was bothering her. She let out an irritated breath. "Black is for Satan, blue is for baptism, yellow is for Jesus, you know." Then she closed her scriptures, crossed her legs, and turned her body so she was facing away from me.

I wondered what her colors were for patience, tolerance, and long-suffering.

* * *

After church, we had an apartment break-the-fast meal with our home teachers' apartment. I found out about it when Luke and his roommate Justin walked by on the way home.

"We'll be over in about an hour?" Luke asked in passing.

"An hour and a half would be better," Rhonda said.

Justin flashed a dimpled smile. "We're looking forward to it."

When the men were out of hearing distance, Sarah whispered, "He is so cute."

"Justin? I *know*," Rhonda said and then added, "and their roommate Landon is pretty dang cute too."

Justin was cute, not that I cared. He had slightly curly blond hair, a build like a quarterback, a win-you-over grin, and a very charming personality. But charming or not, why were they coming over?

"What's going on?" I said, unaware of any ward thing.

"Oh yeah," Rhonda said casually, "our home teachers are coming over, so we invited the whole apartment for dinner. You know, get to know them better."

That explained why Rhonda had left dough rising before we left for church. I'd been thinking about taking a nap this afternoon, but since lunch was doubling as our home teaching visit, there was no way Rhonda would let me out of it. She'd probably send the home teachers into my bedroom if I tried skipping. It was easier to endure it than avoid it.

When we got home, Rhonda was aglow, even in her worn-out, lime-green, terry-cloth apron as she bustled around the kitchen getting ready for lunch. I was reluctant to offer help for fear of being sucked into her entertainment frenzy. So instead, I sat at the kitchen table, my back against the wall, drinking a Diet Coke.

"Okay. We're going to be having pork roast, with . . ." She thought out loud, counting on her fingers.

I tuned her out. How could I get out of this? Dang it. Claire had somehow managed to avoid it by going to her brother's house like she did most Sunday afternoons. If it wasn't for the home teaching, I could make up an excuse about being sick or vegetarian or something. I didn't want to be around boys, men, guys—whatever they were. I was trying to avoid all RMs with raging hormones who thought they needed to get married by semester's end. It'd work out a whole lot easier if Rhonda wasn't my roommate.

"Can I help?" Sarah came into the kitchen after changing out of her church clothes.

"The dinner rolls need to be put on a cookie sheet to rise." Rhonda was quite happy to put her to work. I had suggested Pillsbury Pop Up rolls, but Rhonda had lectured me that that was no way to land a husband. It was not a proper display of homemaking skills, she informed me. I rolled my eyes at her, and Sarah smiled a little.

I thought back to Travis. I had landed a husband. I had even landed a KitchenAid mixer from my parents as a wedding gift. I could have baked him dozens of rolls, and he still wouldn't have stayed around.

"Here." Rhonda plopped a five-pound bag of potatoes in front of me on the table. "You take care of the potatoes." She looked at the clock; we had a little more than a half hour. "I don't want to run out of time."

"What am I doing with them?" I asked warily, still wondering if I could fake a migraine or cramps or something, and quick.

"Whatever you want. Au gratin would be good." She turned the light on in the oven to check the roast.

Where was a box of Betty Crocker's au gratin potatoes when I needed one? "Rhonda, I can't just whip something up with potatoes. I have to cook them first."

She wasn't paying attention. "Whipped potatoes sound good too." She was humming while she stirred a pot of gravy on the stove. She was happy about something, and it couldn't all be about her homemade meal.

"I know," she suggested brightly, "funeral potatoes. Or scalloped potatoes. Those are yummy."

Yummy but time-consuming. Our deadline was fast approaching.

I decided to consult a cookbook. Mashed potatoes were the obvious choice. But maybe there was something a little less ordinary but extremely easy to do with all those stupid potatoes. I knew my mom stuck a cookbook in my designated kitchen cupboard when she helped me move in.

Sure enough, on the top shelf was the homemade, scrapbooked recipe book given to me as a wedding gift. I had loved that book when I was married. I'd consulted it often to render yummy, homemade meals for my man.

"How cute." Sarah noticed it. "Can I see it? Is it scrapbooked? What a clever idea." She took it from me before I could protest. "Did you make it?" Sarah looked through it.

"No. It . . ." I couldn't say it was a wedding gift.

"Let me see." Rhonda grabbed it out of Sarah's hands. "How darling. I want one." She looked at the cover, then opened it to the front page.

"The way to a man's heart is through his stomach?" Rhonda read the inscription and then looked at me, puzzled. "What?"

"It was a gift from a friend," I said, hoping there wouldn't be any need for more explanation. "It'd make a good name for a cookbook, huh?"

"Leave that out. I might want to copy some recipes from it," Rhonda said.

"Oh, yeah, sure." I breathed a sigh of relief.

Mashed potatoes were my executive, albeit unoriginal, decision.

Apartment 307 arrived promptly at 1:30 p.m. bearing gifts of green Jell-O, Ritz crackers, and a pitcher of orange juice. Landon walked in last, carrying what looked and smelled like some sort of tuna casserole. Rhonda raised an eyebrow as he set it on the stovetop.

"Should we get our table?" Luke asked, taking in the seating situation.

"It will be fine," Rhonda said over her shoulder as she took the roast out of the baking dish and set it on a serving dish. I watched in awe as she dumped all the grease down the sink.

"Rhonda, I don't think you're supposed to do that. Won't it clog the sink?" I asked carefully, trying not to embarrass her. All I could picture was a sink full of greasy water clogging the drain.

"It'll be fine." Rhonda turned, presenting the roast proudly. "I know a secret. If you run some hot water with dish detergent, it will wash the grease through the pipes."

I could only hope she was right.

I ended up sitting next to Luke, but the chairs were so close our thighs touched if we weren't careful. Rhonda probably planned it that way because she was sitting on the opposite side of the table, beaming, crammed next to Landon. Justin was at the head of the table, Sarah next to him, straddling the corner closest to where I was sitting. Their last roommate, Christopher, was at the other end of the table, opposite Justin.

"Where's your other roommate? What's her name? Chloe?" Justin asked.

"Claire. She went to her brother's house. He's married and lives in Provo," Sarah said.

"Isn't she from Japan?" Christopher asked. "I served my mission there."

"Wrong girl, Chris." Justin seemed the type to have all the girls checked out. I wondered what their ward directory looked like.

"She does have black hair, but she's not Japanese. She's from Logan." Rhonda provided Claire's background information. Maybe the guys didn't study the ward directory like my roommates did.

"Let's start," Rhonda said enthusiastically. "Thanks for coming. We're happy you're here."

Oh no. Was she going to make a speech? I felt my face grow warm.

"Landon, do you want to pray?" She turned to the object of her affection.

"Sure," he said as we all folded our arms and bowed our heads.

Dinner involved a lot of bumping elbows, moving food on and off the table, and refilling drinks. Despite being crammed together, Rhonda was positively in her glory.

"These potatoes are good," Luke said, taking a second helping.

"Sophia made them," Sarah said.

Luke looked at me. "They're creamy."

"Thanks," I said. Sarah had saved my potatoes by donating her sour cream to the cause.

"But this roast, dude. I haven't eaten like this since I left home." Justin stuffed his mouth with a forkful.

"No kidding," Christopher added.

"Yeah, me too," Landon chimed in.

Rhonda basked in the limelight.

"We have a home teaching message to share. Should we do it now or after lunch?" Luke asked.

Rhonda and Sarah looked at each other. "Now is good. Then we can all have dessert in the living room."

"Sure," Luke said easily and pushed back his chair so he could stand up. He pulled a piece of crumpled paper from the front pocket of his jeans. "I read this scripture when I was having a hard time on my mission, and it impressed me how aware Heavenly Father is of us. I think it's appropriate now because it's easy to get stressed out and overwhelmed with school; it helps me keep perspective. It's Doctrine and Covenants 121:7: 'My son, peace be unto thy soul; thine adversity and thine afflictions shall be but a small moment.'"

That was the pearl of wisdom I needed. I felt a lump in my throat, and my eyes teared up. I took a drink, attempting to calm down and discreetly wipe my eyes. I didn't want to be caught being so emotional.

"I like that," Sarah said.

"Me too. Joseph Smith was so full of wisdom, don't you think?" Rhonda said.

A discussion about Joseph Smith and other subsequent prophets ensued. I didn't attempt to join in. My mind was stuck on what Luke had shared. Were my divorce and the pain I felt about it going to last for a "small moment"? It didn't seem like it right now. I thought of Joseph Smith in Liberty Jail. He was told being there was for his experience and would be for his good. He was facing death. I was only facing single life again, and I couldn't deal with it.

"Hey, are you going to join everyone else in the living room?" Luke interrupted my thoughts.

"Oh." I looked around, not realizing the room had cleared out. "I'm . . . going to clean up the dishes."

"Let me help," he said.

I stood up, trying not to look at him. My eyes were still a little moist. I silently rinsed and stacked the dishes as he brought them to me.

Out of the corner of my eye, I noticed Landon's tuna dish on the stove, untouched.

I picked it up. "Landon's probably going to feel bad that no one ate his food."

"I don't know if I'd want to eat it. He's not the best cook," Luke whispered to me, then looked around to make sure no one else heard.

"Maybe I'll scoop some out and throw it down the disposal so he'll think some people tried it. He might see it if I dump it in the trash," I said, thinking out loud.

"Good idea," Luke said.

I scooped out two good-sized spoonfuls and pushed them into the disposal. With the water running, I switched the disposal on. It made a grrr-ing noise but didn't sound like it was grinding stuff up.

"I don't think it's working right." I switched it off.

That's when I noticed the other side of the sink wasn't so happy. It was filling up with greasy water. I reluctantly reached my hand in to see if the drain stopper was clogged. Nope.

"Crud. I told Rhonda not to do it," I said, mostly to myself.

"What?" Luke asked, stacking the last of the dishes on the counter beside me.

"Rhonda dumped grease down the sink, and now it's clogged. I checked this side, and it's not the drain stopper."

"Do you want me to look?" Luke asked nicely. I stepped aside, and he actually reached down into the disposal, took a little black rubber thing off, and then stuck his hand farther in. He stepped to the other side of me, washed his hands and said, "Okay."

"Okay?" I asked and flicked the switch.

"Wait!" Luke said at the same time I turned it on.

The disposal gurgled, then a big swish of greasy water and tuna casserole came shooting up at me.

"Oh!" I yelled as I raised my hands and looked up from the drain. I had nasty water and debris splattered all over my face and dripping off my hair. So much for Rhonda's secret hot water and detergent trick.

"Are you okay? Here." Luke grabbed a dish towel from the stove handle.

"Eww." I tried wiping the mess off.

Luke reluctantly held up the rubber ring. "I took the splash guard off."

Rhonda came in to see what all the commotion was about. "Maybe I shouldn't have dumped that grease after all." Rhonda chewed on her nail.

I had some choice words I refrained from saying, reminding myself that Rhonda didn't do it on purpose.

Luke went to get some Drāno from their apartment, and he tapped on the door lightly before coming back in at the same time Justin wandered into the kitchen. "What's going on in here?"

"Clogged drain," Luke informed him, pouring the liquid into the nasty water.

"Oh." Justin nodded knowingly.

We waited a few minutes, staring at the sink. There was a sigh of relief when the water made a sucking sound and swirled down the drain.

"Thank you so much," Rhonda said. "I'm going to make you guys some cookies tonight. What would we have done without your help?" She continued with a steady stream of appreciation as she and Justin returned to the living room. Luke hung back a little.

"Are you coming?" he asked.

"I don't think so. I should take a shower."

"You've had quite a mishap today," Luke said.

"But . . ." I paused and took a deep breath. "Thanks for the quote you shared. I appreciate it."

He didn't say anything for a moment. He just stood there looking at me. I felt transparent, like he could see what I was hiding.

"You're welcome," he said simply. "I'm going to watch the movie." He pointed to the other room.

"Thanks for fixing the drain."

"Anytime." He smiled.

As if getting through a meal of reluctant socialization and battling a greasy clogged sink explosion was not enough unpleasantness for one day, I still had to call my mother.

"Hey, sweetie. How are you?" My mother was her typical happy self.

"I'm okay, Mom. How's Dad and Dan?" I tried sounding upbeat.

"We're all good."

"Good."

There was a pause. My mother would love it if I had exciting social events to report, glowing commentaries of how much I loved my classes, anticipation for upcoming dates, but I had nothing of the sort to talk about.

"How was church today? Are you enjoying your ward?" I wondered if my mom was really asking if I *went* to church today.

"Church was fine."

"Are you going to go to family home evening tomorrow night?"

"I sort of have to because it's held here."

"Sophia, you don't have to be so acrimonious." My mother was a high school English teacher. She liked big words and used them often.

I immediately felt bad. "I'm sorry, Mom. I don't mean to take it out on you." Though I disagreed with her. I thought I had a *right* to be so bitter. "So what I meant to say was yes, I'll be going tomorrow night."

"Good," she said cheerfully. "Be gregarious. You're a natural."

"Okay. Thanks for the approbation," I had learned a word or two from her in my nineteen years.

"Are you meeting with your counselor this week?"

"Friday."

"Good. I know it helps."

"Yup."

"Have you been getting the daily spiritual thought I e-mail you?"

"Every day." I usually deleted them, unopened. Occasionally I would open one if I felt an inspirational thought would help that day. Today's was Job 1:21. I didn't even need my index tabs to find the book of Job; my scriptures naturally opened right up to it. The scripture was about how the Lord giveth and the Lord taketh away. But if I mentioned anything about it, my mom would remind me about submitting to the Lord's will instead of my own will.

"Don't forget to get your stuff out of storage."

"Okay, Mom," I said, even though I knew I wasn't going to get to it this week or even next week. I couldn't deal with my real life, never mind stuff in storage from my married life.

"I love you, Sophia."

"Love you too, Mom."

"Call me if you need to."

"Okay."

"I'll let you go now."

"Bye." I hung up before she added anything.

Forty minutes later, my brother called. I never realized what a good guy my brother was until I got divorced. I always considered him the nerdy, embarrassing older brother. He still liked giving me a hard time, but while I was sobbing my way through my divorce depression, he and I had actually become friends.

Friday nights were my parents' date night, and while they were out, I would emerge from my room and hang out with him. Usually, we watched a movie. But there was solace in sitting there with him, not talking but still feeling loved and protected.

"Hey, Sophia," he said when I finally answered.

"Hey, Dan."

"I'm calling to check on you."

"I know." I knew because my mom was predictable. As soon as she'd hung up, she'd probably reported on my progress or lack thereof.

"Mom thinks you're doing better." He sounded hopeful but was more realistic than my mother.

I laughed a little. "I've just become better at faking it, which isn't necessarily a good thing."

Dan chuckled, knowing the sometimes overbearing nature of my mother and her PMA. "So what's the prognosis?"

"Oh, I don't know. I get out of bed and go to my classes. I could be considered functioning."

Good thing Dan was just a guy and not a psychologist so he wouldn't probe any further. "Okay, sis. Just thought I'd get the real story straight from the horse's mouth."

"Ha. Ha. That'd be funny if I were a horse." I tried not to smile, but my brother was unintentionally cheering me up.

"Got it. Note to self: my sister is not a horse."

"Dan, you've got to work on those lines if you're ever going to pick up a girl."

"Okay, Sophia. Note to self: work on pickup lines."

I laughed, just a little. "You should stop while you're ahead."

"Okay, Sophia. Take care of yourself, sis."

"Thank you," I said as I hung up, but what I really wanted to say was "I love you."

Chapter Seven

Conference Weekend

IT WAS THE FIRST WEEK of October when I wandered into the kitchen one morning to find Rhonda with her head in the oven.

"Rhonda, please tell me you are not trying to kill yourself. I could not handle that this early in the morning." I was too tired to muster up proper concern.

Rhonda pulled her head out and immediately looked at her hair. "No, I'm drying my hair."

I plopped down on a chair. "In the oven? Did your blow dryer break?"

"No. I read on a blog if you put mousse in your hair, scrunch it up, and then dry it in the oven, it makes it curlier."

"You do realize your hair could catch fire? Mousse has alcohol in it and is flammable. Putting your head in the oven might not be the best way to achieve the look you want."

Rhonda was nonplussed. "The blog said to put a cookie sheet in first with a gas oven."

"Rhonda. You are putting your head in the oven. Not the best choice. If you want your curls to look different, you should try a different product, not bake your head in the oven. If you light your hair on fire, it will also curl up."

Rhonda reluctantly shut the oven door and turned the heat off. She sat down at the kitchen table looking a little defeated.

"You could try a flat iron or some shaping product," I said gently. But maybe advice coming from me about how to style hair seemed ridiculous since I rarely took the time to do anything more with my hair than throw it in a ponytail.

"I wanted to try something different."

"For school? Do you have a presentation or something?" I was a little enlivened by the idea that I might be able to style her hair the way I thought would accentuate her curls.

"Just in general," she said.

"Maybe someday we can experiment," I said, partly in an effort to fake it to make it.

"Maybe," she replied.

I got the impression she was declining my offer but didn't want to hurt my feelings.

* * *

When I returned from my evening class on Wednesday, there was a message for me in big letters on the white board. FHE brother Tanner (the one who "jokingly" asked me out) had stopped by. I think I knew why.

"I told him we had Relief Society tonight, so if he wanted to catch you, you'd probably be home after eight," Rhonda said as I read the message.

"Thanks, I think."

"If I were you, I would be so excited," Rhonda said, then added, "He's good-looking."

"Hmm."

"Sophia, at least give him a chance."

Why, oh, why did I have to come 435 miles from home only to end up living with my mother incarnate? I didn't want any more motherly encouragement. "He's not my type."

"No one's your type," Rhonda said with her typical tact.

There was a knock at the door. I was grateful for the interruption.

Rhonda opened it. "Oh, hi, Tanner. Sophia's right here." She let him in, smirked at me, then went in the back.

"Hey, Sophia, how are you?" His face reddened a little, and he stuffed his right hand in his jeans pocket.

"I'm okay."

"You know how I was joking, but not really, about asking you out that time at FHE?" he asked.

"Yeah, about that. I'm sorry about the testosterone comment. That was rude of me."

"A few of us are getting together on Sunday morning for breakfast and to watch conference. Would you want to come?"

"That's nice of you, but I can't."

"Oh. Did my roommate Jackson invite you?"

"No."

"Maybe we could hang out some other time, then?" He was hopeful.

"Sorry," I said gently. "Probably not."

He gave me a strange look and backed away.

"Bye now," I said as nicely as I could and shut the door.

Rhonda immediately reappeared. "What did he want?" She was more excited than I was.

"He invited me to watch conference, but I told him no."

"That's too bad. You're always so quick to say no." She frowned momentarily, then she looked at the clock. "Oh. It's time to go to the Relief Society activity. We're meeting Sarah there."

Dang. If only I had been fifteen minutes later, I could have skipped it. "What about Claire?" I asked, since misery loved company.

"She's studying."

"Of course," I said, thinking studying suddenly sounded like a good idea.

* * *

On Friday night, I hid in the laundry room again because Rhonda was having another Friday-night hang out at our apartment. I didn't wait around to see if Bradley was going to show up. I was trying to avoid him. Even I knew it was wrong to hang out with someone just because he was somewhat of a distraction.

Saturday and Sunday were conference. Sarah and Rhonda were going to the Conference Center on Saturday and then spending the night at Rhonda's house and watching the Sunday sessions with her family.

"You should join us, Sophia," Sarah said.

"I don't want to wait in those lines. I'd rather watch it on TV."

"It's not bad," Rhonda said. "It's definitely worth the wait."

"Thanks, Rhonda, but I don't think so. Anyway, I don't mind watching it."

"But you're going to be all alone," Sarah said.

"Claire will be here." Although I could not picture myself hanging out with Claire.

Rhonda looked surprised. "Didn't she tell you? She's going to her brother's for the weekend. His wife is being induced today, and Claire's staying to babysit."

I didn't even know Claire's sister-in-law was pregnant. Come to think of it, I didn't even know what her brother's name was. Too much information was not a problem with Claire.

"I'll be fine."

"Are you sure?" Sarah asked. Sometimes I thought Sarah might be on to me. She was always asking if I was okay as she left for school or when she arrived home from school or any other time our paths happened to cross.

"I will be fine. It's conference weekend. It's time for renewal and rejuvenation." I tried sounding upbeat. I only hoped something in the upcoming talks would resonate with me.

"You're missing out, Sophia," Rhonda said.

"You two go have fun," I said cheerfully, herding them toward the front door. "Besides, I have plenty of things to do." Like cleaning the fridge. Just this morning I found a yellow sticky note on the front of the fridge that said, "Moldy food in fridge. Needs removal." Obviously from Claire. Obviously not my food, since pretty much everything I ate was frozen. But it was a great excuse to use for things I could do.

"Go. Enjoy. I'll be fine." I faked a huge smile for final convincing.

"Really?" Rhonda seemed suspicious.

"Absolutely." I patted them on the back, which was meant to be a push out the door. "Yes. Now go," I insisted, shutting the door and locking it behind them.

The real reason I wanted to be alone was that I was working on a good crying jag. This was the weekend Travis had proposed. One year ago. In front of the fountain of the Salt Lake Temple, after the crowd had cleared from the Sunday afternoon session.

It's easy to guess the rest of the story. I, of course, accepted and was the envy of my roommates. Some thought getting engaged after five weeks was too soon, but he was a righteous returned missionary, and we were in love. It had to be right.

I'd had the last six months to dissect my engagement and any clues I should have noticed about the fate of our marriage. Maybe I didn't pray fervently about it? Maybe I was enticed by my gorgeous, one-and-a-half-carat diamond ring? Maybe I was so excited choosing my dress and planning my wedding I never stopped to consider the red flags along the way? But to my credit, I honestly thought I loved him. Besides, I had told myself, it wasn't too soon. I was so smitten I thought nothing could go wrong.

I had met his parents the week before we got engaged. Boyd and Maxine Duckk. His dad was a prominent lawyer in Salt Lake, and they had a lot of money and a huge house on the hill. Thus explaining Travis's sleek white BMW and Ralph Lauren clothes.

I didn't think anything of it when Travis described his mother as a strong, independent, amazing woman, capable of accomplishing anything she set her mind to.

I didn't think anything of Travis being an only child, thus being the apple of her eye. In short, Travis was her blind spot.

I did think a little when Travis started calling me Fifi early on in our relationship. He explained his paternal grandmother's name was also Sophia, and his mother and Sophia did not get along. At all. Ever. So Travis came up with this "pet name." I thought it sounded like a name for a pet poodle. But I was willing to be his pet. It was easy to dismiss it into the "no big deal" category because at the time, it was okay.

Once we were engaged, I didn't think anything of his parents' newlywed stories. His mother, Maxine, quit college to put her husband through law school. They were dirt poor and worked hard for many years to get where they were now.

They were proud of how they had supported each other and become successful on their own. Boyd Duckk sang praises to his Maxine, the perfect wife, companion, and mother. She was a fabulous cook and housekeeper, and they hoped their only son would one day find a wife to live up to the standard Maxine set. They wished the same happiness and success for us.

Okay, remember I was only eighteen. I wanted to impress them. I wanted them to like me. I could only nod my head and wholeheartedly agree because I wanted to marry their only son. It was easy to tune out Boyd Duckk's speech as I stared into the depths of Travis's gorgeous blue eyes and thought, *I am going to make him so happy.*

After we got married, their wedding gift was taking back that sleek BMW. They claimed they were trying to scale back their material possessions or some stupid excuse like that.

Travis wasn't happy about his parents' sudden decision but didn't argue. After all, he justified, why would we need a car? Everything was so accessible around campus. He didn't take into consideration that I'd be stuck figuring out how to get to and from my two part-time jobs.

His parents also gave us the gift of self-sufficiency, cutting off any funds for Travis's education and lifestyle. Yes, I thought it was mean because it was without warning. Travis was unhappy but again excused their behavior. He claimed he would show them we could do it. We needed to stand on our own two feet, he declared proudly. He didn't mention that not too far in the future he would knock my feet so far out from under me I would feel like I couldn't stand.

My roommates weren't gone for more than five minutes when there was a knock at the door. "You have got to be kidding me," I muttered, wondering who could it be.

It was Bradley.

"Hi." He smiled when I opened the door. "Your bike awaits." Then he swooped into a deep bow.

"What?" I hoped I hadn't heard him correctly. "Did you say bike?"

"Yes. I am here to teach you how to ride a bike."

"But I don't have a bike." About which I was quite relieved.

"Already thought of that." He pointed down to the parking lot, where I saw two bikes.

I felt a little sick. "Are those for us?"

"Yes, they are."

I could tell by his grin that Bradley was pretty pleased with himself. I was not so pleased, but I definitely had to give him points for creativity and effort. "Bradley—" I started protesting.

"C'mon." He didn't let me finish. "Just try. I promise I'll have you home in time for conference. Besides, it'll be fun."

Or funny. As in watching me make a complete fool of myself and possibly knocking my front teeth out again.

He led me down to the bikes. Seeing them up close didn't make me want to try them out any more than when I saw them from upstairs.

"I don't have a helmet," I said in a weak argument.

"I got that covered." He pulled one out of his backpack next to the bike.

"What if I crash and knock my teeth out?" I was looking for a way out because I *liked* the way I looked with front teeth. Riding a bike was s-c-a-r-y. What I looked like riding a bike was going to be even s-c-a-r-i-e-r.

He produced a mouth guard from his backpack.

A football helmet might have been more appropriate protection for me. "You thought of everything," I said in defeat, trying to hide my dismay. "That makes it even harder to say I don't think bike riding is a good idea."

"C'mon. If I bring the bike back now, the guys at the rental place are going to know I was totally shot down."

I hesitated. I didn't want to make him feel like an idiot. "Bradley, I'm a big chicken when it comes to bikes. I *really* don't want to." I couldn't think of a nicer way to say it. I didn't want to get on the bike, and I didn't want to go on a date. I only gave in because he was so darn persistent.

"Are there such things as adult training wheels?" I wondered out loud after a few tries. I might just as well have asked for adult diapers; I was so embarrassed. "Otherwise, this could be very hazardous for me."

He just laughed.

To say bike riding did not go well would be an understatement. I didn't master riding a bike. After many treacherous stops and starts and one skinned palm, I felt like throwing the bike in a big mangled heap on the ground and giving up.

"Come on. You can't quit," Bradley said encouragingly.

Somehow, I did not take encouragement from his words. I wanted to yell and scream and have a little tantrum because I was so frustrated. Then I realized it was not at all about the bike.

Yes, I had a little epiphany out there in the parking lot trying to learn to ride a stupid bike. Somewhere along the line, I seemed to have acquired the attitude that my divorce gave me license to treat people any way I liked. Which was not usually very nice. My mom, telling me that my being so acrimonious was unbecoming was totally true. I owed her a big apology.

I took a deep breath. "I need to stop for now. I am totally getting frustrated, and I might accidentally rip off your head."

Bradley looked alarmed.

"Just kidding. But seriously, I am getting frustrated."

"Maybe we should get something to eat."

I didn't want a break; I wanted an end. And as for eating, well, I was already having a serious helping of humble pie and was worried I might choke on it.

He walked me back to my apartment, where I hoped I could thank him and say good-bye at the door.

"Do you mind if I stay and watch conference with you?" Bradley invited himself in, and I couldn't dissuade him.

I did mind but couldn't be rude enough to come out and say it. So I tried to keep it as platonic as possible and excused myself for a nap as soon as it was over.

* * *

I made sure I called my mother on Sunday evening before my roommates' impending return.

"Did you watch conference?"

"Yes."

"All four sessions? Saturday and Sunday?"

"Yes, Mom."

"What talk did you like best?"

I felt like she was quizzing me. Or maybe I was just in a bad mood from all of my dwelling? "I don't know, Mom. They were all good."

"They were, weren't they?"

"Yes."

"Did you do anything else exciting this weekend?"

I could have told her about Bradley, but that would have been opening a can of worms. Besides, I wasn't all that excited about Bradley.

Chapter Eight
RMs

I COULD HAVE BEEN HAVING a baby right about now, I thought as I held the bowling ball in front of me. Travis had suggested it two months into our marriage. At the time, I freaked out and said no. I wasn't ready to have a baby. Travis was unhappy that I didn't want to go along with his idea, and I was not willing to budge. But really, a man didn't leave his wife because she didn't agree to getting pregnant on a whim, did he?

I had added a block bowling class to my schedule because I thought it would be easy. That was before I knew about bowling techniques. Who knew? I thought all it required was throwing the ball down the alley and hitting the pins. Other than that and the ugly shoes, I was actually enjoying the class.

After my first embarrassing class, where I slipped on the alley part of the floor, set off the buzzer, and accidentally threw the ball backward, it wasn't too bad. I liked it because I could get some anger and aggression out. Every time I sent that ball careening down the alley, I pictured Travis's smile being the pins, and it was the most satisfying feeling when they got knocked down. If it hadn't been so satisfying, I probably wouldn't have returned after the first class. But it turned out that bowling was surprisingly enjoyable.

Of course, it came with its hazards—namely the male population of the class.

I saw it coming before it got here. Well, I should say, I saw *him* coming before he even made it over to me.

"I'm Ethan." He confidently shook my hand.

"Uh, hi?" I didn't want to appear too eager.

"And you are?" He tried catching my eye.

"Sophia," I said but meant, "Not interested."

He was good-looking. Probably the best-looking guy in the class. He looked like a Brad Pitt knockoff with blond hair, blue eyes, and full lips. I couldn't have cared less if he was, in fact, Brad Pitt.

Not. Interested.

"You have quite a powerful throw there. It's a little all over the place but definitely powerful," he said.

"You think so?" I asked cautiously. I knew bowling was the common ground, but then the conversation would turn to our personal lives.

"Definitely. You could blow any of the other girls in the class away with the energy and velocity you put behind your throws."

I wondered what his major was and if he was going to start analyzing my throws using the $E=MC^2$ formula. And what was up with the "powerful" words and banter? I wondered how much energy and at what velocity it had taken him to assess all the other girls in the class and come up with the conclusion that I had the most powerful throw.

"I picture my ex as one of the bowling pins, and, wow, it gives me such focus."

Ethan/Brad took a step back, cocked his head, and wrinkled his brow. "What?" Clearly, he wasn't sure he'd heard me correctly.

"Yeah, I picture my ex, and I can put force behind my throws."

"Have you, um . . . been broken up for long?" Suddenly his air of arrogance became one of caution.

"Couple of months," I said nonchalantly, held up the ball, eyed the pins, and let the ball go. It went right into the gutter.

"Are you ready to move on?" He shifted his weight to his other foot.

I waited for my ball to return. "No. I'm sort of on a self-imposed dating sabbatical."

"What about getting together for bowling? You could consider it doing homework."

I set the ball down and looked at him in disbelief. "I just told you I felt like knocking out my ex. Isn't that a little . . . I don't know . . . psycho to you?" I shrugged my shoulders and looked at him expectantly.

I suddenly imagined him tearing out of the east entrance of the Wilk and running smack into a bus passing on Campus Drive. I didn't need a bus crash injury to Ethan/Brad on my conscience, so I softened up a bit.

"It wouldn't be a good idea. I still have some anger issues." I was hoping that was nice but still enough to ward him off.

He looked sheepish. "Well, I was thinking you would have a good enough time with me that you wouldn't want to do that." He kind of slowed down at the end of his statement.

"You know," I said, "maybe we could just be lane buddies?" Hopefully *buddies* wouldn't give him too much encouragement? *Classmates* might have been a better choice of words.

His body seemed to relax all at once. (Had he been holding his breath?) "Yeah, okay, that's cool. We can be bowling buddies."

Oh. My. He obviously took the wrong meaning from our conversation, but at least he wasn't going to get hit by a bus. I wasn't sure if I had completely dodged the Ethan/Brad dating bullet though. I worried he would be persistent.

When I showed up for class on Thursday, I was apprehensive about Ethan/Brad. I hoped he wasn't planning on partnering up every class.

He wasn't there when I walked into the bowling lanes. I wasn't sure what I preferred. If he'd already been there, I could have easily given him a casual wave and then chosen a different lane. But having him not there made it possible for him to join me.

My problem was solved, not by me but by a nice, slightly awkward, slightly older guy.

He approached me. "Do you want to share a lane?"

"Um." I hesitated. "Okay."

"I'm Ned."

"Sophia."

"It's nice to meet you." He stuck his hand out. It was sweaty. Was he nervous?

I'd escaped the Ethan/Brad dilemma but now faced a new one.

"Do you want to get an ice cream after class?"

I debated. No, I didn't. I didn't want to give Ned the wrong impression. But I felt bad. I could tell it was taking all of his courage to ask me that much.

"Um, I can't." I tried being nice.

He was crestfallen. "I knew it. You have a boyfriend, right?"

"No, that's not it."

"You're not interested?"

Yes, that was it, but it was nothing personal. "I'm not dating right now. Self-imposed ban." His expression kept getting more and more disappointed.

I took pity on him because I felt bad. "Okay, I'll go, but only on a strictly friend basis."

He jumped at the offer. I hoped he didn't think there was still a chance.

"So where are you from?" he asked as we walked to the Cougareat.

"Las Vegas. How about you?"

"Born and raised in Idaho."

"You didn't want to go to BYU–Idaho?" I wondered out loud.

"No."

We stood in line for a couple of minutes waiting to order our shakes.

"What year are you?" he asked.

"I'm a freshman. How about you?"

"Senior."

"So you're graduating this year?" I asked.

"Yes."

There was another pause. I didn't know what add.

He started up again. "What's your major?"

"Um, I don't know yet. What's yours?"

"Computer Science major, Math minor."

It was painful. He was nice enough, but there was no connection. I hoped Ned would feel the lack of clicking and settle for just friends. I could never have too many bowling buddies, right?

"What about horse riding? Do you like horses?" He continued searching for common ground.

I pictured myself getting up on a saddle on one side and falling off the saddle on the other side. I shook the image from my head.

"No. I would fall and break my leg, be trampled, get a concussion or something. Plus, horses scare me. They seem like big, hairy bullies. I'm worried one would step on my foot."

He laughed out loud at my ridiculous fears. "Have you been around them much?"

"No," I admitted. "Horses never were my thing. I'm not much of an animal lover. Dogs make me sneeze."

"So what is your thing?"

I didn't want to get that personal.

"So you like animals?" I said, redirecting the conversation.

"Horses. I grew up on a farm."

"My roommate Sarah likes animals." A lightbulb went on. "You know, you two would have a lot in common. She's a really nice girl. Maybe you'd like to be set up?"

He hesitated. I could tell he was debating. Give up on me and accept the offer or hold out hope that there might be a chance with me.

"She's nice?"

"Very."

"Pretty?"

"She's a cute girl. She's very sweet."

"Sweet as in sweet spirit, or sweet as in *sw*-eet?"

Maybe Ned was not the right man for the job. In terms of guys, I would consider *him* a sweet spirit. He was more nice than handsome.

"Listen, Ned. She is by no means a charity date. But no pressure. I thought since you were both animal lovers, you might hit it off."

"Sorry. I've been set up with a couple of weirdos before. I want to make sure she's normal."

"No worries," I reassured him. "She's quite normal." I only hoped he was.

"Okay, then, I'll give it a try."

"Give me your phone number, and I'll have her call you."

"Okay." His enthusiasm was evident.

* * *

I was remiss in talking to Sarah about Ned until Rhonda reminded me the next night. It wasn't something she said but what she was doing. Usually, about this time on Friday, she was baking a batch of cookies for the Friday-night hangout. Instead, Rhonda was in a frenzy.

"What's wrong?" I had suspicions it had to do with a boy, but there was the slim possibility it didn't.

"I invited a guy over for dinner, and I burned it. Dang it!"

"You have a date? What about the standing Friday-night plans?"

She looked at me like I was crazy. "A date is more important."

"Is it Landon?"

"Landon? No. I'm not interested in him anymore."

I wondered if his tuna casserole had changed her mind. "Who is it, then?"

"Darren," she said dreamily.

"Darren?" I hadn't heard of him before. "How did you meet him?"

"Oh, we haven't officially met yet. I found him on Facebook."

"You haven't met him in person, but he's here at BYU, and you met him online?"

"Yes. Isn't that so romantic?"

BYU had a male population of I don't know how many thousands, all readily available to meet in person, and Rhonda was meeting people online? "Be careful, Rhonda. What a person presents to you isn't always how that person really is." I should know.

"No, he's a nice guy. But I don't know what to do about dinner. I wanted to make a good impression."

"What about going out to dinner?"

"I don't want him to feel obligated to pay. And I can't afford it."

"You know, Rhonda, you don't have to cook to impress him. You can still get married even if you don't cook."

She looked at me, incredulous. "How would you know? You don't cook, and you're not married."

If she only knew. "Well, Martha Stewart cooks, is a good cook, and she's divorced. So, see? Cooking doesn't seal the deal in marriage."

"I disagree. I think it's important. It could make or break the impression I give him."

"Can you make something different?" I couldn't blame Rhonda for wanting to make a good first impression. I had been like that with Travis. But I had a different perspective a year later and definitely a different opinion from Rhonda.

"He's going to be here in an hour. What am I going to do?"

I knew what I'd be doing in an hour: laundry. But since there was no rush to hit the laundry room, I could spare some time to help Rhonda out of her predicament.

"Okay. Go get ready, and I'll work on dinner."

"But you don't know how to cook," she wailed.

"Rhonda, please. Give me some credit."

She reluctantly gave in and took a shower.

I found two identical frozen dinners. Chicken with creamy cheesy sauce with pimentos and green peppercorns. Crisis averted. Pop them in the microwave, and viola! Dinner. I made a batch of Minute Rice to serve with it. All while Rhonda was in the shower.

Sarah came home right about then. "What are you doing? Are you having company?" She seemed to perk up at the thought of my entertaining someone.

"Oh, no. Not me. Rhonda. She's freaking out. She has a date, but she burned dinner and didn't have a backup plan. So I made her some frozen dinners and instant rice."

"That was nice of you." Sarah surveyed the alternate dinner.

In the back, I could hear the shower shut off.

She then rolled her eyes. "Presentation is very important to Rhonda. She thinks how she presents her food is a reflection of herself."

Presentation. Sarah's comment made me stop for a moment. Presentation was very important, even to me. Not that I presented myself very well lately with my yoga pants and my messy hair, but the way other people presented themselves to me was important. When my mom suggested something, all super happy and upbeat, my first reaction was to bristle against it. But if my counselor, Dave, suggested something, I was usually willing to at least consider it. If a guy came up to me all cocky and arrogant, I was immediately turned off. But if the guy seemed humble and kind, I could deal with it better.

"Maybe it would help if I set the table," Sarah said.

"She probably would appreciate it," I agreed.

After Sarah set the table with our apartment's finest melamine, she stepped back to admire her work. "What do you think?"

"It looks nice."

Sarah looked at me. "This has been kind of fun, hasn't it?"

I nodded. It had been kind of fun. Just a little. Which reminded me. "Hey, Sarah, there's a guy in my bowling class I was thinking of maybe setting you up with. What do you think?"

"Sure, why not? Would it be a double date with you?"

I laughed out loud at the suggestion. "No, probably not with me. But I'm sure Rhonda would be willing to do it with you. As we can tell," I motioned to the table, "she likes to date."

Sarah nodded in agreement as we went to see if Rhonda needed help. Having Sarah point out the importance of the evening from Rhonda's perspective made me a little more willing to help her make the good impression she so desperately wanted.

"Is there anything else you need help with?" I asked. She stood at the vanity, doing leg lifts. Rhonda did leg lifts every time she was at the vanity. Whether it was drying her hair, brushing her teeth, or applying makeup. Even with the new perspective for Rhonda's point of view, I still found her multitasking funny. Exercising while getting ready for a date? Seemed like a contradiction, in my opinion. She was already dressed, her hair in a towel, and she was applying mascara.

"I could flat iron your hair. I think it'd be a good look for you," I said.

"Um, I don't know. I was going to use my hot rollers."

Big hair. Smooth hair. I would encourage the smooth hair. "Let me try a little bit, and if you don't like it, you can use your hot rollers."

"I don't have time. I still need to figure out dinner."

"We have it all taken care of," Sarah said.

"Yeah," I said. "I made some chicken with cream sauce over rice, and Sarah set the table. You can wow him with your cooking next time."

"It's all done?" Rhonda's expression did not hide her astonishment.

"Yeah, unless you want help doing your hair."

"Thanks, Sophia, but I'm going to use my hot rollers. Thank you, guys, for helping me with dinner though. That was so nice."

"Sure, no problem," I said.

I think Rhonda was surprised.

I think I was a little surprised.

I was also a little surprised a few minutes later when I overheard Sarah and Rhonda talking at the vanity. I was in my bedroom gathering my dirty laundry, not paying much attention until I heard the word *divorced*.

"Divorced?" Sarah sounded surprised and interested.

My ears perked up. I held my breath and waited, my heart pounding wildly. Were they talking about me? Had they found out somehow?

"Yeah, Claire says he's like twenty-three and already divorced."

Phew. It wasn't me. It could be anyone.

"How does she know him?"

"He's in one of her classes she's a TA for," Rhonda said vaguely.

"Wow. Weird. I guess even Mormons get divorced."

How little they knew.

Chapter Nine

Intervention

SUNDAY AFTER CHURCH WE HAD a roommate meeting scheduled. Apparently, there were some unresolved issues needing to be addressed. I wasn't sure what they were, but weighing what they might possibly be against my own issues, I figured they would pale in comparison. I planned to sit back and tune it all out for the time it took to iron out the minor infractions that naturally happened when living with others.

I had no idea I'd be blindsided.

Rhonda called the "meeting" to order. "There are a few things we'd like to discuss with you, Sophia."

With me? Wait a minute.

Sarah noticed my shocked expression. "We're concerned," she said gently, touching my knee.

"The crumbs are enough to drive me insane, Sophia!" Claire broke in. She had left me a yellow sticky note about it once, stuck to the counter where the toaster had been. I crumpled it up and threw it away, then swept the crumbs off the counter and into the sink. It wasn't a big deal.

They were concerned about crumbs on the counter? Really?

"Crumbs?" I asked in disbelief.

"Well, it's not just that, Sophia." Rhonda jumped in.

Claire continued with her rant. "I don't understand why you leave crumbs all over the counter. Is it too hard to pick them up?"

Why was Claire verbally attacking me over some stupid crumbs? Sometimes I decided to mix things up a little and *toast* my Pop-Tart. The crumbs were a result of moving the toaster in and out of my cupboard. I usually did a quick sweep of the counter but seemed to have missed a few. "I'm sorry, Claire. I didn't realize it was such a source of—" I searched for an appropriate word—"discontentment to you. I will clean up after myself better." I figured the apology would end the part I played in this roomie meeting, but Claire continued her tirade.

"What about the bathroom?" she asked, referring to the bathroom we shared.

"What about it?"

"It never gets cleaned. It is so disgusting I don't want to use it."

"And?" I wasn't sure where she was going with this.

"What Claire is trying to say, is—" Sarah started to say.

"Why don't you clean it?" Claire cut her off. "You're home all day. You have nothing else to do."

I bristled against her observation. "How would you know? You're hardly ever here."

Claire's eyes narrowed. "I know how you are."

How was I? I wondered. But we were getting off track. "Last I checked, Claire, you use that bathroom too. Why is it my responsibility to clean it?"

"You use it more." Claire was very worked up. She was shaking her head while passionately flailing her arms. "I barely use it."

She was kidding, right? She was quantifying who should clean the bathroom by who used it more? *Really*? Why hadn't she gone to her brother's house today?

"So what are you proposing, Claire? I clean the bathroom three Saturdays and you clean it one Saturday every month?" Sarcasm was dangerously close to taking over.

"I want you to take responsibility for your messes." Her eyes were ablaze with emotion.

I wanted to keep her from going all psycho over the cleaning issue. But thinking she might not receive it in the right spirit, I simply said, "Okay. Point taken. Anything else?" I was getting defensive. How stupid and petty for her to get so worked up over nothing.

"Well, actually, yes. There is something else," Rhonda hedged a little.

Great. What else? I couldn't think of anything else I could possibly be doing wrong. I kept to myself and minded my own business. Was Rhonda going to bring up the socializing issue she always nagged me about? Did she think it was serious enough to have a roommate meeting over it?

"We're worried about your weight," Sarah said quietly.

"My weight?" I repeated. Why? I wasn't overweight. I wasn't underweight. Sure, I had lost weight since my divorce, but I wasn't *worried* about it.

Rhonda agreed with Sarah. "You're very thin."

"You never eat," Claire said, a scowl on her face.

She seemed to know an awful lot for someone who was never home. Were the other roommates getting together and having secret early morning apartment meetings while I slept in? Why would *Claire* think I never ate?

I managed a laugh. "You think I'm anorexic?" That's what they suspected? Didn't we just get finished talking about all the crumbs I left on the counter? I refrained from rolling my eyes.

I pointed a thumb at Claire. "Shouldn't you be worried about her? She's the one who counts her crackers. I'm not worried about my weight. So don't you worry, girls. I'm not anorexic. I eat. Every day."

"It wasn't anorexia we were worried about," Sarah mumbled, staring at the floor.

Gosh. Spit it out! I was getting hungry with all this talk of food.

Rhonda took over. "We were thinking more like bulimia."

I laughed. "I hate throwing up. It's definitely not bulimia." I hated throwing up more than I hated Travis. Throwing up was one of the more shallow reasons I didn't want to get pregnant.

"Then what is it?" Claire demanded. She was at the end of her patience.

"What is what?"

I knew what they were looking for. They were looking for a reason. They were looking for an explanation. They wanted to know what was wrong with me. All valid questions. But none I was willing to answer or explain. I had worked too hard guarding my secret to tell them the truth.

"What is the problem?" Claire asked again.

I though it through very carefully. Telling them would open a whole other can of worms. But what could I say that would quell their concerns?

Aha! "I didn't want to come to college. My family made me. I didn't have much choice in the matter."

"That's it? That's all?" Sarah's words came out as a gush of relief.

"You don't want to be at BYU?" Rhonda openly expressed her surprise.

"Are we done now? I need to get to my brother's." Claire's concern was evident. I could tell what *she* was worried about. But that was okay; I wanted her to go.

As Claire stiffly stood from the couch and walked away, I followed her into our bedroom.

"Claire, you know, I feel like you don't like me. Did I do something?" I didn't think I had, but Claire never seemed very friendly toward me. Not that she was a warm, fuzzy person to begin with.

"I have a plan for what I want to accomplish in my life, and part of that is getting into graduate school. I am paying for school myself and need to maintain the scholarships I have. I don't have time for distractions and drama."

I looked at her, confused. "I don't understand."

"Sophia, you just scream drama queen, and I don't want to get caught up in your drama. I have enough stuff to deal with at home and at school."

I hadn't realized I was affecting her life in any of the ways she'd mentioned. "I'm sorry, I . . ." I didn't know quite what I was apologizing for.

"I get that you're having a hard time or whatever"—she looked at her watch—"but I just don't have time for anything but school. And now I need to go."

She whisked by me and left me sitting on my bed in awe. Wow. I knew how serious she was about school, but having people skills also went a long way in furthering your success in life. She reminded me of my ex-mother-in-law, with her bossy and blunt personality. I decided it was best to stay out of her way and wait the school year out. I didn't know how else to deal with someone like Claire.

When I heard her leave, I went back into the living room. Sarah and Rhonda sat on either side of me on the couch.

Sarah hugged me. "I'm sorry, I didn't realize you weren't enjoying school."

"You know," Rhonda said, "it gets better. It's only October. You're still adjusting. I had a hard time when I was a freshman. It was very overwhelming. But we'll help you get through it." She also gave me a hug.

"Don't worry, you can do it," Sarah said.

I had only revealed the tip of the iceberg about my problem, and it had released a flood of goodwill, advice, and shows of love and concern. How would they react if they knew the truth?

Sarah and Rhonda continued their stream of advice.

"Maybe if you got out more, you would enjoy yourself more."

"We could try and make things less contentious in the apartment."

"What about having apartment prayer?"

"We should set up some rules."

"Maybe we should call them guidelines."

"Claire's opinion about cleaning responsibilities is a little extreme."

"Maybe a chore chart would help."

I tuned them out. I was exhausted. And I hadn't even called my mother yet.

Chapter Ten
Confessions

By Friday I was quite ready to go to my counseling appointment. I needed to tell someone about my intervention. If I wasn't so mad about it, maybe I would have found it funny.

Dave, my counselor, sometimes doubled as my personal cheerleader and was there to talk me off the ledge, so to speak, when I felt like my life was too much of a train wreck. It was like I was attending a pep rally. So far, I seemed to like talking to Dave.

He reminded me of a big Ewok. I would have said teddy bear, but from the moment I stepped into his office, it was quite obvious he was a Star Wars fan. There was Star Wars memorabilia decorating the tops of his bookshelves and little figurines on his desk.

My parents would have approved of him, since they were Star Wars fans themselves. Every couple of months while I was growing up, my parents would have a Star Wars–themed family night. My mom would make chocolate tortilla chips named Darth Vader chips and make huge cinnamon rolls named Princess Leia buns. We would sit and eat and watch the trilogy together.

It was fun when I was younger, but as I became a teenager and Luke Skywalker didn't seem so cute anymore, I lost interest. My parents and brother, on the other hand, still fully enjoyed a Star Wars night, complete with namesake Star Wars treats.

I settled into my chair, anxious to start my session. "My roommates staged an intervention on Sunday."

"Did they now?"

"Yes, they sure did. They seem to be under the impression that I am bulimic."

"Are you?"

I shook my head vehemently. "Most definitely not. I hate throwing up."

"What do you think prompted this?"

"My behavior. They are trying to figure out what's wrong with me."

"Did you tell them?"

"No way."

He leaned forward in his chair. "What's the worst thing that could happen if you told someone?"

I thought about it for a minute. If I told someone, I was admitting it was real, that it was true. I told him my secondary concern instead. "It would get passed around the ward. I don't want to be labeled or judged."

"So you see it as a stigma?"

"Yeah."

"Maybe if you told one of your roommates about your divorce, you could start trusting others again."

I furrowed my brow. "You don't think I trust people?"

"Do you?"

Did I? I didn't think not telling my roommates about my divorce showed a lack of trust in them. I thought it was more a reflection of my not wanting to accept it.

"I don't think I know them enough to trust them with that information yet."

"Have you made any effort to get to know them?"

"No. Yes. I mean, I don't completely ignore them, but I'm not interested in hanging out with them."

"Why?"

"Because if I'm friends with them, it's harder to keep my secret. Eventually, it would come out that I'm divorced."

He smiled encouragingly. "And would that be so bad?"

I slouched back into the chair, my shoulders drooping. "Haven't we been over this already?"

"I want you to think about confiding in someone."

I was exasperated. "But if I tell someone, I'm admitting it's over."

"You don't want to admit it's over? Why?"

"Because I hope it isn't. Maybe there's still a chance." I shrugged. "Maybe he will realize he made a mistake."

"Do you think he made a mistake?"

"Yes."

"Do you think *he* thinks he made a mistake?"

I couldn't emphatically answer yes to that. I chewed on my lip instead.

"Sophia, are you being realistic?"

"I know you don't think I am, but . . ."

"Has he called you since the divorce?"

"No."

"Texted? E-mailed? Has he tried to have any sort of contact with you?"

"No."

"So what does that tell you?"

"That I'm stupid to keep hoping he's going to change his mind."

"I wouldn't say *stupid*. But I think you need to consider that it's really over."

Hearing that made me want to cry. I wasn't completely ready to let go. "Sure, no problem. I'll get right on that." I felt defeated. In my head, I knew I needed to move on, but I was having a hard time getting my heart to cooperate.

"Sophia, maybe if you confide in someone, it will also help you accept that it is over."

That's exactly the reason I didn't tell anyone.

"Have you thought about journaling? I think it will help you sort through your feelings."

No. I didn't think about journaling. "I bought a journal," I told him. But I had absolutely nothing written in it. I didn't want to journal because writing it down made it so much more real than just thinking it in my head. On good days, I could convince myself I was moving on. On bad days, there was that glimmer of hope that we might get back together. I *was* trying to move on, but a tiny, itty-bitty part of me still loved Travis. And that same itty-bitty, tiny part of me secretly hoped maybe, somehow, he might still want to work it out.

* * *

After my jovial meeting with the counselor, I had a lot on my mind. Did I still love Travis? Did I want to get back with him? How could I stop loving him just because a piece of paper said he was no longer mine to love? But at the same time, I hated him for hurting me. I didn't know what I wanted. Did I want to hold on and hope or try to move on and have a little faith that there was something better in store for me?

Originally, Travis said he needed space and time. I earnestly tried to give him that by not calling him (too often) or texting him (too much).

But what kept me in such a state of ambivalence was something I hadn't told my counselor. It was the one phone conversation that had given me just enough hope to hold on. It had been barely a month since *that day*, and the papers had just arrived in the mail, needing only my signature to finalize the divorce. I called him, begging and pleading with him to change his mind.

When it was obvious—painfully obvious—he was not going to change his mind, I finally conceded. "Fine, okay. I'll sign them." Then, in a moment of bravado, I added, "But you are going to miss me and be sorry you ever left me."

To which he murmured, "Maybe I will." Then he let out a breath. "But I don't think so."

So I kept waiting for the day when he would realize he *did* miss me and *was* sorry he left me. Because maybe he would be.

Could you blame me?

* * *

Rhonda greeted me at the door when I got home, with Sarah right behind her. I was so deep in thought, they scared me. I was nervous they might launch another roomie meeting/intervention.

"Aren't you supposed to be in class, Rhonda?"

"I came home early." She was almost giddy. She wouldn't be giddy about an intervention. What could be so exciting and important that Rhonda would skip class?

"The ward talent show is tonight. Remember?" She did the clapping in succession thing and then said in a singsongy voice, "We need to figure out what we are going to do."

"You're not serious, are you?" One look at Rhonda's face and I could tell how serious she was.

What was I thinking questioning her seriousness of this activity?

"I know. How about we do a roommate dance, like a choreographed jazz routine?" Rhonda said.

Me dancing was a scary thought. I'd be the one who would misstep and fall off the stage. "No way," I said, clearing my throat. I did not want to make a spectacle of myself. "No. Especially in front of people. No." I shook my head adamantly.

Sarah was not on board either. "I don't like to get up in front of people."

"What about Claire? Is she going to be a part of this whole talent routine thing?" I asked. Misery loved company, and this was definitely going to be an exercise in misery. I couldn't imagine Claire up on a stage dancing any more than I could see Sarah or myself.

"Oh, I doubt it. She'll probably be studying like she does every Friday night," Sarah said.

"Wait. Wait. I've got it." Rhonda was not to be dissuaded. "How about we sing a song? Maybe from a musical, like *Pocahontas*."

I burst out laughing. "You want us to sing a Pocahontas song? It's a Disney movie."

"What's wrong with Disney movies? I like Disney movies." Rhonda looked wounded.

Sarah stared at Rhonda, speechless.

I attempted to soften the blow. "There's nothing wrong with them. I like them too. I just don't want to be in front of the whole ward singing 'Just Around the River Bend.' I was kind of hoping you'd be the token roommate and do something to represent us all."

Sarah was quick to jump on board. "I agree with Sophia."

"Well, that's no fun." Rhonda pouted. "We need to do something together."

"No. We could just be inactive," I said, since that was my original plan.

"You never want to do anything. You're a killjoy."

I was about to argue with her, telling her I didn't appreciate the personal dig, when I realized it was true. I was the cynical voice. It was not her fault I had failed at marriage.

"You're right. I am," I said, agreeing solemnly, then went to my bedroom.

Rhonda came in a few minutes later to apologize.

"You're okay," I told her. "It's not about the talent show."

"What is it, then?" Rhonda said almost demandingly.

"I don't want to be up in front of everyone, especially if we're singing. I'm not that great of a singer or dancer." In fact, none of us in the apartment was a great singer. I could imagine us up there slaughtering the song. No thanks.

"We can do something else. Come on, come help us plan." Rhonda put her arm around my shoulder.

I needed an excuse, and I needed one fast. If I didn't, Rhonda was sure to get me on stage one way or the other.

"I should get dressed," I announced, since I was still in yoga pants. Rhonda left me alone and went back to the kitchen.

I rummaged through my closet and found a white cotton button-down shirt I hadn't worn all semester. I had jeans somewhere. Where were they? I found one pair in the back of my closet. When I pulled them on, they slid down to my hips. I threw them back into the depths of my closet.

I finally settled on a black skirt that didn't look too dressy. Honestly, I had no idea what I had for clothes in my closet. I had accumulated quite a collection of comfy clothes that I usually opted for, leaving the other ones untouched. So many clothes, so little motivation to wear them.

I joined the other two back in the kitchen. Sad to say, they had decided to go with a *Pocahontas* song. All the more reason to avoid the social. It ended up working out better than planned when I opened a fresh can of Diet Coke at precisely the same time Rhonda wondered out loud if we'd be able to find feathers for headpieces. I started laughing, promptly choked, and consequently spewed soda all down my shirt. "I can't believe I did that," I said loudly, getting their attention. "This is going to stain. I better go wash it."

"Oh, yeah, it will," Sarah said, offering me a napkin.

"I should change." I went back into my bedroom, changed back into my yoga pants, and quickly gathered my laundry. If I made a fast exit, maybe I could escape being any part of tonight's talent. I purposely left my cell phone in my room.

"Try to hurry, or you'll miss the talent show," Rhonda said as I was leaving.

"Don't wait for me. I don't want you to be late." I avoided committing to showing up.

I let out a sigh of relief as I headed for the stairwell. Looking forward to laundry wasn't the most exciting thing to do on a Friday night, but anything was better than participating in the ward talent show. Plus, there was always the risk of running into Bradley at the activity. Not that that was a bad thing, but I didn't want to be paired off with him for the evening if he was there. I was trying not to encourage him.

"Hey, Sophia," Luke greeted me as I walked into the basement laundry room. Other than him, it was empty. It was the perfect hideout.

"Luke, hi." I wanted to be alone, but Luke was an okay enough guy.

"Are you ditching the talent show?" He smiled easily.

"How did you know?" How *did* he know?

"That's why I'm here." He laughed.

"Um, yes, but don't tell on me, please. My roommates were going to perform a Disney song."

"My apartment was invited by a girl's apartment to do a spoof on *Twilight*. Either that or sing a song a cappella wearing togas. Not exactly my thing." Luke rolled his eyes.

"Your secret's safe with me."

He jokingly let out a big breath. "Thanks for sparing me."

"The laundry room is a pretty safe place to hide out on a Friday night."

Luke gave me a questioning look. "Do you come here often on Friday nights?"

"I've started to. Otherwise, Rhonda is always trying to get me to join her standing group hang-out thing or set me up on a date."

"Oh yeah." He nodded. "Your allergy to testosterone."

I blushed a little. I might never live that comment down. "Something like that."

"Oreo?" Luke took a package out of a grocery bag.

"I'd love one. Oreos are my favorite."

"Mine too. Although, there will be ice cream sundaes after the talent show. You could show up in time for dessert."

I cringed. "No, thanks, I'm trying to avoid the activity altogether. I prefer Oreos anyway."

"Me too." He held out the package of Oreos to me. "More?"

"Sure, thanks."

Oreos made doing laundry better, I decided.

Chapter Eleven

Scary

HALLOWEEN WAS, WELL, SCARY.

My Halloween plans included not dressing up and not going out. Instead, I had a date with my laundry. Rhonda, on the other hand, had plans.

The smell of popcorn accosted me when I entered the apartment. Rhonda was up to her elbows in a mound of caramel popcorn covering our countertop.

"Quick. Grab the saucepan off the stove. It's going to burn," she said without even a glance.

I moved the pan. "What are you doing?" I asked.

"Making popcorn balls, of course."

Yes, it was Halloween, but was she expecting trick-or-treaters, or was she having a get-together?

"Could you dump that over there?" She pointed a sticky hand to the counter next to the sink. There was another mound of popcorn on top of wax paper.

How long had it taken her to pop all this popcorn?

I carefully poured the hot caramel mixture over the popcorn heap. "What's this for?"

"A treat."

"For what?"

"The get-together. Sarah's going out with that guy, Ned, you set her up with, and I invited someone from my math class and few others. We're going to that huge corn maze. You should come."

"I don't know . . ."

"Gosh, Sophia. Lighten up; live a little. Don't you ever want to have fun?"

"Is this another intervention?"

"Come on." Rhonda stomped her foot in frustration. "Why is it like moving a mountain to get you to go out?"

"There's more to life than boys and dating, cooking to impress, and getting a ring by spring."

"Like what? Tell me what more you have in your life? You never seem happy. You never do anything." She waited. "Wouldn't it be nice to have some harmless fun for once?"

I considered it for a moment. She did have a point.

"Okay. I'll go."

"Great. You wait. It's going to be so fun."

I didn't share her enthusiasm, but maybe getting out would be good for me. And I had an excuse to bow out early, since I needed to do my laundry.

I started reconsidering my decision when Rhonda appeared from her bedroom in a full Snow White costume. Was her date coming as a prince? "Hurry, Sophia, you need to put on your costume."

"You're wearing a costume to the corn maze? Why?"

"It's Halloween. It's part of the fun."

"I'm not completely convinced about the fun part."

"It will be. Besides, Bradley's coming."

Rhonda probably thought she was doing me a favor by inviting Bradley. And maybe in a different life, I would have appreciated it. But I didn't need help encouraging Bradley, I needed help *dis*-couraging Bradley. Nicely, of course.

Claire made a surprise appearance, coming home earlier than usual from campus. She took one look at Rhonda in her Halloween costume and stopped dead.

"Are you having people over *again*?"

"No, we're going out," Rhonda said easily.

"Good, 'cause I need to go to bed early. I have to take a test at the testing center tomorrow morning." She changed her clothes before heading into the kitchen to eat a sandwich, then started gathering her book bag up again.

"What are you doing?" I wondered.

"Going back to the library to study." She slung her bag over her shoulder and left.

Claire was acting strange. She hadn't ever come home to change her clothes to go back to campus to study, that I knew of. Was she meeting someone?

* * *

We ended up with eight of us going. Which meant two cars. Bradley offered to drive and led Sarah, Ned, and me over to a rugged jeep with big wheels.

"Wow," I said. "You don't mess around with your vehicles."

"I need something that can do all the things I want to do."

"Like what?" Sarah asked.

"I do a lot of hiking and camping and rock climbing. I want to be able to drive over rugged terrain and not get stuck."

"Cool." Ned nodded in approval.

"I've taken this Jeep everywhere—Grand Canyon, Jackson Hole, Bend, Moab."

"Moab's cool." Ned continued the conversation while I tried to figure out where Bend was. I'd never heard of it before.

"We should go for a weekend. It's still warm during the days."

"I haven't ever been to Moab. I hear it's very pretty. Isn't that where Arches is?" Sarah said.

Bradley was in his element. "Yeah, it's awesome. You can go hiking, biking . . ."

All the stuff that endangered my life. After my failed attempt at skiing, I tried to be brutally honest with people about my outdoor skills, or lack thereof. More confirmation that I was so not the girl for him.

The wait in line at the corn maze was about half an hour. Bradley carried the conversation, holding everyone's attention with stories of rock climbing and river rafting and wanting to live in the jungles of South America doing humanitarian aid. His stories were fascinating but still not enough to make me interested.

Once in the maze, Bradley held back from the group a little. "I know a short cut," he said and went the opposite direction of the group.

"Are you sure?" How would he know? Had he done this before?

He smiled and reached out for me. I think he wanted to hold my hand. "How?" I kept both hands firmly planted in my coat pockets but let him guide me by the elbow.

"My internal GPS." He tapped his forehead.

I think his internal GPS got all screwed up by some gigantic magnetic force field because he only succeeded in getting us lost.

"Wrong again." He laughed as we came to a wall of corn stalks for the second time.

I wasn't finding this all that fun. Maybe if we had stuck with the group, we wouldn't have kept running into dead ends. "I hope the others aren't worried about us."

Bradley walked next to me. "How about we ditch this lame party when we get out and go have dinner at Thanksgiving Point?"

I said the first thing that popped into my head. "But what about the popcorn?"

Oh my gosh. Did I really just say that?

"Who cares about the popcorn?"

"How will Sarah and Ned get home?"

"They can squeeze into the other car. It's not that long of a drive."

"That's not nice of us to bail."

"C'mon," Bradley said. "Let's go someplace where we can be alone."

I started laughing, mostly to hide the fact that I was getting a little annoyed. "We are alone, remember? We're lost in a corn maze."

I started retracing the path we had just followed. The whole corn maze fun was fading quickly, and I was ready to rejoin the others.

"Hey, wait up." Bradley jogged up to me. "What's the hurry?"

"We should find the others." I hoped I didn't sound too impatient.

"Sophia."

I stopped walking and turned. "Yes?"

He put his hands on my arms. "I don't want to find the others." He tilted his face and leaned into me.

I took a step back, stunned. "What are you doing?"

Bradley looked surprise. "I thought I was kissing you."

"Don't do that." I stumbled over my words.

"Why not?"

"Because *that's* not what *this* is." I shook my head.

His voice took on a hint of anger. "What is *this*?"

"I don't know. We hang out a little . . ."

"You've got to realize how I feel."

I chewed on my lip. "No, actually I don't."

"So you're leading me on?"

"No. Nothing like that." I thought back to my interactions with him. I had always been nice but not flirty.

"Let's go find the others," Bradley said, walking past me.

Driving home was quiet and awkward, to say the least.

Rhonda was directing the group toward our apartment as we piled out of the cars. Bradley stayed in his jeep with the engine running. Sarah and

Ned climbed out, obviously sensing by the quiet drive home that something was up.

As soon as they were out of hearing range, I started to apologize. "Bradley, I'm sorry, I . . ."

"Whatever, Sophia." He scowled at me and put his Jeep in gear.

I shut the door and watched him drive off. Gosh, I'd attempted to do something fun and had somehow screwed it up.

I skipped out on having popcorn treats, gathered my laundry, and gave Rhonda some lame excuse about Bradley having to go.

Luke was folding his laundry, almost ready to leave when I arrived.

"You're late," he said jokingly.

I chose a machine on the opposite row from him. "You would not believe the night I've had." I started dumping my laundry into a machine.

"Bad night?"

"Yeah, that's one way to put it."

"What happened?"

"Rhonda planned this group thing to go to the corn maze and then eat caramel popcorn after."

"That doesn't sound so bad."

"But she invited this guy who thought we were on a date."

"You went on a date?" Was that alarm in his voice?

"Not on purpose. There's a reason I do laundry on Friday nights." I let out a huff of air. "So Rhonda can't convince me to go do something 'fun' with her." I made quotation marks in the air with my fingers.

Luke had an amused smile on his face.

"What?" I asked, suddenly feeling self-conscious.

"So would you classify it as your worst date ever?"

"No. My worst date was going to a guy's prom when I barely knew him."

"Why did you go with him, then?"

"Well, it was kind of a favor to my dad. He was the son of my dad's coworker. My dad bribed me to go by promising to buy me something I'd wanted for a while. I was a lot more—" I almost said shallow, that being the truth, but instead decided to go with a more positive word. "Immature then and thought my dad would buy me a car."

"You got a car out of it?"

"No. I got an iPod. And a bad night."

"What happened?"

"What didn't happen? We went to an expensive restaurant, where he insisted we order hors d'oeuvres. He ordered shrimp scampi, which gave him garlic breath. Then he forced me to try some of his shrimp, which, come to find out, I have an allergy to. My lips swelled up like Angelina Jolie on collagen, and my tongue started itching. I didn't know what was happening until the waiter came over, took one look at me, flipped out, and called an ambulance. Long story short, I got a shot in the leg and never made it to the prom. He still wanted to go, but I had to talk him out of it. It was terrible. Especially since everything in high school seems like it's the end of the world."

"It's been a long time since high school. I'm halfway to my ten year reunion. I never went to prom."

"Never?" I was surprised. "Why not?"

He shrugged a shoulder. "I was too shy to ask anyone, and no one asked me."

"Honestly, you didn't miss out on anything. Prom is highly overrated."

"Thanks. I feel better now, I think."

"So how about you? Any bad dates?" I sat on a table by the washing machines.

"I went on a double date with Justin that went downhill quickly."

"I want to hear."

Luke held up his hands, trying to explain. "Okay, so you need to know Justin will go to great lengths to pick up and/or impress a girl."

"Okay."

"Justin was showing off and thought he could slide down the rail of the RB stairs in his socks. But instead, he lost his balance, fell over backward, and split his head open. We ended up taking him to the emergency room instead of going to the Brick Oven."

"That's embarrassing."

"Yeah, especially since Justin was bragging to the girl about what a great snowboarder he was. Obviously, he was exaggerating his abilities."

"He seems like he can be quite charming."

"He used to set me up on double dates with him, but . . ." He trailed off.

"You prefer to do laundry now instead of going out?"

"Yeah, something like that." He cracked a smile.

"I'm right there with you."

Chapter Twelve

Reminders

FIRST BLOCK WAS ENDING, AND I felt a little sad taking the final for my bowling class. I had come to enjoy it enough that I even considered taking another bowling class. As expected, the final was a breeze. Ned made a point of thanking me for helping him score, meaning, being set up with Sarah. It sounded like a cheesy line I would have used last year while unabashedly chasing Travis.

I stopped by Bradley's house on my way home, hoping to catch him. I felt bad with how things had ended on Halloween and wanted to apologize again. And maybe even clarify.

A roommate answered the door.

"Is Bradley home?"

"Nah, he's gone."

"When will he be home?"

The guy shook his head. "Sometime after Thanksgiving."

"You mean he's already left for Mexico?"

"A couple of days ago."

Huh. I forgot about him leaving. "Okay, I'll catch him when he gets back."

"Okay," he said and closed the door.

Guess I could put off that apology for a couple of weeks. I admit I was a mildly relieved.

Sarah came home from school with a newspaper in her hand. "I'm going out with Ned tomorrow, so I was thinking I'd get a haircut. Do you want to get a haircut with me?" Sarah asked, sounding apprehensive. "There was a two-for-one coupon in the *Daily Universe* today. It might be fun. If anything, it'll be cheap."

A haircut. How long had it been since my last one? Dave would approve. He was always telling me I needed to make an effort to start feeling better. Maybe a haircut would help.

"Sure, let's get haircuts. Why not?"

Sarah seemed pleased that I'd agreed to join her. And it was actually fun. I shouldn't have waited so long to do something nice for myself.

But cute hair could only do so much, as I came to discover later in the day when an unexpected knock brought me out of my usual haze.

"Sophia?" A guy stood at our door. Did I know him? He looked familiar.

"Yes?" I asked cautiously.

"I'm Logan. Apartment 205." He pointed vaguely over his shoulder. "Uh, we got a letter I think is yours." He held out a mangled envelope that had been forwarded several times.

I looked closer. It was for me but was addressed to Sophia Davis Duckk at the address where Travis and I had lived. It was from Gretchen Clark, my old roommate. I wondered why she wrote me an actual letter instead of e-mailing, only to remember it had been months since I had checked my e-mail account. There was a "return to sender" in Travis's handwriting, a "forward to" that went to the mission office, another "forward to" that went to Gretchen at a different address from the return address, and yet another "forward to" to my parents address. And my mom's handwriting forwarding it to me. It looked about as good as I felt: battered.

"Yes, it's mine, thank you." I started closing the door.

"Hey, wait." Logan pressed on the door.

I opened it back up.

"My friend is having a party tonight. Would you like to come?"

"Thanks, but . . . now's not a good time."

Logan smiled what would have been a charming smile in any other situation. "You sure? It's going to be fun."

"I'm very sure."

"Well, okay. Uh, see you around."

My attention immediately went back to the letter. Gretchen and I became instant friends last year, and I missed having her for a roommate. But like everything else after *that day*, I'd neglected keeping in touch.

I ripped open the envelope, but Rhonda arrived home right then. "You know, you look so much better when you do your hair."

"If that was a compliment, thanks, I think."

Rhonda set her backpack down and opened the fridge. "So why was Logan Reese here?"

Rhonda would have the whole ward directory memorized.

"He dropped off a letter." I held up the envelope, then thought of my name on the front and quickly folded it over in my hand. "It was sent to the wrong apartment."

"It looks like it got sent by the wrong mail system. How was it sent? Pony Express?"

"No, just sent to the wrong place."

"So who's it from?" Rhonda was always curious.

I couldn't say an old roommate. A missionary friend would be an easy enough explanation, but Rhonda would launch into the detailed questioning. Was it a guy? Was he my missionary? Was I waiting for him?

"A friend on a mission." I tried to sound vague.

"Do you secretly have a missionary you're waiting for? Is that why you're always so mopey?" She tried catching a glimpse of the envelope.

"No." I laughed, trying to lighten things up while also trying to surreptitiously put the letter out of sight. "I don't have a missionary."

Rhonda stared at me. Her eyes narrowed a bit. "Are you sure?"

I snorted. "Very."

She continued staring at me. She probably imagined I was hiding some secret love affair from her. Such a romantic. Unfortunately, my secret was very unromantic.

She sat down at the kitchen and pulled her laptop out of her book bag. That meant she was here to stay for a while. I wasn't going to get the privacy I needed to read my letter with Rhonda looming around the apartment.

I figured the only place I would get any privacy was down in the laundry room. Sure, I could read it in my room with the door closed, but I hadn't heard from Gretchen in forever, and last she knew, I was still married. So I had no idea how I would feel after reading what she wrote. And Rhonda was close enough to hear me if I was crying. Besides, it was Friday night, and Rhonda was bound to have some people coming over to hang out.

I couldn't get my laundry together fast enough. The letter was burning a hole in my pocket. I was excited to read it but also felt a little trepidation. Hearing from Gretchen brought back so many memories from last year.

I chose a washing machine on the back row so I could hide if anyone else came in.

Dear Sophia,

Oh my gosh, married woman! How are you? I still can't believe you are married now. I've tried e-mailing you a few times but have never heard back, so I thought I'd send a letter.

I love New Zealand. It is beautiful. I am still learning how to be a missionary, but I am excited to be serving the Lord. I truly feel blessed. Even though this is an English-speaking country, I have culture shock. I feel bad saying I'm homesick, but I am.

Being a missionary isn't what I thought it'd be. I thought the work would be so easy, with people lining up to be baptized. Some days we don't teach anyone. My expectations were so different from how it is. I get discouraged very easily.

But enough about me. How are you? Are you guys doing well? Do you just love *being married? Gosh, I am so jealous. Travis is such a great guy. And what a babe. You caught a good one. You two are going to have gorgeous babies. Speaking of babies . . . Any babies????*

I crumpled up the letter and threw it across the floor. Granted, she had no idea what had happened, but how would I ever respond to it? *Dear Gretchen, my marriage is over. I feel like a complete loser. My life is a train wreck.* Really. I couldn't believe what had become of me while Gretchen had been on her mission. How had I let this happen? Where had I gone wrong? What had I done to deserve this? I wasn't a bad person.

I started to cry. I didn't get why my happily ever after had gone so wrong. My whirlwind romance had ended almost as quickly as it had started. How had I become so pathetic that I was sitting on the floor in a basement laundry room crying unabashedly about my failed life?

I paused to take a deep breath. I sniffed and wiped my eyes with my sleeve. Then I banged my head against the washing machine. Not hard enough to give myself a concussion but just enough to feel it. I banged it a few more times. I felt . . .

"Hey, are you all right?"

Luke. I should have guessed he'd show up.

I straightened up a bit and wiped my eyes, not bothering to hide it. It was obvious I was crying. "Yeah, great." I sniffed.

"You got your hair cut. You don't like it?"

"No, it's not the haircut."

"Letter from your boyfriend?" Luke gestured toward the crumpled letter on the floor.

"No." I sniffed again. "I don't have a boyfriend."

"Your missionary?"

I snorted. "I would hope not, 'cause it's from a sister missionary."

"Yeah, then I would hope not either." Luke nodded in agreement.

"I'm sorry. I just need a moment, or a day, to get over it."

"Okay." Luke looked uncomfortable. "Uh, are you doing laundry too, or do you just like to hang out in the laundry room?"

"No. I'm doing laundry. What about you? Do you always do laundry on Friday nights, or do *you* just like to hang out here?"

"Someone recently let me in on the fact that Friday night in the laundry room is the best kept secret of this place." He winked at me.

I don't know, I thought. Maybe the best kept secret was the nineteen-year-old divorced girl in the ward.

I stood up and dusted myself off, collecting my crumpled letter on the way and shoving it in my front pocket. I wished Luke had shown up a little later. I wanted to wallow in my grief alone. But if I went back to my apartment, I ran the risk of Rhonda, and she would bug me about why I was crying.

Luke. Rhonda. I weighed my options. Luke seemed like the better choice for company. Besides, maybe this time he wouldn't hang around waiting for his laundry to be done. Maybe he would. Maybe he had Oreos.

Chapter Thirteen
Thanksgiving

THANKSGIVING WAS UPON US, AND I was not feeling thankful.

I should have gone home for Thanksgiving. I could have hidden under my own covers, in my own bed, in my own room. But I made the decision to make no decision and thus ended up making no plans to go home.

The truth was I didn't want to face my parents, who were under the impression I had snapped out of my funk and was back to normal. Whatever normal was. I couldn't handle going to church in my home ward on Sunday and having members kindly asking how I was doing. Or how I was feeling. Or how I was getting along.

Because I was getting along okay, I guess. I put on a good act, but truth be told, I was still trying to put the pieces of my broken heart back together.

"You can come home with me," Rhonda said.

"Oh, no. I'll be fine." I managed to be chipper. "I have a big . . . floral design . . . project I need to do. I keep putting it off. This is the perfect opportunity to finish it without any distractions." Unfortunately, I wasn't all that motivated to do it.

Sarah was heading home to Colorado. "Come," she offered kindly, telling me her parents wouldn't mind. I gave her the same excuse I'd given Rhonda. Sarah questioned me with a doubtful look but accepted my reasoning.

Claire was already packed when I saw her. Unlike the other roommates, she did not offer to take me. I wouldn't have accepted anyway. "Going to your brother's house?"

"Actually, my mom's for the weekend."

"Oh yeah, how has she been feeling? Is she better now?" I'd never heard anything more about her mom being in the hospital.

"She's fine." The look on Claire's face was almost one of confusion. As if she wondered why I was even asking about her mother.

"Well, she was in the hospital that time . . ." I trailed off.

Claire shook her head. "She's fine now."

"So have a great long weekend and enjoy." I gave her a half wave and went into the living room. Trying to carry on a conversation with Claire was as difficult and painful as pulling teeth.

I finally got everyone on their way, repeatedly assuring them I'd be fine on my own, with the company of my school projects. I felt relieved as I shut the door behind Claire, the last one out, and locked it.

Alone at last.

I waited a few minutes to make sure no one came back for forgotten items before I started my own private pity party. I deserved a good cry; Travis and I had gotten married the Saturday after Thanksgiving, and this weekend would have been our one-year anniversary. To celebrate, I planned to have a movie marathon, starting out with *Hope Floats* and following it up with *Dear John*. After that, I'd see if I felt like I had cried enough or if I needed to find another tragically sad movie to watch.

Hope Floats had been my mother's, which made absolutely no sense, since its subject went against her positive nature. Maybe because the title contained *hope*, she thought it was a happy movie.

I had just finished watching the part that always made me cry when the doorbell rang.

Who could that be? I hoped it wasn't Bradley back from Mexico. I certainly was not answering the door since it'd be obvious I'd been crying.

I decided to ignore it instead.

"Sophia?" called the knocker. Great. It was Luke. I figured as EQP, he was making sure everyone had a place to go for Thanksgiving dinner the next day.

I didn't want to be seen looking like this. The last time he saw me I was crying in the laundry room. How did he always manage to find me when I was crying? And I definitely didn't want to be invited to some Thanksgiving dinner where only the leftovers of the ward were attending.

I made a split-second decision. I dropped to the floor and started army crawling along the edge of the couch. My plan was to crawl by the front door and make it back to the bedrooms without being seen. I was barely to the edge of the couch when I heard Luke tap on the sliding glass door. "I can see you," he said.

I looked up at him watching me. Next time, I needed to remember to close the curtains *before* starting a pity party.

Well, dang. How embarrassing. I couldn't ignore him now. And it'd be awkward the next time he came over to home teach. I guess I had to suck it up and answer the door.

"You caught me," I said as I opened the door. Might as well just admit I was crying.

"What are you doing in there?" He looked at me with suspicion. Then he noticed my wet face and asked, "Are you okay? You're crying."

"I was watching a sad movie. You know, a chick flick, tear jerker."

"Sorry to have interrupted."

"It's fine." I put on a smile, though I really wanted to get on with my pity party, alone.

"Are you going to be here for Thanksgiving?"

"I'm here all weekend."

"Do you have someplace to go for Thanksgiving dinner?"

I knew it. He was here to invite me to Thanksgiving dinner. "Well, yes, yes, I do have plans. I'm going to . . ."

"Rhonda said you had no place to go."

"She sold me out," I said, but it didn't come off in the joking manner I'd intended it to.

"She's worried you won't get out at all," he said, excusing her.

"I don't mind not getting out."

"So that's why you're hiding out in the laundry room every Friday night."

I laughed at his argument. "So are you."

"Touché." He sort of nodded his head in defeat, then tried a new approach. "How about coming to our Thanksgiving dinner? A bunch of us are getting together. Besides, I'm going to need your help cooking the turkey. C'mon, you know it's going to be fun."

Fun. Cooking a turkey was anything but fun to me. It brought me back to last Thanksgiving. Maxine had invited us for Thanksgiving dinner. When I called to thank her and ask if there was anything I could bring, she said, "How about the turkey, honey? That would be great." Before I could protest, she said, "Gotta go, dear, bye." I was left speechless with the responsibility of the main course dumped in my lap.

"Lucky you, cooking the turkey," I said dryly.

"That's why I need your help. I have no clue how to do it. I'm hoping you've had some experience."

Some experience? As a matter of fact, I did. My only experience cooking a turkey had ended up with a trip to the emergency room with food poisoning for Travis and both of his parents. I declined partaking of the holiday bird after having to stick my hand in his I don't know exactly which cavity of his body it was, to pull out the giblets, which luckily saved me from getting sick.

"I do know if you don't cook a turkey right you can get food poisoning."

"Like I said, I need your help."

I wasn't going to be much help. "I'm not the best person for the job. I almost killed someone last time I cooked a turkey. I'm talking emergency room and everything."

"I don't believe you. I think you're still trying to get out of coming to our humble dinner." He knew very well what I was trying to do.

I gave in. "I'll try and help, but you've been warned. So don't ask me to drive you to the emergency room at 1:00 a.m."

He still thought I was joking. "I'll take my chances."

Unfortunately for him, I wasn't.

* * *

I was almost late for Thanksgiving dinner because my brother called to check on me. Knowing it would have been my first anniversary, he was worried I wouldn't be doing well. I was worried too.

"Hey, Sophia, how are you?"

"Well, I've been better," I said cautiously. I never knew if my mom was standing right next to him, interpreting his one-sided conversation into misconstrued information.

"Better than May, or better than August?"

"I'm not curled up in a fetal position in my bed, if that's what you're asking."

Dan laughed. "That's exactly what I was asking."

"Then the answer to that would be no."

I heard Dan exhale. "Then that's something to be thankful for on this beautiful Thanksgiving Day."

Dan had learned PMA from my mother about as well as I had. "Is Mom standing right next to you? Putting you up to this?"

"No, no. I did this on the sly. But that's not to say she won't call you later to ask how your Thanksgiving was. She'll probably even guilt you for not coming down here to spend time with us."

I honestly didn't know if I could handle as much thankful cheer as my mom could dish on a day like today when I was supposed to be thankful and grateful. "Well, you know, I have that school project and all—"

"Excuses," Dan cut in. "You can't fool me, sis. I know you're avoiding Mom." I could tell he was smiling as he said it.

"All right, okay. I'll confess. I couldn't—"

"It's okay, Soph. You don't have to explain it to me. I just wanted to make sure you were okay."

And that was why I loved my brother.

* * *

Dinner was set for 2:00 p.m. Luke said there would be six people total—him and me; Justin; Shunske, a guy from Japan; Scott, a guy I didn't know; and Rachelle from the apartment downstairs from us. According to Rhonda, Rachelle was twenty-eight years old, a nurse, and desperately trying to get her "Mrs." degree.

When I arrived at two, I was relieved to see no one else was there yet. Luke was in the kitchen, looking very stressed and a bit confused. Something smelled very, very bad.

"What is that awful smell?" I set my chocolate cake on the table, my unconventional donation to the dinner party. Making a pumpkin pie was almost as gross as handling raw turkey. Instead, I opted for chocolate.

"I know it smells bad. Landon, for some strange reason, stores pans in the oven. I didn't check before I turned the oven on, and there was a pan in there. Then my mom called, and I didn't realize something was wrong until the smoke detector went off. A plastic spatula melted in one of the pans. I threw it all away."

I laughed. "Sounds like a kitchen disaster I would have. You've had a busy morning."

"It's been insane." He continued. "I tried to air it out in here, but it was freezing with the windows open. I hope Tom the Turkey doesn't smell like that when he comes out."

"I'm sure it will be fine." I was trying to be positive because, for his sake, I wanted it to be fine.

He checked the bird. "Tom isn't getting very brown."

"How long has it been in there?"

"I put him in about two hours ago. There is one of those pop-up buttons that tells me when he's done."

"I don't think two hours is long enough. Unless it's the size of a Cornish game hen."

"A Cornish game hen would have been easier. It was good to get him out of the freezer this morning. That darn bird took up the whole thing."

Did he say what I thought he said? "Wait. You just took the turkey out this morning?"

"Yes."

"You didn't let him defrost in the fridge?"

"No. Was I supposed to?"

"You didn't defrost him at all? You put him in frozen?" This could be as bad as my turkey disaster.

"Yeah. Is that wrong? He was frozen when I bought him. I figured you're supposed to cook it frozen. You know, like frozen lasagna."

"Oh, my. Did you take the giblets out?"

"The what?"

Thanksgiving dinner was officially ruined for me. "You know, the body parts they stick in the turkey's . . . cavity . . . like the liver, neck, and heart?"

"Why would they stick those in there?" He scowled.

"I think some people eat them."

"Gross."

I agreed. "It is, but don't you think it's even grosser that the giblets are still inside Tom's cavity while he's cooking?"

"That's a problem, huh?" He sounded resigned.

"I think so," I said gently. I felt bad for him. Here he was trying to provide a dinner for the students who had no place else to go, and his dinner would not be worth eating.

"Maybe I could pull out that stuff out and then put the bird back in to cook. What do you think?"

"It might still be frozen inside," I said, cringing. "I don't want to reach my hand in there to find out."

Luke agreed. "Nope. Me neither."

"Maybe we can pull it out when the bird is done and not say anything to the others," I suggested.

"I'm not sure there's going to be any others. Shunske stopped by and said some girls invited him over for their dinner. Rachelle left a message that someone called in sick so she had to work. Justin went to a friend's house to watch the football game. He said he'd be back but didn't say when. And Scott wasn't sure if he'd make it; he has a sinus infection. I encouraged him to stay in bed."

"So it's going to be you, me, and Tom?"

"If Tom makes it. He's not looking so good. I might have killed a dead bird."

It was nice not to be the only one to ruin a turkey. "Don't worry. I told you about my turkey. Maybe give him an hour? Turn up the temperature or something?"

"It's worth a try."

The temperature thing worked really well . . . at burning the outside of the turkey. When we pulled the bird out, he was very crisp on the outside and still frozen on the inside.

Luke looked at the bird in dismay, then stabbed it with the carving knife, disgusted. The knife broke off at the tip when it hit the frozen center. "Would you settle for a turkey sub at Subway? My treat?"

"I would love a turkey sub at Subway."

"Later we can go sledding on the turkey."

"It probably would still be frozen."

"I'm sorry about dinner. I'm kind of embarrassed," Luke said.

"Don't be." I knew how he felt. "At least no one went to the hospital."

"I thought you were joking."

I shook my head. "I wish I was, but no."

"But no one got fed either. Some Thanksgiving dinner."

"No one has to know. Let's just discreetly dispose of the body in the Dumpster and not tell anyone." That sounded like a good plan. I was all for keeping secrets about one's failures.

"As long as we don't get caught with the evidence," Luke said, livening up a bit.

"Who's around to see us?"

"Right." Luke seemed reassured.

We took the turkey outside to the Dumpster. After looking around to make sure there weren't any witnesses, we threw him in.

"I think our clandestine mission was successful," I whispered.

"And if it wasn't, I am in no way claiming to know anything about a turkey in the dumpster." Luke whispered back.

"And I'll back up your story."

"Deal."

Chapter Fourteen
Build Relationships of Trust

WE WALKED UP NINTH EAST to the Subway shop across from campus.

"I hope you don't mind walking. My truck starter died yesterday, and it won't be fixed until Saturday because of the holiday."

"That's okay. Exercise and fresh air are supposed to be good for us, right?"

"Yup," Luke said. "Sorry again about the turkey."

"Turkeys are overrated, and the meat is always dry," I said.

"So, um, how's school going?" Luke asked.

I scowled. "School. It's going."

"So I take it it's not going very well?"

"You could say that."

"Why not?" Luke pressed. "Hard classes?"

I rolled my eyes. "I just finished taking bowling on the block, and I'm currently taking Floral Design, Living with Plants, and Intro to Interiors."

Luke looked straight ahead with his hands in his coat pockets. "Very demanding," he mused.

"Please." I snorted. "How pathetic am I if I'm having a hard time with classes like those? I am so unmotivated. I probably shouldn't have come back to school."

"Come back?" Luke was quick to catch my slip. "I thought you were a freshman."

Whoops. How could I have let that out of the bag? "I am a freshman." I tried not sounding flustered.

"But you were here before?"

There was no way around it. I was going to have to explain. "Yes," I began carefully. "I went fall semester last year, took off winter semester to work, then went home spring and summer, and came back this fall. I feel like I'm out of the groove. I conveniently forgot what it was like going to school and living with roommates and doing the whole BYU thing. It's been a little overwhelming."

"Roommates can be a challenge," Luke said.

"Like Rhonda clogging the drain."

Luke just smiled but said nothing.

"Or Claire being so uptight."

Luke shook his head. Maybe in agreement?

"Or Sarah . . ." I thought for a moment. "Well, Sarah's just nice."

"Like Landon leaving frying pans in the oven?" Luke said, and we both laughed.

When we got to Subway, we found out it was closed. "We're not having much luck with turkey today." He looked around. "That convenience store next door looks open. Maybe they'll have something."

"Of unknown origin," I finished. I was surprised how easy it was for me to talk with him.

He grinned. "Maybe it's safer *not* buying a sandwich from a convenience store. Would you settle for turkey Lunchables?"

"Maybe they'll have Oreos for the dessert."

Sure enough, we found turkey Lunchables *with* Oreos in the refrigerated section. Luke grabbed two.

"Is that going to be enough for you?" I eyed the kid-sized package. "They're awfully small."

"You're right." He took three more. "Two for you, two for me, and one just in case we're still hungry."

We sat on a bench under the eaves outside the store and continued our conversation while we carefully balanced our Lunchables on our laps.

"Do you have a hard time with your roommates?" I was curious. Luke seemed like a pretty easy-going, affable guy. I wondered if roommates ever rubbed him the wrong way.

"Not so much my roommates. On my mission, there were definitely some companions who annoyed me. One elder, Kerlan, always had to do things his way. We never saw eye to eye, and we were together for three very long months. At least roommates are not companions. I can leave the apartment if someone's getting on my nerves. Or go to campus."

"Or the laundry room," I said.

"Or the laundry room. Another good choice," he agreed.

"Did you know your roommates before you moved in?"

"Just Justin."

"Just Justin?" I repeated, emphasizing the repetition.

"Yeah. How about you? Did you know your roommates?"

I shook my head. "No, I didn't know any of them."

He gathered his trash. "Are you ready to go?"

I nodded and stood.

It was so still outside. The sky was gray, and it had started snowing. The quiet made me nervous. I had the urge to keep babbling about inconsequential things so the conversation wouldn't turn personal.

I continued with the earlier conversation. "Sometimes I look at my roommates and wonder how I ended up with them. Rhonda is so completely opposite of me. She's a little too zealous for me."

"She seems nice enough. And makes good cookies."

"Oh, she is nice and has a good heart. Just too boy crazy."

"Justin's a little girl crazy. Actually, he wants to be married within a year. A postmission goal."

I almost shared my opinion about his goal but decided against it. "So was he your roommate last year?"

"No. We were mission companions. He was my last one before I went home." Luke seemed a little quiet.

I relaxed. Missions were a safe conversation topic because most guys at BYU had served a mission and were more than eager to share their great spiritual experiences. "Where did you say you went on your mission?"

"London, England. You know, a foreign mission where they speak English."

"Cool."

"Do you want to go on a mission?"

"I don't think I can." It slipped before I thought my wording through properly.

"Why not?"

"I meant, I don't think I could *do* a mission. You know, handle it. I, um, don't think I will. I know it's supposed to be a great experience and all, but it seems hard." I needed to stop rambling. I was going to end up giving away my secret. "Was your mission hard?" I diverted the attention away from myself.

"Yes, it was hard. It was a lot different than I expected." Luke stuck his hands in his coat pockets.

"Why?" I was taken aback. For Luke being elders quorum president, thus equaling a spiritual giant in our ward, I expected the typical, enthusiastic response of "I'd go back in a heartbeat," or "It was the best two years of my life." I was expecting hours of stories, and maybe even a testimony.

"I didn't start off as a very good missionary."

"I find that hard to believe, Luke. You're so good . . ." And spiritual and nice and active in the Church.

"In the MTC, it's easy to be good. Everyone is trying to be good there. But then you get out in the field, and you're left to govern yourself, and sometimes it was easier with some companions than with others to follow the mission rules. When I got there, my trainer was awesome. We got along great and worked well together, played basketball on P-day with our district. Then my next companion was completely o.p."

"O.p.?" I couldn't remember if Travis had mentioned that. All he ever talked about was what a great missionary he was.

"Off the program. You know, breaking the rules. We'd sleep in, go recreational biking instead of tracting, hang out at members' houses for hours. He'd even gone to movies with one of his other companions. He wanted to do anything but missionary work. He was going home in two months, and he was dead."

"Dead. As in done?" I remembered Travis using that term.

"Yeah. We didn't get any work done those two months. He should've gone home when I arrived for all the good we did while we were together. I tried being the good missionary, but he never seemed influenced by my opinion, and I gave up and gave in."

"That doesn't usually happen on missions, does it?"

"There are a lot of surprising things that happen on missions. Even as a missionary, I thought I'd go out and it'd be so easy, right? After all, I was on the Lord's errand. Yet it was so different than I imagined. Missionaries are human. There are still temptations, weaknesses, shortcomings, frustrations.

"One day I woke up and realized I wasn't the missionary I wanted to be. I had to change if I wanted my mission to end differently than the direction it was headed. So I did. I started doing what I was supposed to and things were going really well. Then my dad passed away while I was there."

"Your dad passed away? Wow. I am so sorry. What happened?"

"Blood clot."

"Luke, that had to be horrible."

"Yeah, it was pretty bad. I ended up leaving my mission early. I felt guilty for not finishing, but I was close to my dad, and it hit me pretty hard." He played with his zipper pull. "That's something I can't ever go back and change."

I knew exactly what he meant. "But look what kind of person you are now. You are EQP, and you're a great home teacher."

"EQP?" Luke looked confused. "Is that like *GQ* or something?"

"Elders quorum president."

"That means nothing. I feel like I need to make up for being such a slacker missionary. That's why I do EFY. I figure if I can help any of those boys realize how important being a good missionary is, maybe the ripple effect will teach some of the people I never taught."

"That's a worthy cause."

"I wish I had done it right the first time. I wouldn't feel like I was always trying to make up for lost time." He looked so sad. Then his expression softened. "Sorry. I'm unloading my crummy missionary guilt on you."

"We all have regrets. It's nice to know I'm not the only one." Without going into details, I wanted to make him feel better. For the first time in months, the positions were changed. I actually wanted to console instead of be consoled.

"I don't talk about it with my roommates. They think I'm being humble, like I did my best but still feel like I could've done better. But having my dad die when I was there was so hard. I was mad at everyone. I couldn't understand why something like that would happen while I was serving my mission. I was gobsmacked."

He was *what*? "Sorry to interrupt, but you were gob-what?"

"Gobsmacked. The British use it to mean completely shocked."

"Got it." That's how I felt about my divorce.

He continued. "It took a long time to not feel that way. I eventually realized it wasn't a punishment; it was just one of those things that happens in life. I guess one of those experiences that would give me experience and be for my good. But because my roommates haven't been through something like that . . ."

"They don't get why you feel that way. I think mine worry I'm Jack Mormon." I didn't mean to interrupt, but I felt such relief I started to choke up. I didn't have to beat myself up for being so angry about my situation—Luke had experienced the same feelings.

"Why would they think that?" He seemed surprised.

"Because I'm cynical. And negative. And I seem downright inactive sometimes."

"I'm sorry. Did one of your parents pass away?" Luke wouldn't know what I was talking about, would he? "Is that why you always seem so sad?"

I couldn't lie to him. I mean, I could, but strangely, I didn't want to. I had someone, albeit unknown to him, whom I felt connected to through our losses. But he had caught me crying too many times to blame it on emotional movies.

"No. I'm sorry. Now I'm the one unloading. BYU was hard last year. A lot of changes. A messy break up. It was a big adjustment."

"I've never thought of you as inactive. You just seem to keep to yourself."

"So it's a good thing Rhonda's my roommate. She tries to socialize enough for both of us."

"Yeah, Justin's the dating king in our apartment. He has a two-date rule. If he hasn't kissed her by the second date, he won't ask her out again. Crazy, huh? Oh, and get this. You want to hear something weird about Landon? But you can't tell anyone."

"Hey, my word is good. After all, I know about Tom the Turkey, right?"

"Landon has a genuine cubic zirconia ring in his drawer. If he meets the right one, he's going to give her that as a promise ring. Isn't that funny?"

"So he's going to propose with a fake diamond ring?"

Luke chuckled. "I know. Can you believe it?"

"What is the marriage going to be like if it's starting out with a fake diamond ring? Doesn't that seem a little weird that he already has a ring?"

"I feel sorry for the poor girl who accepts. Landon's a good guy, but he's in too much of a rush to get married." Luke paused, then said, "There's something I've wondered about since the first family home evening."

I broke out in a little sweat. "What?"

"Which of those two things was the lie? I know you said neither, but was that true?"

"No, really. Neither. They were both lies. I couldn't think of anything to share, so I made up two lies."

"We didn't believe you. My roommates decided you went on stage at a rock concert."

"Nothing quite that exciting has ever happened to me. Which reminds me, you got skipped because of me. What were you going to say?"

"My brothers' names are Matthew, Mark, and John, or I was born with six fingers."

"My guess is that your brothers' names are Matthew, Mark, and John."

"You are correct."

"No! Your parents named you Matthew, Mark, Luke, and John?" It was almost too funny to be true.

"Yup, my parents did that to us. Growing up, we always had the books of the New Testament sung to us. I don't like that song anymore."

"You were traumatized."

"Yes, I was. But it gets even better," Luke said.

"What?" I waited. It reminded me of when Travis told me his major was premed. I suggested he could be a podiatrist. That would be pretty funny, right? A podiatrist named Dr. Duckk. At least I thought it was hilarious. Travis, on the other hand, did not see the humor in it. At all. It didn't matter anyway, because right after we were married, he had a career crisis. He wasn't sure that premed was his passion and changed to prelaw.

"My sister, the next youngest after me—her name is Leia."

"No!" I gasped. "Like Luke and Leia from Star Wars?"

"Yup."

"But why? Why would they do that?"

"My parents made a deal. If it was a girl, my dad named the baby. If it was a boy, my mom named the baby. If it was the other way around, I might have been named Fox Mulder from *The X-Files*. Talk about traumatizing."

"I prefer Luke," I decided.

"Me too," he said. He looked at me in the way that always made me feel like he could see through my facade.

"What?" I asked, uncomfortable.

"Nothing." He shook his head. "I've never seen this side of you. You've never been much of a talker, even over laundry."

"Hmm," I said without looking at him. It was true. This was the most personal conversation I'd had with almost anybody, besides Dave, since returning to school. It was surprising, but I felt comfortable talking to him. But missions and names were a lot easier to talk about than my former life as a married woman.

"Should we have a piece of your chocolate cake?" he asked as we walked up the stairs toward his apartment.

"Sounds good to me."

He opened the door to see Justin chowing down on the cake, eating right off the serving plate.

"Hey. Luke. Sophia. Have you tried this cake, dude? It's, like, delicious. I haven't ever tasted a cake as awesome as this. Mmmmm." He dug his fork in again.

"No, uh, we haven't yet." Luke stared at Justin chewing a huge mouthful.

"Hey, save some for us," I said.

"Oh yeah, sorry. No one was here, so I figured it was leftover from the dinner. And, dude, where's all the turkey? I want to make a sandwich. I'm starving."

"We sort of didn't cook it right," I said.

Justin stabbed the cake again. "You mean there is no leftover turkey?"

"Nope." Luke shook his head.

"How about," I said lightly, "you let me cut you a slice. Maybe even get you a plate." I gently removed the cake from Justin's grasp.

Luke took down a plate from the cupboard and handed it to me.

"Hey, Sophia," Justin said between bites. "You up for going to a movie tonight?"

I tilted my head, surprised. I wasn't expecting that. "Thanks, but no. I have things I need to get done, and I'm pretty tired." I picked up the cake.

"That's too bad. It'd be fun."

"Not with me, Justin."

Luke stopped and looked at me, an expression of perplexity crossing his face.

"Here, I'll walk you home," Luke said, opening the door.

He didn't say anything during the short walk over to my apartment. His silence again made me feel like I needed to say something. "You never got any cake," I said as we came to my apartment. "Do you want to come in and have some?"

"I'd like that." Luke nodded.

Inside, Luke and I sat across from each other at the table as I cut two slices.

"You make an awesome chocolate cake," he said after his first bite.

"Thanks."

"Can I ask you something?"

"Yeah."

"Did you tell Justin no because you don't like him or because of last year?"

I shrugged. "Both. I'm not interested in dating Justin. He's a good guy, but I don't want to date him."

We were silent for a moment, except for the sound of forks scraping on plates.

"Another piece?" I asked, not only because he finished his piece but also to break the silence and steer the conversation somewhere else.

"I want to say yes because it's so good, but I probably should get going." He stood and pulled his coat on.

I kind of wanted him to stay a little longer. I wasn't sure why though. "Do you want to take a piece home?"

"That would be great." He waited by the doorway as I wrapped a slice. "Thanks for the cake and the company today and the . . ." He trailed off.

I handed him the cake. "Clandestine mission and the confidentiality," I added.

"Yes. And please promise you will never talk about Tom the Turkey ever again."

"I won't say a word." I paused. "And if you'd return the favor and not say anything about my being a returning freshman, I would appreciate it."

"No problem. Have a good night, Sophia."

"Thanks. You too."

When I shut the door behind him, I still had that weird feeling. I couldn't immediately put my finger on it. Without even realizing it, I'd actually had a good time. I didn't feel like watching any more of my sad movies.

Instead, I went out to the Dumpster and took pictures of the turkey.

Chapter Fifteen
Resolve

THE SEROTONIN RUSH RESULTING FROM the unintentional good time I had on Thanksgiving came to an abrupt end on Sunday. Rather than being uplifting, church brought me back to the reality that all was not well with my universe. It seemed contradictory to the nature of church, but everything I heard struck a nerve, one that had been raw and exposed for way too long.

The first speaker in sacrament meeting was Simon, the guy who always talked about his moped. On this occasion, he had his arm in a sling.

"I was riding along on my moped the other day, and I wasn't paying attention because I had too much on my mind and ended up rear-ending the car in front of me. I flipped over my handlebars and landed on the trunk of the car and broke my collarbone.

"Life is like that. We're mopedding along, and we're too busy to pay attention. We're too busy to take time to pray. We're too busy to listen to the Spirit. We're too busy to read the scriptures. Then bang. Something hits us, or we hit something, whether it's a car or a trial, and suddenly we realize how out of touch we are. Sometimes we need to be literally hit over the head to force us to pay attention to our spiritual lives."

I got lost in my own thoughts, contemplating whether I was mopedding through life. I didn't think I was. My problem was more that I had been cruising through life and been hit by the moped. Or maybe plowed into by a Mack Truck would be more appropriate.

Relief Society was the real clincher. The lesson was talking about having an eternal perspective. The teacher read a poem by Carol Lynn Pearson named "The Lesson." I had never heard the poem before but could easily relate. It talked about how a child needed to learn to walk and how difficult that seemed at the time. But then it compared that to how we, as children of God, get frustrated while we're here on earth learning to "walk."

Tears instantly burned in my eyes. My chin was quivering, threatening to give my emotions away to anyone who happened to look at me. I tried breathing slowly, hoping the lump in my throat would go away. I knew what it felt like to cry and be frustrated because of the lesson I was trying to learn. Or be taught. The emotion in the poem was exactly the struggle I was experiencing.

I discreetly wiped my eyes while deciding what to do. I could try to make it through Relief Society, or I could jump up and run out like I wanted to do—but at the risk of making a scene. In the absence of all my roommates, would anyone even notice my quick exit? My third option was to compose myself, dry my eyes, and calmly walk out of the room. Tom the Turkey served as my distraction to rein in my emotions until I could calmly leave. When I finally made it out of the building, I headed home.

The clouds were a gray blanket in the sky, and it was lazily snowing. It had snowed long enough to leave a white cover a couple inches thick. How had the snow built up so fast when it seemed to be snowing so slowly? If the slow, steady downfall kept at it long enough, it built up to something significant, I thought. Kind of like the slow, steady pain that just kept snowing down on me.

I stopped at my apartment and changed before going outside and ending up at the park behind the apartments. The snow was untouched there. Mine were the only tracks in the field as I made my way onto it with no particular destination in mind. My coat was thin, and I didn't have a hat or gloves on, but I was only slightly aware of the biting cold air against my wet cheeks.

After stumbling forward a short distance, I sat down. I put my bare hands in the snow, needing to feel something other than the same sadness I always felt. I wanted to feel something, even if it caused me pain, as long as it was a different pain. My burning cheeks and stinging fingers made me feel alive as I felt the cold against my skin.

Then I gave in to the crying. This lesson was too hard. I didn't know if I'd ever learn it. Yet deep down inside I knew this wasn't how life was supposed to be. God didn't want me to be unhappy. I truly believed that. My unhappiness was the consequence of Travis's decision to leave.

But it was my choice whether I continued down the painful, pathetic path I was on or whether I chose a different path. The problem being, a different path would require effort on my part.

But it wasn't simply a matter of changing my mind and my attitude. It would take time for both grieving and healing. Maybe now was the time. My depression wasn't going to go away because I wanted it to, no matter how much positive mental attitude my mom preached to me. It was like Dave always said: you gotta want it before things are going to change. Maybe I finally wanted it.

I'm not sure how long I was out there before I heard someone call out, "Hey, don't they teach you anything in Vegas?"

I looked up to see Justin lumbering toward me.

"You're supposed to wear a *winter* coat when it snows."

I didn't want him to catch me crying, so I did the only thing I could do: I pretended to stumble and face planted in the snow so I could use it as an excuse for my watery eyes and red nose. I sniffled and shook off the snow. "Yeah, I should have a warmer coat."

He helped me up. "Are you trying to catch pneumonia? You could have hypothermia or frostbite, and I might have to perform CPR on you."

"You don't treat frostbite with CPR." I rolled my eyes. Normally, I would have found Justin funny.

"Well, come on." He grabbed my arm, leading me home. "Let's get you out of the cold. It's almost time for us to come home teaching."

I had forgotten about that. Were any of my roommates even back yet?

Justin continued good-naturedly. "It's the last Sunday of the month. Luke always gets 100 percent. Besides," he smiled at me and winked, "Rhonda promised apple pie."

"What time is it?" How long had I been out there?

"It's 12:15. I stayed late after church. You might have been a frozen little snow angel if I hadn't seen you when I drove in."

It hadn't been that long. Maybe fifteen minutes. Maybe twenty at the most. I would have eventually felt cold enough to go in, right? I wasn't so far gone that I would have let myself freeze to death, would I? Was I crazy thinking the cold felt good?

Justin kept up the one-sided conversation as we climbed the stairs. I was too lost in my own thoughts to pay attention to what he was saying. We stopped at the top of the stairs, and he let go of my arm.

"We'll be over around three. I can't wait for some pie."

I shook my head and rolled my eyes yet again. I hoped Rhonda was not back so I wouldn't have to account for being all wet.

The apartment was still empty when I opened the door. Good. A few more minutes alone to savor . . . to savor what? My aloneness? My misery? My pathetic pity parties and dwelling on my failures? Sitting in the snow had made me realize one thing: I wanted to feel something different. And getting frostbite was not the answer.

I took a shower to warm up. I sat down in the tub as the hot water streamed over me, and I gave in to my emotions again. I wanted it to go away. I was so sick of trying to figure out where it all went wrong and what I could have possibly done differently so the outcome would have been different. I was in a bad place, and I didn't want to be there anymore.

I thought hard about my options. I could give up and go home. No one would think any less of me. After all, I had been through a really rough time. But then my mother would provide a steady stream of helpful ways to make lemons into lemonade and look at the bright side.

I could stay here at BYU. I could stay and make an actual attempt at going to my classes and not moping through my days. I needed to start caring about my appearance and start socializing a little more. Maybe I needed to give Bradley a real chance. Maybe there could be something there if I didn't always keep him at arm's length. I wasn't foolish enough to believe a new relationship was going to help me get over my old relationship, but maybe I needed to try. I didn't know exactly how all this was going to happen. But one thing I did know was that I was ready to put the past behind me. I was the only one who could make things change. I could, and I decided I would.

Chapter Sixteen
Run-In

I SHUFFLED AROUND THE APARTMENT in my hot-pink kitty pajamas and slippers. My attire reflected the rough time I'd had over the weekend.

Claire set the tone of the day with a yellow sticky note on the thermostat. "Temp. too high. Keep at 68." I felt like throwing away her pad of yellow sticky notes. She was hardly ever here, and she still drove me nuts. Not what I needed first thing in the morning.

My misery was my own. Everyone else I saw looked jovial. It had snowed almost a foot during the night and appeared to be an exciting addition to everyone's day. Outside the kitchen window, I could see a couple tossing snowballs at each other.

To me, it was just one more nuisance. I needed to go to the health center because I was out of antidepressants. Since they seemed to be helping, I wasn't ready to stop taking them just yet. Even just getting out of the apartment before noon was a small improvement, right? I had already talked myself out of going to class and had decided to go to the bookstore instead. I liked to peruse it for unnecessary junk to buy for reasons unknown other than it was appealing at the time.

I also needed to buy a new fat novel to pretend to read. If anyone was keeping track, I should have finished *Les Misérables* by now. Gretchen had been an English major, and between her and my mother, the English teacher, I had a large mental list from which I chose my books to "read." I figured it gave credibility to the idea that I was actually doing something while I was at home all day.

Maybe this time I would try *War and Peace* or a thick Dickens book. I'd considered *Anna Karenina* but was afraid my roommates might think I was planning on throwing myself onto railroad tracks.

I was not considering death. I wasn't that far gone.

But I was considering buying some fudge for a little pick-me-up.

As I got ready, I became more and more annoyed about the snow. Being from Las Vegas, I didn't have snow boots because it only snowed there once every six years, but I found a pair in the hall closet that looked abandoned. They were a little too small but would do. And if my boot situation was not bad enough, I didn't have a winter coat either.

Actually, I did have one last year, but somewhere between premarried, married, and postmarried life, I had lost track of it. I had lost track of a lot of things between married and postmarried life. Since my marriage, I think I had pretty much just lost it.

A friend drove me back to Vegas the day Travis dropped the divorce decision on me. My mother and brother came to Provo about a month after *that day* and picked up some of my belongings. What hadn't fit in the car was put into storage in Provo. I hadn't cared about any of it until now, despite my mom's reminders to get my belongings out of storage. Nothing like a snowstorm to prove my mother right.

Instead of a coat, I put on a fleece pajama top over my T-shirt and then pulled a thick hoodie over that. I didn't look great, but hopefully I would be warm enough.

Then I headed out for medicine and some useless, pick-me-up shopping at the bookstore.

So far from my random shopping sprees, I had accumulated a girl's BYU baseball cap, a package of glitter pens, and a floral journal with absolutely nothing written inside—yet. I had also collectively purchased three tubes of mascara, two pressed powder compacts (one with light-shimmering accents), and five satiny lip glosses in various colors for whenever I felt well enough to put makeup on. And finally, a toiletry bag for the makeup I had bought but not used and some bright red nail polish that I painted on once and promptly picked off within an hour.

While at the bookstore, I meandered my way to the fiction section and looked in the classics. I stuck with my original idea and chose *War and Peace* solely for its thickness. I knew I could borrow books from the library to pretend to read, but buying things felt so good. It made me less lonely in some weird, probably sick way.

I talked myself out of the fudge and instead chose a Diet Coke, Twizzlers, a french manicure set, a tube of silk-infused lotion because it smelled good, and matching shower gel. And a new bath scrubby because it was a pretty pink. My arms were so full I wished I had grabbed a shopping basket.

Oh, and I needed antifungal cream. I seemed to have developed a small case of athlete's foot resulting from sleeping with my socks on.

I managed to grab the cream with my left hand, but since I didn't want to parade to the register with antifungal cream in plain sight, I stopped at the end of the aisle to readjust my armful of stuff. With the cream hidden safely under the rest of my items, I headed for the checkout.

And promptly crashed into someone.

The lotion slipped from my grasp and landed with such force, its top popped open and silk-infused lotion splattered the carpet. And the shoes and bottom of the jeans that stopped abruptly in front of me.

I bent down to pick up the lotion. I wasn't sure if I should try to clean up the mess or just apologize. "I am so sor—" I started saying as I stood up, only to stop.

There he was, standing right in front of me. Travis. The moment I had envisioned a thousand times was not at all how I envisioned it. Any cool, collected behavior I had imagined went out the window, and I was left speechless.

"Fifi? Wow. Did you forget to get dressed?" That's what he had the nerve to ask me, never mind calling me by his pet name.

I knew I didn't look my best. It wasn't like I was planning on running into my ex-husband today. It was quite obvious by the kitty cats that I was still in my pajamas.

I stared at him in disbelief. "You're still here?"

Travis looked confused. "Yeah. Where else would I be?"

"But . . ." I stammered. "You transferred to the U." That was a major reason for my agreeing to come back to BYU. He wouldn't be here.

"Nah, I changed my mind."

Typical. "So you're commuting every day from Salt Lake?" Part of his rationalization for transferring was we could live with his parents and save money. I had not been thrilled with *that* idea.

"No. That'd be stupid. I moved back into Jake's condo."

Jake was his old roommate.

He looked at my outfit again. "Are you sick?" I doubted he was saying it out of concern.

I brushed my hair from my face and squared my shoulders. "I'm fine." I just wasn't recovering very quickly from being taken by complete and utter surprise.

I then realized the girl standing next to him was *with* him because she took an uncomfortable step back.

"Who's she?" I looked over the girl, who had been picking at her zipper pull, not looking at me.

Her head snapped up.

I narrowed my eyes, suspicious. "That's kind of quick, don't you think?"

"Fi . . . Sophia, she's just in my study group." He sounded defensive.

"Oh." I felt a little defeated that I couldn't use that as a reason to be mad at him. The real reason I was mad at him was that I hadn't heard from him yet. But then, I reminded myself, I shouldn't be trying to pick a fight. "Sorry, I, uh . . . Do you maybe have a minute we could go someplace and talk? I've been thinking—"

"I have class at the fieldhouse." He cut me off before I could finish.

Then he was off, and I was left frustrated. Frustrated with myself, frustrated with him, furious that I had not said what I wanted to say. Frustrated that I couldn't even have a few minutes of his time.

I dumped all the stuff I was holding on a shelf in a random aisle and headed for an exit. I started crying before I even made it out the door.

On the way home, I had a "should've, could've, would've" conversation with myself about all the things I should have done differently. I couldn't believe he was still here at BYU. I couldn't believe I ran into him. I should've looked better. I should've found out what exactly he was doing with her. I should've been more insistent. He could've made time for me. Shouldn't he have been happy to see me? Shouldn't he have realized he wanted me back?

I didn't have answers to those questions. All I knew was that it was easier trying to move on when I thought he was going to the U of U. Because I really was trying to get over him. But seeing him today brought out a whole bunch of emotions I was trying to ignore.

The apartment was empty when I got home. Thankfully. I was saving the real breakdown until I was at least behind closed doors. I sat down on the couch, laid my head back, and cried. Gosh. Why couldn't I get on with my life instead of hanging on to Travis? Hadn't I just decided yesterday that I was moving on? And here I was, backsliding again. Why was it so hard letting go? But most of all, how could someone I had loved so much hurt me so badly?

The last question brought on another round of tears. Which Sarah happened to walk in on.

"Sophia?" I could hear the alarm in her voice as she sat down next to me. "What's wrong?"

I wished I hadn't been caught crying. "Do you ever have one of those days when everything is just wrong?"

"Of course. We all have them."

"That's today."

"What happened?"

I smiled weakly. "I woke up."

"Yeah, I know what you mean."

"I went up to campus in my pajamas, and a guy asked me if I forgot to get dressed."

"That wasn't very nice."

"No, it wasn't. I probably wouldn't have looked so ridiculous if I didn't have three layers on top and looked like a stuffed sausage. I need to buy a winter coat and some boots."

"You don't have stuff for winter?"

"Not yet. We don't have much of a winter in Vegas."

"I'll take you shopping this weekend if you want. But for now, I was thinking I needed to go buy some chocolate. How about it? Want to come?"

Although the voice in my head resisted the invitation, I was reminded of my mother's advice. Maybe going out with Sarah and thinking about something else would help me feel better. "I know how to make some delicious chocolate sauce for ice cream," I said.

As we drove to Smiths, I only half listened to Sarah because I was formulating a plan. Seeing Travis today made me decide our marriage deserved a second chance. I not only bought what I needed for chocolate sauce, but I also bought ingredients for Travis's favorite dessert, chocolate éclair pie. That would be my excuse to go over to his apartment. He couldn't brush me off forever. And the next time he saw me, I was going to look good, have a pie, and make him wish he had never left me.

"What about calling your mom? That always helps me," Sarah said while we were enjoying our ice cream.

"The ice cream will make me feel better," I declared.

"How come?"

"My mother is the queen of positive mental attitude. Her idea of cheering me up is singing 'The Sun Will Come Out Tomorrow' over the phone. So I'd rather self-medicate with ice cream and chocolate sauce."

"Oh." I think Sarah was surprised.

It probably seemed like a contradiction for me to have an optimistic mother.

"You know, if you're ever having another bad day and need to use my car to go buy more chocolate, I won't mind."

"Thanks, Sarah. I appreciate it."

* * *

I made an emergency appointment with Dave for the next day because I couldn't wait until the end of the week to see him. It wasn't like I could hash this out with my roommates.

"Travis is here!" I said before I even shut the door to his office.

"By here, you mean at BYU?"

"Yes." I plopped down in my chair.

"How do you know?"

"I saw him. I literally ran into him at the bookstore."

"How did that make you feel?"

I gave him a look of disbelief. "Are you seriously going to ask me all those feeling questions?"

"Yes, I am. Plus, I'm curious to know what happened."

Dave didn't need to do all this prodding. I would analyze it to death on my own because I had gotten good at that since the divorce. That's what I did over the summer when I used to stay in bed all day. "I was shocked. I felt like someone punched me in the stomach. He was supposed to be going to the U."

"Did you talk to him?"

"Yeah, kind of, but not about anything important. I wanted him to give me a few minutes of his time, but he was too busy."

"Too busy or didn't want to?" Dave folded his arms.

I shifted in my seat. "Probably both. He said he needed to be somewhere and didn't have time."

"What's your take coming away from that interaction?"

"Well, he wasn't able to talk then, but he said maybe some other time."

"Do you think he meant it or was just saying that for an easy getaway?"

"I hope he meant it. I would like to talk to him."

"What would you say?"

"I'd see if he wants to get back together."

"Sophia," Dave said gently. "Remember how we've been talking about being realistic, accepting that you're divorced, and moving on? Do you think he's having doubts about his decision?"

"Seeing him again wasn't like I thought it would be. He didn't exactly react the way I imagined in my fantasies."

"How so?"

"I thought if he saw me again, he'd be happy to see me. Tell me he was sorry. Tell me he missed me."

"So you want him back?"

"If I had the chance, yes."

"What if he told you he made a mistake and he wanted you to take him back? Would you?"

"Yes. I want my marriage to work. He broke my heart, but I love him."

"Even with everything he's put you through? The depression, the sadness, the heartbreak?

Sophia, you have given up almost seven months of your life wallowing about a man who left you, who divorced you."

One thing about Travis, he always seemed to get his way. "I didn't want to get divorced. I wanted to work things out. I am still willing."

"But Travis isn't."

I didn't reply right away. I needed to let my emotions settle. "It is unbelievable to me that he could be over me so easily."

He leaned forward a little bit. "So what are you going to do about it, Sophia?"

"I don't know. That's why I come to you."

"I can think of a couple of things you could do."

"Like what?"

"What do you think your options are at this point in your life?"

I wished he would just come out and say it instead of making me work for the answer. "I don't know."

"Think about it. If you don't want anything to change, what should you do?"

"Continue to wallow."

"Right."

"If you want things to change, what can you do?"

"Wait until Travis is ready to talk about giving our marriage a second chance."

"If you think he would consider giving your relationship another chance, maybe you should confront him and ask him. Then you'll know for sure where you stand."

Confront Travis? I didn't have the guts. What if he rejected me twice? Maybe he already had. Seeing me on Monday didn't exactly make him sway and wilt and grab my leg and beg me to take him back.

"I don't know what else to do."

"You mean other than wallow and hope he'll be back? I thought part of the reason you were coming to counseling was so you could move on with your life."

I didn't know how to move forward. I was trying, but I seemed to keep backsliding.

"Sophia, you should start journaling. Writing down your feelings will help sort them out. Then bring what you've written with you next week, and we can discuss it. How does that sound?"

I snorted. Journaling? More like tunneling. I could dig a hole deeper than I was already in.

"What do you say? Are you willing to do it?"

"I could try." I was less than enthusiastic.

"Remember what Yoda said."

"Yeah, yeah, I know. There's no such thing as try." I was exasperated.

"Don't be too excited."

"I won't."

"You gotta want it, Sophia. You gotta want it," he said.

Sometimes I wasn't so sure I wanted it.

Chapter Seventeen

A Momentary Lapse of Reasoning

IT ALL STARTED INNOCENTLY ENOUGH. I mean, who decides, "Today I am going to totally lose it. Heck, I have nothing better to do"? I even put some lip gloss on for church, attempting to make a small change to move forward with my life.

Last Sunday, the first counselor in the bishopric, Brother Redding, stopped me in the hall when church was over. "Sister Davis, we'd like you to speak next week about overcoming trials."

Oh, the irony. "I can't speak in sacrament."

"It's only for seven minutes."

I shook my head. "No. I can't."

"Why don't you think about it? You'll do just fine, don't worry."

His reassurance and confidence in me were in vain.

"Really," I reiterated.

But he must have taken my "Really, I can't do it" last week as "Really? You'll think I'll do fine?" because when I sat down next to Rhonda for sacrament meeting today, she looked at the program and said, "You're speaking today?"

I was busy looking around, wondering (maybe worrying) if Bradley was back yet. "What?"

"You're in the program. See?" She pointed to the third speaker.

Sure enough, there I was.

"You didn't tell us you were speaking," Sarah said, sitting down on the other side of me.

"I told him no," I said out loud. This was wrong. I was not getting up there. No way. Name on the program or not, I didn't care. I was not talking today. "Excuse me," I said calmly. I didn't want to alarm my roommates or clue them in that I was, in fact, escaping. They might come chasing after me once they saw me walking out the exit instead of walking up to the stand.

"Where are you going?" Claire asked, sounding put out as I squeezed past her into the aisle.

"I suddenly have a talk to prepare for," I said over my shoulder and took off.

Brother Redding was in the foyer when I found him. "Sister Davis, I'm looking forward to your talk today." So happy, so pleasant, so completely mistaken. There wasn't going to be any talk today.

I stopped briefly, my heart pounding. How could he have done this to me? I told him no. "Look. I told you I couldn't talk about getting through trials. I just got divorced, and I can barely get out of bed. There is no *way* I'm getting up there to talk about it!" I rushed past him but not before registering the look of complete shock and disbelief on his face. Was I going to be struck by lightning for yelling at a counselor in the bishopric?

I burst out the exit and walked briskly away from the building. I didn't want to make a scene by running. Smart choice. Luke was walking toward me.

"Hey," he said. "Aren't you going in the wrong direction?" He stopped to talk. "I need to go back to the apartment," I said and kept walking. I certainly was going in the wrong direction. For the whole stupid semester, I had been going in the wrong stupid direction. I should have gone in the direction my gut was telling me—which was not the BYU direction. How could I let my family convince me to come back here? As if I could pretend I was just fine? As if I could pretend to be like other students, getting an education and hoping to find love along the way? What was wrong with me? What was I thinking?

This was a bad idea right from the beginning, when my mother practically peeled me off my sheets to drive me back to Provo. Why had I agreed? Why hadn't she, my own mother, known that I was not going to be able to do it? That I would not be successful at getting on with normal, everyday college life? I was so stupid. Stupid. Stupid. Stupid.

Then there was Travis. This was all his fault. He had totally and completely screwed up my life. And I had just let him walk away. I had to make him see how wrong he was. I decided I'd go see him and make him realize he was completely and utterly wrong.

When I reached the apartment, my heart was racing, and my head was spinning. I could take Sarah's car. Should I go? I debated for a second, reconsidering my decision. Did I have the courage to go see him? I knew where he lived. So now I had absolutely nothing standing between me and confronting Travis.

I brushed my hair. The last time I saw him I had been such a mess. Why would he want me back if I looked like the creature from the Black Lagoon? Makeup. I needed makeup. And regular clothes, not just yoga pants and a T-shirt. And pie. I was going to make him that pie I kept meaning to. When I showed up with a chocolate éclair pie and me looking fabulous, he would wonder why he ever left me. That was what I would do.

I finally found a pair of jeans that fit still folded in the bag my mom had packed, shoved way under my bed. Jeans and a skinny, scoop-neck shirt. What was not to want?

I made the pie in record time. I may have also made a little bit of a mess, because I wasn't exactly careful whipping the vanilla pudding with the milk and Cool Whip. It's hard not to splatter when you're in a hurry to beat the heck out of something. The chocolate topping had barely cooled before I spread it over the pie, but it was good enough. I just wanted to get there.

I went ahead and borrowed Sarah's car without asking. She had offered it before, so I hoped she didn't mind my taking it. I just needed to get where I was going and get everything straightened out.

Then I headed over to Travis's without a thought in my head of any possible repercussions. I was surprised to see Travis's white BMW parked prominently in front of the building. His parents must have given it back to him after the divorce.

I knocked on door 2B.

His former/current roommate Jake opened the door. "Fifi?" he said incredulously.

I handed the pie to him as I pushed past him without being invited in and ignored the other two guys sitting on the couch. "I need Travis," I said.

"Travis, dude," Jake yelled, looking me over, then eying the pie, not knowing what to do with it.

"Yeah?" Travis came down the hall in shorts and a T-shirt. His hair was rumpled. Had he been sleeping? Gosh, how I missed running my hands through that hair.

"Fi?" His voice did not hide his shock. "What are you doing here?"

I rushed toward him. "You were wrong." The words tumbled out before I could edit them, especially considering we had an audience. "I want another chance. You didn't give it enough time."

"Sophia. Stop."

I threw myself at him and wrapped my arms around his neck, and he smelled . . . oh, he smelled so good. "Travis, we need to try again—"

He pushed me away, breaking my lock around his neck. "Cut it out," he said. "We're not doing this."

He turned and walked back down the hall, and I stumbled after him into his bedroom.

When he shut the door, he turned to me. His expression was not full of love and understanding. "What do you think you are doing coming here? Embarrassing me in front of my friends? How can I be any clearer? I don't want to try again."

"Wait, Travis, wait. Don't say that," I begged.

"But I don't. I don't want to try again. I don't want to be married to you. It was a mistake."

I couldn't believe what I was hearing. This wasn't the way the conversation was supposed to go. He was supposed to realize he was wrong. He was supposed to realize he missed me. He was supposed to realize he wanted me back.

"Why? Why would you think that? Travis, I love you. I want us to be together."

He gave me a hard stare. "I don't."

"Please don't say that. Please take me back," I begged.

"Are you too stupid to understand? I don't love you."

Tears lined my eyes, and I was overcome with anger. "How can you not love me anymore?" Tears streamed down my face.

"I just don't."

"So that's it? It's over?" A sob escaped.

"Sophia," he hissed. "Get it in your head. It's been over for a long time."

"And you think it's okay to just change your mind and walk away? How can you be so selfish?" I screamed.

"Keep it down."

"I don't care." I finally found my spine and stood up to him. I took a deep breath. "Travis," I said as calmly as I could, my hands held out helplessly. "I'm sorry. I don't want to cause a scene. I just think—"

"Sophia, we're divorced." He pronounced *divorced* slowly. "I made it so simple for you. All you had to do was walk away. So get on with your own life, and stay out of mine."

"Simple? Was it that easy to walk away?" I was infuriated. "There's someone else, isn't there?"

"So what if there is? You're not my wife anymore," he angrily retaliated.

"And you think she's the right one?"

He didn't completely answer my question. "The right one's out there; it's just not you. Now get out."

"Oh, you mean your delusion of the perfect Mormon wife?" Bitterness conquered my tears momentarily.

"Sophia." He shook his head and clenched his teeth. "We've been divorced eight months. Why don't you get it?"

Good question. Why didn't I get it? The divorce itself should have made me get it. And yet, here I was. Sobbing and crying, holding on to the man I hated so passionately yet thought I still loved. Here I was, begging him to give me another chance that he so obviously couldn't care less about considering. I was wasting my time, but most of all, I was making a fool of myself.

What was wrong with *me*? It was no longer a question of what was wrong with me in the sense of why he didn't want me. What was wrong with me that I didn't get it? *Walk away!* my mind screamed. *Walk away with what little pride I have left.*

"Oh." A hiccup escaped. Pride kicked in. I had to get out of there fast.

I pulled open the door as hard as I could, feeling satisfied as it slammed against the back wall. "I hate you!" I seethed at him.

I headed for the front door. When I reached the living room, his roommates were suddenly engrossed in the TV infomercial about super absorbent towels. *And* they were eating my pie. Just digging in with forks. How dare they. I had brought it for Travis, but there was no way he was getting it now.

"That's mine." I snatched it away from them. Jerks.

I grabbed the doorknob, ready to leave, but stopped. Travis made his way slowly into the living room. His roommates were openly staring at us. I wiped my eyes, protectively holding the pie plate.

"Get out, Sophia."

I looked at him one last time. The man I had loved. The man I was supposed to spend all time and eternity with. I was overcome with hatred.

And just because I was feeling mean and nasty and hateful, I yelled, "I hope you get testicle cancer, you jerk."

"It's testicular. And that's highly unlikely," he said smugly. So arrogant.

"Yeah, well, whatever. I hope you get cancer."

"Whatever, Sophia. Go away." He obviously couldn't care less.

"By the way, I lied about your hairline. It *is* receding." Maybe I could hit him where it hurt: his vanity.

Travis scowled at me.

I slammed the door behind me, but it didn't shut, just bounced back open.

"Dude, she was your wife?" I heard one of the roommates ask. I slowed down.

"Yeah. It was the most miserable time of my life," Travis said.

"I wouldn't mind being miserable like that."

As I walked past his pristine car, I dumped what was left of the pie on it and smeared it all over the hood. With the chocolate filling, I spelled out *liar* on the windshield. I wiped my hands on the front of my jeans and stepped back to admire my handiwork.

Payback felt good.

Chapter Eighteen
Divulgence

I COULDN'T CALM DOWN AS I climbed into Sarah's car. I was almost hyperventilating. What was I *thinking*? Had I been that stupid the last eight months, wanting him back? A fog had lifted, and I could finally see what everyone had been trying to tell me. It really *was* over. I had held on to that tiny scrap of hope because I didn't want to accept the truth. Just call me Sophia, Queen of Denial.

I drove home rather recklessly. I prayed I wouldn't be pulled over by a cop. But with the bad behavior I'd displayed so far today, I didn't think I was entitled to asking for favors. I probably should have asked for forgiveness instead.

Speaking of forgiveness, I'd have to ask Sarah's forgiveness for taking her car without asking. My timing was such that I pulled into the parking lot when everyone was arriving home from church. Sarah looked completely surprised when she saw me driving her car.

"What is going on, Sophia? We thought you ran home to get something for your talk, but you never came back. And why are you driving my car?"

"Why are you crying?" Rhonda said, joining in the inquisition.

"I'm sorry, Sarah. I should've asked. I had to do something . . . And I can't believe . . ."

I started heaving and choking up again. Even though I loathed Travis, the idea of moving on was overwhelming. Where did I go from here? What a fool I'd been.

My roommates looked at me, confused. "What are you talking about?" Claire threw her hands up in frustration. My ramblings were surely confusing her.

"I can't talk about it." Tears ran down my cheeks. I was creating a scene but didn't care. Some people slowed as they passed; others stopped and openly stared. Wouldn't there already be gossip because I bailed on my sacrament talk? Why not add some hysterics to the rumor mill and let them come up with a good story. Maybe it would be entertaining, even to me.

I dropped Sarah's keys in her hand and ran past my roommates, ignoring the onlookers, into the apartment.

I locked myself in my bedroom and burrowed under my down comforter. I was so stupid! I hated Travis! I hated myself for making a fool of myself.

There was a knock at the door. "Sophia, can we come in?" It was Rhonda. "We want to talk to you."

"Go away, Rhonda. I want to be alone," I said from under the covers.

"But what's wrong?" Sarah sounded like she was talking through the crack at the bottom of the door.

"I just need some time to think," I said slowly and emphatically.

It was getting hot under the blanket. I flung it off and sat up. I was too keyed up to sleep anyway. Instead, I pulled out the framed wedding picture from the back of my closet and threw it against the cinderblock wall. It shattered into tiny shards of glass. I wasn't quite satisfied yet. I hit it repeatedly against the wall until the frame was completely flattened and misshapen.

"Did something break?" Sarah was alarmed.

"Let us in," Rhonda demanded, banging on the door.

"No. Go away." The picture of us as a happy couple had fallen out. I plucked it up and ripped it into teeny, tiny pieces.

"What is her problem?" I heard Claire say. I was surprised she had even gotten involved. "She's such a drama queen. I can't wait around for her to open the door. I've got to get to my brother's."

So much for concern. But whatever. I wouldn't want Claire consoling me.

"Please. Sophia, please let us in," Sarah begged through the door.

"I want to be alone," I said tersely.

"We need priesthood!" I heard Rhonda say. It sounded like she was running for the front door. She sounded frantic.

That stopped me for a minute. What did she mean by priesthood? What was a priesthood holder going to do? If they'd just leave me alone, I could sort it out myself.

Next I pulled out the loose pictures from under my mattress and ripped them into little pieces. I considered lighting them on fire and burning them to ashes. Was this what "letting go" felt like? Maybe it wasn't so bad. Maybe

I should have tried it a little sooner. I was looking for something else to destroy when there was a knock.

"Go. Away." I was quite irritated by my roommates' concern. Couldn't they give me a few minutes alone so I could have my tantrum in peace?

"Hey, Sophia?" It wasn't my roommates; it was Luke.

Poor Luke. How'd he get sucked into this? He probably had no idea what to do next. I almost felt worse for him than I did for me.

I opened the door a crack.

"Can I come in?"

I felt bad for him, being asked to deal with the hysterical girl. I could imagine the scene Rhonda caused running from the apartment, waving her arms, screaming for priesthood.

"You're the priesthood?"

"By default of being your home teacher."

"Aha."

"So can I come in, or do you want to tell me what's wrong through this little crack in the door?"

I debated. Did I want to talk about it? And did I want to talk about it to him? "I don't know . . ."

"You do realize," he whispered, "if you don't let me in, everyone will be listening around the corner." He nodded in the direction of the kitchen. My roommates were most certainly standing at the doorway, straining to hear what was being said.

"Good point," I whispered back, defeated, then stepped away from the door and let him in.

He glanced around, uncertain, but said nothing. His eyes rested momentarily on the shards of glass that still littered the floor. I'm sure I looked like a mad woman, with crazy hair and mascara most likely trailing down my cheeks. I wiped under my eyes.

"Can I sit down?" He motioned to the end of my bed.

I nodded. I sat at the head of my bed against the wall, with my pillow on my lap. I took a deep breath, but when I let it out, it sounded like a shudder.

"What's going on, Sophia? Are you okay? Your roommates are pretty worried."

"I know." I didn't look him in the eye. "I—"

A knock at the door interrupted me. "Sophia? Luke can't be in there." It was Rhonda again.

I'm sure my expression reflected my annoyance. I stood up, wiped my eyes with the back of my hand, and opened the door enough to address her. "But you're the one who sent Luke back here."

"I know, but I thought you would talk in the living room. You know guys in the bedroom are off-limits."

I was in the middle of having a breakdown and had locked myself in the bedroom. Why would she think I would talk to Luke about it in front of everybody? "Okay," I said and shut the door. I leaned against it and looked at Luke. "Apparently Rhonda wants you to resolve the situation, just not in here."

"Do you want to go for a drive?" Luke asked, his voice quiet.

I thought about being in such confined quarters to spill all my secrets. It made my skin itch with claustrophobia. "I don't know."

Luke brightened and stood up. "I know where we can go."

I stayed where I was. Was he thinking of going to his apartment? Were his roommates more lenient about having the opposite sex in the bedroom? I didn't know if we'd get any more privacy over there. "I don't know. Maybe this isn't such a good idea."

Luke smiled slowly. "Trust me on this, okay?"

And for some reason, I did. I silently followed him out of my room and my apartment. I didn't look back to see if inquiring minds wanted to know and were curious enough to bother watching. When we walked past his apartment door without a word, I began to wonder where we were going. We went down the two flights of metal steps and into the confines of the laundry room.

I looked around the familiar room, making sure that it was indeed empty. It was dim and quiet, deserted in observance of the Sabbath.

Luke flipped the switch, and the lights flickered on. "What do you think? Is this enough privacy?"

I shut the door behind him to avoid any lurkers. I wasn't sure if my roommates had gone as far as following behind us. "Not as comfortable as sitting on my bed, but sure, it'll do."

I sat on a utility table pushed against the wall and leaned my head back and closed my eyes momentarily.

Luke sat next to me but far enough away to give me my space. "So, what's up?"

"I don't even know where to begin," I said without looking at him.

"It's going to sound cliché, but the beginning would be good."

Where was the beginning? The talk at church this morning? The beginning of the semester? Travis telling me he wanted a divorce? Where did this whole mess start? I shook my head and looked at my hands.

"You left church kind of suddenly today," he prompted.

"I was asked to talk in sacrament," I said. "They wanted me to talk about overcoming trials, but I told them I couldn't."

"That's what this is all about? You had a panic attack? You don't like speaking in church?"

"It wasn't the talk. It was the topic."

"Overcoming trials?"

"Yeah."

"Because you've been having a hard time with school?" Luke was fishing for information.

To tell or not to tell? That was the question. I looked at Luke, and the tears started again. Nice, sweet Luke. Other than Dave, he was the person I confided in the most. He had seen me crying. He never hit on me. He made sure I didn't spend Thanksgiving alone. I felt like he truly cared about what was going on.

"Remember how I told you over Thanksgiving that last year didn't go very well?" I took a deep breath. I couldn't believe I was going to tell him.

"Broken heart."

"Yeah. Broken heart. Actually, there's a little more to it. I guess a lot more to it." I picked at a piece of fuzz on my shirt before sneaking a glance at him.

He stared at me, waiting. "Okay?" He looked apprehensive.

"I . . . um . . ." I took another deep breath. "I got married."

"Married?" His surprise was obvious. "You're married?" He looked away before looking back at me. "And here I thought you were going to tell me someone died or something."

"No, nothing so serious."

"Married," he repeated thoughtfully, almost to himself. "That definitely changes things. I mean . . ." Then he stopped. "Do I need to go talk to the bishop?"

"Why would you have to talk to the bishop? For hanging out with a divorced girl? Oooh, big sin."

"Wait. You're divorced? You're not married; you're divorced?"

"Yes. That's why things didn't work out so great last year. I got married, and four months later, I got divorced."

"I don't know what to say, Sophia. I mean, I'm glad someone didn't die, but . . . wow."

"I know. It's not something you hear every day. There aren't a whole lot of nineteen-year-old divorced Mormon girls out there. I haven't told anyone here, except you. Not even my roommates. I haven't been able to get past it, or through it, or over it. So instead, I sit around feeling sorry for myself, being pathetic."

Luke gave me a consoling look. "Don't be so hard on yourself, Soph. You're not pathetic."

I snorted.

"Seriously, Sophia, give yourself some credit. You've been trying, right? You had a great, memorable Thanksgiving. I think that counts . . . What could be better?"

"My ex-husband getting testicular cancer," I muttered.

A pained look crossed Luke's face. "Oh, don't say that. Just thinking about that makes me cringe. Remind me never to get on your bad side. I don't want you cursing me with anything like that."

"Don't worry. It's highly unlikely I would ever wish that upon you."

"Thanks, I think."

"Seriously. I don't go around wishing horrible sicknesses on everyone I'm mad at. I'm just so angry with my ex right now. I went over and saw him today. I hadn't really seen him since the divorce."

"So," he said, "you went and saw your ex-husband, and that's why you're so upset?"

"Yeah. I thought maybe there was still a chance for us. But there isn't."

"Do you still love him?" Luke asked in a quiet voice.

"No. Yes. I don't know. I thought I did, but I've been lying to myself. Gosh, I'm so stupid! I made a complete idiot of myself." I started crying again.

"He doesn't want to get back together?"

I shook my head. "No, he doesn't. I hoped for so long we'd get back together. And now I don't know what to do."

"Um, are you asking me for advice, or do you just need to vent?" Luke asked.

"I don't know. I've spent so much time loving him and hating him, and now I don't know what to feel."

"Better?" Luke said.

"What?" I wasn't sure what he meant.

"You want to feel better, right?"

"Yes. I do. I don't know how though."

"Well," Luke said, "with all my vast psychological experience, I'd tell you to, um, watch Dr. Phil or . . ."

"It's okay, Luke, I'll figure it out," I said, letting Luke off the hook. That's why I went to Dave.

"Sophia, I don't know what to say. But I don't think people are going to think any differently about you or judge you because you're divorced."

"Do you think differently?" I asked quietly, dreading the answer. Now that Luke knew, what did he think?

"I'll admit I'm surprised, but it doesn't make me think . . ." Luke seemed to be searching for a way to say it. "Any less of you."

"I don't want people talking about me." My chin quivered, and my eyes filled up with tears again. I wiped my eyes with the back of my hand and took a couple of deep breaths.

"No one needs to know," Luke said simply, decided.

"You won't say anything?"

"Why would I?" he said. "It's your decision who you tell."

"I'd appreciate it." I paused. "I'm sorry, Luke."

He looked at me like I was crazy. "About what?"

"About dumping all my emotional baggage on you."

"It's fine," he reassured me.

"Are you sure?"

"Yes."

"Thank you," I said.

"You're welcome. Anytime."

"Um, before we go, can we agree on an explanation?"

"Easy. You freaked out about talking in sacrament, right?"

"Right. And thank you again."

He reached out like he was going to touch my leg but then pulled back and rested his hand on his knee. "No problem. If you need anything, Sophia, call me or come by. I mean it."

He was so sincere I started to cry yet again. "I will."

"I'm going to check on you." He made it sound like it was a threat.

I managed a weak smile. I thought about throwing myself across the table and giving him a long, hard hug. Considering the jerks guys could be, including my ex-husband, Luke was one of the good ones. In fact, I almost could have kissed him at that moment. Whoa. Where did that come from? Did I just admit to thinking that?

"Are you going to be okay?" Luke said as he got up.

"Yeah, I think so." I wiped my eyes as I stood up to walk out with him.

He gave me a pat on the shoulder. "Really. I'm just a few doors down if you need to talk again."

"I know. And I appreciate it Luke."

He opened the door of the laundry room, and we left in silence. I looked around as we walked up the stairs to the third floor. Nothing looked any different. Nothing had changed physically in my surroundings, but things felt very different. Maybe it was just the weight lifted from sharing the secret I had been carrying around for too long.

"Thanks again," I said as we approached his door. I had the same urge to hug him but decided against it.

"See you later, Sophia."

"Bye, Luke." I managed a small smile and gave a wave good-bye. As his front door shut behind him, I took a deep breath. Wow. I had just told someone I had been married. Wow.

I slowly walked to my apartment. I knew I'd get the third degree as soon as I walked in, but I'd have to face it at some point, and since I had no place else to go, I pulled on my emotional big-girl pants and opened the front door.

"Sophia, thank goodness you're back," Rhonda said immediately, jumping off of the couch.

"Are you doing okay?" Sarah followed up.

"I'm exhausted," I said instead of facing the onslaught of questions. "I'm going to lie down for a while." I left without anymore explanation. Taking a nap was so much easier than dealing with real life, or at least Rhonda.

My cell phone's buzzing woke me up a couple of hours later. I chose to ignore it because it was my mother and I couldn't handle any encouragement right now.

The only reason I came out later was that Luke stopped by to check on me. Otherwise, I would have hidden in there until the next morning or until I had to unlock the door to let Claire in. I was able to reassure my roommates that it was something like a panic attack that caused my odd behavior this afternoon and that I was doing much better now.

The next day when I was up on campus, I printed a picture of Tom the Turkey in the dumpster, glued it on cardstock, and made Luke a card. Inside I wrote, "Thanks for keeping my secret. Sophia."

Chapter Nineteen
Acknowledgments

I MADE ANOTHER EMERGENCY APPOINTMENT with Dave.

"Another pleasant surprise. What's up?"

"I did something incredibly stupid yesterday," I said, sitting down.

"Like what?"

I took a deep breath. "I went over to see Travis."

"To talk to him?"

"More like beg him to take me back," I admitted sheepishly.

Dave's eyebrows shot up. "Oh. How did that go?"

"Other than my making a complete fool of myself and realizing you've been right all along, it went great."

"What do you mean by realizing I've been right all along?"

I hated to admit it, mostly to myself. "I haven't been realistic. At all. He totally was not interested in getting back together or giving our marriage another try."

"How does that make you feel?"

"Like an idiot."

"Sometimes, Sophia, in the grieving process, because this was a loss in your life, it takes awhile to get through the stages. There is not any set time for any one stage. It seems like you've held on to the denial and isolation and depression, but now you're getting into the acceptance stage, and once you've begun to accept the situation for what it is, you will able to move on in your life."

"So you're saying it's okay that I went over there and made a complete fool of myself because now I can move on?"

"What I'm saying is, maybe that's what you needed to do to finally accept that it is over."

"Well, yeah, I finally get the part that it's over."

"How does that make you feel?"

"I don't know. I feel like I'm in limbo. I'm no longer holding on to him, but where do I go from here?"

"You go forward."

"But I don't know what's in front of me."

"No one does. But you'll figure it out."

I thought about that for a moment. I wasn't so sure I would. It didn't make me feel any less lost.

"Maybe it will help you move forward by telling someone your secret."

"I already did."

His surprise was evident. "You did? Who?"

"My home teacher." I recalled the memory of Luke standing at the door, unprepared for what he was about to hear.

"Why him?"

Good question. Why did I tell him? I knew the answer right away. Because I felt safe with him. "I trust him. He gets me."

"How do you feel about him knowing you're divorced?"

"Kind of relieved. Kind of unsure what he thinks about me now."

"So it wasn't so bad telling someone you're divorced?" He smiled.

"I had a moment of weakness."

Luke stopped by later that evening. "I wanted to check on you, make sure you're hanging in there."

"Hey, yeah, I do feel a little better. I, uh, have something for you." I suddenly felt self-conscious about giving the card to Luke.

"I hope it's not a Christmas present 'cause I don't have anything for you," he said jokingly.

"No. Don't worry. Hold on just a second." I ran back to my room and grabbed it. Claire was on her bed, talking on the phone. I had no idea why she would be home at this time of day. Maybe she wasn't feeling well. But maybe with the semester winding down, she was actually relaxing a little. Who knew?

"Because technically I am still your TA," she said. Was she arguing with one of the students in her class?

Sarah and Ned were in the living room hanging out on the couch. Not wanting to talk in front of them, I pulled my coat on and stuck the envelope in my pocket. "Can we . . . ?" I motioned to go outside with my head. "Can we walk for a minute?" I chewed on the corner of my lip. I wondered what Luke's reaction would be now that my news had had time to sink in. I felt vulnerable.

"Here. I wanted to give you this," I said once we were outside. I pulled the card out and handed it to him.

"Thanks." He started opening it.

"No. No." I waved my hands, trying to stop him. "It's just to thank you. But don't open it now."

"Okay. I'll save it for later." He put it in his back pocket.

We walked for a few minutes before either of us said anything. I was trying to decide if I should just address my meltdown or if I could think of something else to talk about.

Luke broke the silence. "You're doing okay though? Recovered from Sunday's . . ."

"Drama?" I filled in for him. "I feel . . . relieved."

"I bet." He paused. "I'm sorry, Sophia. I kinda get the sadness now."

"Yeah. My deep, dark secret," I said.

"That had to be hard."

"Yeah, it was."

"When did all this happen?" he asked.

"We met at the beginning of school last year and got married right after Thanksgiving. He told me on April first he wanted a divorce, and it was finalized a month later."

"You've had a very busy year."

"It doesn't seem like I've been divorced for eight months, but I feel like I should be over it by now."

"You don't just get over something like that," he said gently.

"But I wish I did."

He turned and faced me. "It does get better, Sophia."

I didn't mean to, but I started crying. "I know, but when?"

He stopped and put one hand on each of my shoulders as if squaring them up and bent down to look me in the eye. "I think you're on your way. Don't you? Sunday was sort of—what do they say?—your closure. You confronted him, and now you can move on."

"I wish it wasn't so hard." I sniffed.

He took a step back, letting go of my shoulders. "I'm sorry," he said, slowly starting to walk again, and I followed him. "I don't mean to minimize it. I know it's hard. There are still some days I totally miss my dad."

"Yeah," I agreed.

"Hey, do you want to get something over at Stan's hamburger place?" He looked across the street at it. We had walked five blocks, and I hadn't even realized it. "Stan makes a mean Oreo shake, and his fry sauce is to die for." Luke was laying the temptation on thick.

"All right. Sold," I said as we walked in and sat down in a booth.

We both ordered Oreo shakes and some fries. It was quiet for a few minutes. The lack of conversation compelled me to start babbling to break the silence.

"So how do I bridge the ginormous gap from feeling crappy to feeling happy?"

He started laughing. "I guess that's one way to put it."

"But you know what I mean, right?"

"Yeah, I know. I think it just takes time," he said, then added, "and it does get better."

Somehow, it was easier to take his sort of pep talk than my mother's.

Chapter Twenty
The Truth of the Matter

As if all my drama and excitement weren't enough, Rhonda got a new calling, and Sarah got engaged. It was a relief to have Rhonda released as FHE cochair, but it created a new problem, since she was now on the Relief Society committee in charge of activities. It was not completely surprising, given her propensity for baking, hosting, and socializing.

I wasn't completely shocked about Sarah's engagement either; things did tend to move rather quickly at BYU. I should know. Ned was nice enough, but I was worried that it was too fast. I felt like Sarah was up and marrying the first man who came along. Just like I had. This was one instance when we needed Claire to leave a yellow sticky note saying "*Don't do it.*" But if Sarah was happy, I was going to be happy for her.

"Congratulations! Are you so excited?" I asked when we were alone.

She didn't immediately answer me with a resounding yes.

"Is something wrong?"

"No. Why would you think that?"

"Just your reaction. But maybe I'm reading into things."

She hesitated for a moment. "I expected this fairy-tale proposal and had dreams of an amazing wedding."

"What do you mean?"

"Oh, I can't believe I'm admitting this. The way Ned proposed was disappointing."

I thought back to what she had told me about him proposing at a little restaurant. "You mean he didn't ask you over dinner?"

"No, he did. But the little restaurant? It was McDonald's."

"He proposed at McDonald's? For real?"

Sarah frowned. "Yeah. I'm talking Big Mac and fries. Totally unromantic, huh?"

"Yeah. I could see why it wasn't the proposal of your dreams."

"Then my mom told me we would have to have the reception in the church cultural hall. I don't want to have a fern in the basketball hoop." Sarah cringed.

"Maybe it won't be that bad," I said.

"My brother's reception was at a nice banquet hall, but that was because his wife's parents paid for it. My parents said there wasn't money for that. Then my mom asked if I wanted her to make my wedding dress."

"She must sew pretty well."

"No, that's the problem. She doesn't. I had to learn the hard way. She made my prom dress, and I totally hated it. It *looked* homemade."

"Oh," I said slowly. "I see what you mean."

"So it's not so much Ned as it is everything else. It's just not this magical fairy tale I imagined it would be."

I thought of my checklist for Travis before I got married: attractive, smart, charming, and rich. I thought I was living the dream because I was getting everything I'd ever wanted. Yet, look where it got me. I was now living in a crummy, single-student housing apartment, going through the motions of living, and being divorced and broken at nineteen.

I debated telling Sarah the truth about my recent behavior and my short-lived marriage. But that was my bad experience. It didn't mean her marriage would turn out the same way.

I could *not* tell her, but I could still caution her to consider wisely.

"Sarah," I started carefully, "just make sure you're going to be happy."

"I'm happy with Ned. It's all the wedding stuff I'm disappointed about."

"You just got engaged, Sarah. You don't need to figure out all the wedding plans in one week. It takes time, and maybe circumstances will change. You just never know."

"Are you sure you're only nineteen?" Sarah asked.

I was surprised by her question. "What?"

"You just seem to have this bigger understanding about life than I do."

I think that was called experience. I tried to downplay her observation. "I think we have these dreams, but reality changes them into something different. The marriage is so much more important than the wedding, don't you think?"

"See. That's exactly what I'm talking about. You're so profound."

"Profound," I repeated, then rolled my eyes.

We both started laughing.

* * *

Bradley called later that day while I was walking home from campus. Funny, with as much as I had told myself I should give him a chance, I hadn't thought much about him while he'd been gone. I had heard through the grapevine (meaning Rhonda) that he was back, but with all that had been going on in my life, I hadn't even given a thought to calling him.

"Hey, stranger," I said in greeting. "You're back?"

"Yeah, I've been home about a week and a half. I looked for you at church but didn't see you."

So he had been back that Sunday. "I had to leave early."

"Weren't you supposed to talk?"

I cringed thinking about it. "There was some miscommunication about that."

"Oh."

"So how have you been?"

"Busy. Make-up work, graduation stuff, you know."

"How was your trip?" I thought it was better to start with small talk than jumping into the apology I owed him.

"It was good. I was wondering if I could stop by? Are you home?" he asked.

"Give me about five minutes; I'm almost home. I'm just going to be studying for my finals, so I'll be there."

"I'll see you then."

I wondered what was up. He seemed anxious.

He was waiting for me at my door when I arrived.

"C'mon in," I said as I unlocked the door. "Have a seat." I motioned to the kitchen table. "Do you want something to drink?" I let my backpack drop to the floor and went to get a Diet Coke.

"No, thanks."

I opened my drink and sat down across from him. "You know, I felt bad about what happened at Halloween. I went over to talk to you, but you had already left for Mexico. I wasn't trying to—"

"It's okay, Sophia," Bradley cut in. "I realize I was kind of rushing things. You don't need to apologize."

"See," I started to explain. "I was . . ." I debated if I should tell Bradley about my divorce but quickly decided against it. "I was in a pretty serious relationship last year, and it didn't work out. It's made me overly cautious about getting involved with someone else."

"It was me. I'm sorry."

I was glad to have the apology out of the way. "So tell me about your trip. How was it?"

His face lit up. "It was awesome. I loved it. I learned so much, and it's totally the kind of thing I want to do for a career."

"Keep volunteering for Habitat for Humanity?" How would he support himself?

"No, but working with some sort of organization that does that kind of work. And because I wanted to learn more, I signed on to do a three-month project in Peru. Cool, huh?"

"What about getting a job after graduation?"

"Doing this helps build my résumé. I can always find a job later. Or maybe I'll join the Peace Corps."

I didn't know what I wanted to do with my life, but it was definitely not join the Peace Corps. Roughing it like that would be way too rough for me. I would hate living that way.

He continued before I could respond. "I was wondering if we could keep in touch while I'm gone. I'd like to see you when I get back. I'll be doing river guides close to Moab this summer, and it's not too far from Vegas."

I thought about what he had been doing over the last couple of weeks and what he was doing the next three months and for the summer. "Bradley, the things you are passionate about are things I am not interested in."

"Maybe if you gave them a try . . ." he said.

I took a deep breath. "We're two different people, and I know from experience that you can't force a relationship. I will never be a girl who wants to rock climb, river raft, or camp. Building houses for people living in poverty is so admirable, but it is not me. And it never will be."

He looked somber. "You don't think there's a chance?"

I frowned. "You can't force a connection," I said gently.

He seemed resigned to my reasoning and stood to leave.

I gave him a hug and said good-bye to Bradley Benson.

Chapter Twenty-One
PMA

AFTER THE WHOLE FIASCO LAST weekend, all the realizations, the talk with Luke, the promises to myself to move forward, I decided to take some personal responsibility. Telling Luke felt like a burden had been lifted, and I was ready to make some of the changes I needed to in my life.

With my new attitude came a new sense of purpose. This was the first day of the rest of my life. Right? All that positive mental attitude and stuff. So I decided to go jogging. It was a bright, sunny day, and I was going to give it a go. Exercise produced pheromones? Or maybe it was hormones? No. Serotonin? Melatonin? Dopamine. No, wait, it was endorphins. Yes. Endorphins.

My plan was to walk up Ninth East (warm up, you know. I didn't want to overexert myself since it'd been over a year since I had jogged last), then jog around the perimeter of campus. That plan lasted maybe seven minutes.

Oh. My. Gosh. What was I thinking? I hated jogging. That was why I never did it. It hurt. And I was out of breath in like two minutes. I kept on though, convincing myself it would get easier.

But it didn't. By the time I reached the fieldhouse, I was completely winded. The Brick Oven restaurant was down the street, and pizza aroma filled the air, suddenly making me hungry. *Maybe I should rest at the Brick Oven.* No. I was going to be strong. I was going to finish jogging.

I went into the fieldhouse to get a drink of water and walked out the door leading to the south side of campus, congratulating myself for even trying to jog, when I saw *him*. I had just rounded the slight bend of the sidewalk and saw Travis and his roommate Jake walking toward me. Talk about bad timing. I hadn't showered today. I looked like I had just rolled out of bed, because I had, and I didn't want him to see me. Or smell me. Attempting to jog could work up quite a sweat. Never mind how embarrassed I was about my recent visit to his condo. Really? Could my luck be this bad?

My options were limited. I could turn around and run back to the fieldhouse, I could hold my head up and walk by . . . or I could hide.

Hiding sounded like the best choice for his imminent approach. I wasn't close enough to the parking lot to hide there. But . . . above me was the sidewalk that ran along the edge of the hillside mostly hidden by trees. Mostly hidden by trees sounded ideal. The bad thing was I had to scramble up the hill through the bushes and trees to reach it and hide myself in time, and I didn't realize how scratchy and difficult it would be.

I stopped behind a bare bush a few feet from the higher sidewalk and stayed down, hoping he wouldn't notice me.

I could make out bits and pieces of their conversation about a football game. Then Travis's cell phone rang.

"Hey, I'm gonna take this. I'll catch you later." He waved good-bye to Jake and stopped to answer his call.

Even though I couldn't hear him clearly, I could tell by the way his voice changed that the caller was female. He used to use the same sexy voice with me.

"How are you?" Travis schmoozed.

I caught the word *building*. Big help.

"How about I meet you there? I can't wait to see you."

What? He was meeting a girl? I knew there was someone else! I was tempted to follow him and find out who she was, but that seemed more like stalking than moving on.

I waited until he was gone before I stood carefully, planning to climb the rest of the way to the sidewalk and take the stairs down so I could avoid poking my eye out on a tree. But my ponytail got caught in a branch. As I turned to pull my hair from the branch, I scratched my eye with another branch.

I finally untangled my hair but then tripped on a root, landed on my knee, fell forward, and slid to the bottom of the hill, taking a small sapling with me. I hoped no one from the grounds department happened to witness the destruction I had caused. I was covered in dirt, and my hair had come out of the ponytail. A stranger walking by offered a hand to help me up and made sure I was okay. I think my pride was hurt more than anything.

I limped my way home, reprimanding myself for doing something so ridiculous. As luck would have it, I ran into Luke walking to his truck in the parking lot. I was thankful it was him and not Mr. Outdoors Man Bradley.

"Sophia? Are you okay?"

"Sure. Why?" I tried downplaying my current state and acting like I had no idea what he was talking about.

"You have twigs in your hair." He pulled one out to show me. "And a scratch on your cheek. What happened to you?"

I caught a glimpse of myself in the side-view mirror of his truck. I looked ridiculous. "I was attempting to jog but had a fight with the bushes and lost. What are you doing?"

"I'm tired of studying, so I thought I would take a break and get a slushie. Do you want to get one with me?" Luke asked. "You look like you could use one."

"Could I make it a Diet Coke? It's kind of chilly for a slushie—for me, that is."

He opened the door of his truck for me. "How did you end up in the bushes?"

"I saw my ex, so I hid." I felt like an even bigger idiot saying it out loud.

"You hid in the bushes?"

"Well, yeah. I'm still kind of embarrassed about going over to his place, making a fool out of myself, smearing chocolate pie all over his car—"

"Wait a minute," Luke said, cutting me off. "You smeared chocolate pie all over his car? You didn't tell me about that. Wow, Sophia, you were . . ."

"A crazy woman. Yes, I know," I filled in for him.

"I was going to say upset, but okay. Why did you smear pie on his car?"

"I made him his favorite pie and brought it with me, but since things did not go so well and I was mad, I dumped the pie on his BMW."

"I would have hidden in the bushes too if I had dumped pie all over someone's car."

"It's weird. I don't see him all semester and I've seen him like three times in the last two weeks."

"I think I'd pick a different jogging route."

"I think I'm just going to give up jogging."

"Good idea," Luke said, then out of the blue added, "I had a mission companion whose uncle got struck by lightning when he was jogging."

"Did he die?" I blurted out before thinking.

"Yeah." He shook his head.

"Wow."

"I know what you're thinking. I mean, who gets struck by lightning? That only happened in the days of Ben Franklin, right?" He looked at me, waiting for my response.

"Actually, yeah. That is unbelievable."

Luke nodded. "Crazy, huh?"

"It's just so shocking."

"Literally," Luke said soberly.

And I started laughing again. I tried catching my breath. "I'm not trying to make a joke out of it. I'll just stop talking now."

Luke looked at me, his eyes bright. "There's another reason to not go jogging. It can literally kill you."

I relaxed a little. "That will be my new reason to not jog. I might die."

"That's what I think too. Okay, we're here," he said as we pulled into the convenience store.

"So are you ready for finals?" he asked as he grabbed two large, thirty-two-ounce cups and studied the slushie machine.

"I'm as ready as I'm going to be considering how difficult Floral Design and Living with Plants can be," I said jokingly, then cleared my throat, trying to be serious. "I think Intro to Interiors will be my hardest final."

Luke filled his cup. "But of course you're going to ace them."

"I'd be happy if I just passed them." I looked down at the floor, thinking about how much I had slacked this semester. I noticed my shoe was untied and bent down to tie it, knowing I'd probably trip if I didn't.

I stood as Luke turned, holding both cups in his hands, and I hit his arm, making him dump one drink down the front of my hoodie and drop the other one on the floor.

"Sophia! Sorry. I didn't see you there . . ."

"No, it's okay. I'm sorry. Bad timing." I shook the drink off my hands.

He grabbed a bunch of napkins, trying to mop up the mess. He went to blot my sweatshirt, then stopped. "Oh, um, sorry, I didn't mean to . . . I mean . . . I'll, uh, mop up the floor."

"Let me help." I stepped, slipped on the wet floor, and went down. I was about as graceful as a newborn calf trying to stand for the first time.

"Give me your hand." Luke reached out to help me up. I slipped again and pulled him down with me. He ended up sitting next to me on the floor, the bottom half of one leg in the puddle. I knocked a couple of cans off the bottom shelf as I was trying to stabilize myself.

I stifled a giggle.

The store attendant brought over a mop and told us in a huff not to worry about it. Clearly, he wanted us out of the store.

"Let's go." I grabbed the arm of Luke's jacket and carefully stood. "I'm not thirsty anymore."

He got up after me and headed for the exit. "Sorry," he said to the store clerk, backing out of the store and handing him some money as he went. "Keep the change."

Once we were outside, he started apologizing to me. "I'm sorry, Sophia. I didn't mean to dump the drinks all over you." Luke opened the passenger side door for me, then looked behind the backseat. "I might have an old towel to dry off better."

"Please. I slid downhill on my face today. What's a little spilled slushie compared to face sledding?"

"Are you sure? Look at your sweatshirt; it's a mess. Will you take a rain check on the drink? I'll wash your sweatshirt if you like." He produced what looked like an old T-shirt and handed it to me.

"It's fine, Luke. I'm sure I'll see you in the laundry room on Friday. If you want, you can wash it in one of your loads."

"I won't be there. I have a final that night. Unless you want to meet me in the laundry room tonight," he said. "You know, add an element of excitement to your evening."

"I can't say I have that much dirty laundry yet," I said hesitantly. I wasn't sure if he felt that obligated to wash my sweatshirt or was trying to ask me out. I was hoping it was the first one because I didn't want Luke to go there. I felt a certain kinship with him after Thanksgiving. But I didn't want to lose that because of feelings. Burning turkeys and dumping drinks were safe situations, since they didn't require any attraction from either party.

"I think I've butchered all of my attempts to add excitement to your BYU experiences."

"I don't know why I'm telling you this, because it will tell you how pathetic my life is, but those have been highlights considering how I've been feeling the rest of the time."

He gave me a strange look, like he was trying to register the seriousness of that remark. "I guess I'll take that as a compliment."

"It is a compliment. And you should take it. I don't give out compliments very often."

He grinned. "Well, okay. I don't completely get it, but I'm glad I provide some amusement."

I gave him a friendly jab with my elbow. "Me too."

It wasn't so much amusement that he brought; it was more a sense of feeling normal. Even if it was fleeting.

If only I could tell him how much it *really* meant to me.

* * *

I was glad that I would have my finals over by the end of the week. I took two of my finals on the first day of exams. But there wasn't much to be tested on in Floral Design, and Living with Plants was pretty easy. The day after that I would take my final for Intro to Interiors, and then this semester would be officially over for me.

I did okay on my first two finals. I didn't think I failed them, but I didn't ace them either. I should have put a little more study time into the Intro to Interiors final, but I wasn't too stressed. I was just happy to be done with them.

When I came home after my last final, Sarah gave me an early Christmas gift. It was a book about learning to crochet, and it came with a starter kit, including the hook and some yarn.

She blushed as she handed it to me. "I thought this might be something you'd like. They say using your hands helps with . . ." She trailed off.

I think she wanted to say depression. Or maybe sadness? Whatever she thought, her intentions were right.

"Thank you." I hugged her. The girl on the front of the kit was wearing a dang cute scarf with little flowers on it. I wouldn't mind knowing how to do that. Maybe I'd give it a try. You know, give it a whirl or a knit and a purl or stitch . . . or whatever the proper terms were. If anything, it'd give me something to do over the break.

Luke stopped by on his way up to campus. "I'm making good on the rain check for the Diet Coke I owe you." He handed me a bottle.

"Perfect timing. I just got home from taking my last final."

"That's great. My last one is tomorrow. Then I'm heading home. How about you?"

Always making sure everyone was taken care of. "I'm going home. I leave in two days. Sarah's giving me a ride down to the I-70 junction to meet my mother."

"I could've given you a ride home. I drive right through Vegas," Luke said.

"I had to force my mom to agree to this plan. She was determined to come get me. But less time driving with her means less time answering questions about how things are going."

"She gives you the third degree?"

"Yes. About everything," I said. "I know she means well."

It was quiet for a moment.

"So you're going home tomorrow?" I said.

"Yeah. I'll be at home for Christmas and then probably come back on the twenty-ninth or thirtieth. The holidays are hard on my mom since Dad died. So we don't celebrate a whole lot. After Christmas, my mom is flying up to Portland to visit my sister's family for a couple of weeks."

"On your way back through Vegas, if you need a break, you should stop by. It's about a half hour detour, but if you wanted to . . ." I said.

"Maybe I will. Vegas is almost halfway, and the break would be nice. If you're sure it's okay."

"I'll warn you, my mother will probably completely overreact that you're a boy *and* you're visiting. She tends to jump to conclusions. So I apologize in advance."

"I'm just your home teacher stopping by to see how your Christmas was. How's that?"

"Perfect."

Luke was the perfect home teacher.

Chapter Twenty-Two
The Gift of Giving

SARAH'S GIFT WASN'T THE ONLY book I got. *All* of my Christmas presents were books but not the kind I would even pretend to read. I think my mom cleaned out the divorce section at Deseret Book.

Then there were my mom's upbeat questions.

"Are you dating?"

"Did you like being back at school?"

"Jeanie Bergers's son is back from his mission. Maybe you two should go out?"

"Are you eating? You're so thin."

"Are you exercising? It helps with your mood."

"Do you go outside? You look pale."

"Have you made any New Year's goals? It's a fresh start."

"Maybe you should go to the single's ward New Year's Eve dance."

The constant flow of inquiries was suffocating me.

Crocheting was my only respite. I felt like my mother was lurking around every corner, lying in wait for me to pass so she could launch another question attack. It was easier to hide out in my room crocheting than ward off another one of her assaults. I was thankful to have an activity that kept me busy.

I think my mother assumed my being in my room so much meant I was reverting back to my old habits of staying in bed all day. "You need to do something with yourself. If you're just sitting around doing nothing, you're going to start getting depressed again."

"I am doing something, Mom. I'm teaching myself to crochet." I couldn't tell her I was avoiding pep talks and things of that nature, but added for good measure, "And I have all those books to read." Maybe I should give one of them a peruse. Maybe there would be some helpful advice.

The day after Christmas, my mother took care of my need, or perceived need, to do something with myself by volunteering me to babysit without consulting me.

"Cali Hanson in the ward, the one I visit teach, had a baby two weeks ago and needs some help," my mom said as she returned home from somewhere—probably visiting teaching.

"Oh," I said, not sure why she was telling me this.

"Three hours a day, three days a week for the next two weeks. She pays ten bucks an hour."

"That's generous."

"I told her you would do it," my mom said, not looking at me because her head was deep inside the fridge.

That's where she was going with it. "What? I don't want to babysit. I . . ."

My mom turned and faced me. "You what? Are you too busy? You are not going to sit around till you go back to school. Get over yourself, and go help someone who needs it."

It looked like I didn't have much say in the matter. But that was typical of my mom. I was so glad she didn't try to pull this last year while I was permanently in bed; it might have turned to violence.

I had never met Cali Hanson. She'd moved in sometime while I was at school. When I went over to her house the next morning, I felt sheepish and juvenile as I stood on the front porch of her custom home waiting for her to answer her huge oak door.

"Hello?" the lady who opened the door said. Maybe she was the help. She wasn't too much older than me and was wearing fleece pajama pants, a T-shirt she obviously slept in, and a telltale bed head flat spot in her hair. Not to be mean, but she was bordering on looking haggard.

"Hi." I felt ridiculous. "I'm Sophia. I'm here to help Cali?"

"You're not fifteen," she blurted out, studying me.

"No, I'm not," I answered slowly, thinking this was about to get weird. "I'm nineteen."

She squinted her eyes in the sunlight, then shook her head. "I thought your mother said you were fifteen." She stepped back from the doorway and opened the door wider to let me in.

As soon as I was in, she turned and walked through the living room. I gathered that she was Cali. I shut the door and took in the huge front room with all the curtains drawn. It was empty except for the Christmas tree. I slowly walked to the kitchen, which was also dark and overrun with dirty dishes. Cali had made her way back to a couch in the adjoining family room and had sunk deep down in the cushions, holding a little bundle in a blanket. I assumed that was the baby.

"Have a seat." She motioned to a spot for me to sit.

I sat on the edge of the love seat.

"Did your mom tell you what I was looking for?" she asked.

It sounded like an interview question, and I was under the impression this was not an interview but an assignment. "She said you needed someone three days a week for three hours a day." I parroted back the information my mother had told me.

"My husband travels for business. Depending on how things go, I might need you for more or less time on those days."

"Okay." I was still wondering if she was screening me for the job or if the job was mine.

"Do you have any experience?"

"I babysat when . . ." I trailed off. I was going to say "when I was a teenager," but technically, I *was* still a teenager. "When I was in high school."

"Okay, here's Joy." She stood up with the blanketed lump, walked over to me, and deposited it into my arms, then said, "I need to get some stuff done upstairs. There's a fresh bottle on the counter when she wakes up, and then there's formula if she needs another bottle. She only drinks one to two ounces at a time. Make sure you burp her. Diapers are over there." She pointed to a package at the edge of the couch that looked like it had been attacked by a dog. "Wipes are next to it, and the TV remote is there. Don't worry about answering the phone, help yourself to whatever food is in the kitchen, though I don't even know what's there, and feel free to try one of those baby things back there." She was referring to a swing, a bouncy chair, and some other baby contraption I couldn't identify.

"Okay." This was bizarre.

"If anything pressing comes up, my bedroom is the one with the double doors to the right of the stairs. Just knock." She headed upstairs and shut her door.

I sat there wondering what I was supposed to do. She didn't ask me to do the dishes, and I didn't want to step on her toes by assuming she wanted me to do them. Behind the couch, a laundry basket peeked out. When I took a closer look, I found a huge pile of laundry overflowing from two baskets hidden back there. Wow. I wasn't quite sure what to make of the situation. Should I hang out, hold the baby, and watch TV? Should I put the baby down and clean up? What exactly was she paying me to do for the three hours I was there?

After sitting and holding the baby for thirty minutes and doing absolutely nothing, I decided it'd be okay for me to tidy up a bit. Joy didn't seem like she was going to be waking up anytime soon, so I set her in the corner of the couch and started setting up her swing.

It took me a few minutes to get it up. I strapped the baby in and went to work.

The kitchen island was cluttered with empty water bottles, Diet Coke cans (I guess we had something in common), and empty boxes of Lean Cuisine. I threw everything away and took out the trash. I found the garbage can in the garage. While I was in there, I took a moment to look around at their stuff. There were two bikes and several plastic bins labeled "Christmas." That was about it. Either they were minimalists or very boring.

Back inside, the baby snoozed away. Upstairs, I heard absolutely no movement or sound. My thought was Cali was sleeping too. She looked like she could use the sleep. She could seriously pass for the walking dead.

I swept, replaced the trash bag, and did the dishes. By then, the baby started stretching so I assumed it was time to give her a bottle.

After I fed, burped, and changed her, I heard the blaring beep of what sounded like an alarm clock. A few minutes later, Cali stumbled down the stairs, bleary eyed, with the indentation of a pillow seam on her cheek. I was right; she *had* been sleeping.

"How'd it go?" She looked around a little.

"Good. I just fed her, changed her, and put her back down." I gestured to the baby happily tucked in the seat of the swing, busily sucking on her pacifier.

"You did the dishes?"

"I figured while the baby was sleeping I might as well do something. I hope that's okay?"

"Yeah," Cali said.

I stood. "Is there anything else you need me to do?"

"That's all for today. You can still come tomorrow, right?"

There was almost an edge of desperation to her voice, like a child making sure her parents were coming back to pick her up from the babysitter's.

"Uh, yeah. Same time?"

"Yes. And if it's okay, I'll pay you for the three days on Thursday?"

"Sure, no problem."

Cali sort of plopped onto the couch, so I figured I'd see my own way out. "See you tomorrow." I half waved and started toward the front door.

"Yeah, tomorrow," Cali said dully.

Once I made it out the front door and into the sunlight, I felt like I had left an alternate universe. What was the deal with Cali and her dark and dingy castle? I'd have to ask my mother, but I wasn't expecting to get much dirt since my mother always saw the best in people.

The next day was almost identical to the first day. Cali unenthusiastically answered the door, I followed her into the family room, then Cali went upstairs. The one thing that was different was the baby was happily rocking in the swing.

I started working as soon as Cali's bedroom door shut. From what my mom told me the day before, Cali wasn't taking to motherhood like she thought she would. She was tired all the time and overwhelmed. I got that. It's hard to have energy when you hate your life. And laundry certainly was not on the top of the priority list when you had no energy. So I figured the least I could do was her laundry. Most of it was baby clothes, burp cloths, and blankets. In the middle of folding, I stopped to feed Joy. She happily went back in her swing, and I kept tidying up.

When Cali stumbled down the stairs after three hours, she looked around at the now-picked-up family room and said, "What happened to the laundry?" It almost sounded like an accusation.

"I folded it."

To which Cali started crying.

"I'm sorry. I hope I didn't offend you. I just thought I should—"

"No, I'm sorry." She held her hands out helplessly. "I'm not usually like this. I'm a lawyer. I go to court. I handle big cases and big clients . . ." She trailed off.

I wasn't sure again where she was going with this line of explanation.

She slumped into an arm chair. "And yet I can't seem to handle a six-pound baby. What is wrong with me?" Tears streamed down her face as she wiped them with the back of her hand. She sniffed. "I'm sorry." She sounded a little bit calmer. "I'm overwhelmed, my hormones are crazy, and I'm a crying wreck."

"It's okay," I murmured awkwardly.

"No, really, I'm not so . . . crazy. My husband took last week off and was on baby duty the whole time. But he had to get back to work this week, and I just can't seem to pull myself together and function. I just want to sleep . . . and cry." She started crying again.

Wow. Holy moly postpartum emotional woman.

"I'm sorry," she started again, wiping her eyes and sitting up straighter. "I'm probably scaring you from ever having children. Or ever coming back here. Like I said, I'm not usually like this."

I'd hate to see her on a *really* emotional day. And it wasn't that I was judging her either. I was not one to talk; I was a mess last year.

The next day she was still not doing well. Cali answered the door with glassy red eyes. Then she sobbed the whole time. Even being upstairs behind closed doors, she was loud enough that I could hear her. Besides hearing her, I was an expert on the signs and symptoms of crying.

When she emerged from her room three hours later, red and blotchy, I took a chance and broached the subject. "Cali, what's wrong?"

She flopped down on the couch, rubbed her eyes, then she shook her head. "Just a bad day."

Here came the part where she might get defensive. "But every day I've been here seems to be bad. Is it the baby?"

Her words gushed like a dam breaking. "And getting up all night. And I hate breastfeeding. And giving in to giving her a bottle. But every good Mormon mother is supposed to *love* breastfeeding. But I don't. And I hate my husband right now because he's not here. But I know he needs to work. And I love Joy, but I don't love being a mother. This is not what I thought it was going to be like."

Obviously, there were a lot of issues going on here that were outside my realm of expertise on crying, heartbreak, and depression. I didn't know what to say. So I said the first thing that came to my mind. "Do you want me to stay a little longer? Maybe you could take a nap," I suggested gently.

She was like an obedient child. "Yes, thank you. I'd like that very much." She stood and walked toward the stairs but paused on the first step. "If she needs . . ."

"I got it, Cali. Go take a nap."

Cali slept for another three hours. I hoped she would pay me for the extra hours. But more than that, I hoped she would wake up renewed and refreshed and feel better.

She didn't wake up a new woman, but she did look better. I had a strange realization about how bad I wanted her to come down those stairs showered, kempt, and happy. Was that how my parents felt last year? Every day hoping their little girl, who was not so little anymore, would emerge from her bedroom the girl they sent off to college just months before? It was a helpless feeling not being able to fix someone else's life.

I offered to find something for her for dinner, but she showed me her freezer full of frozen dinners. "I'll be okay. My husband comes home tonight and has tomorrow off."

"Are you sure? I'm pretty good with the microwave."

She smiled a little. "Yeah, I'm sure."

For her sake, I hoped she would be okay.

I was surprised how going to Cali's made me feel. My mother was right. Helping Cali made the days go faster and me feel better. The extra money didn't hurt either.

Cali looked a little better the next week. Maybe she took a shower or got more sleep. Either way, making Cali feel better was my mission this week.

I came armed with ideas and suggestions to get her out of the house or at least out of bed that might—and hopefully would—make her feel better. I suggested shopping. Nordstrom, Macy's, heck, even Target might do the trick. She shot them all down. I suggested seeing a movie. She wasn't interested. Next on the list was going out to eat. Another no. This was getting hard. Had I been this difficult? Probably. At the time, I'd thought it was just my mother nagging me, but I didn't understand the helpless feeling she must have had watching me struggle or the urge to fix it. So I kept on with Cali. I asked about a mani or pedi? No. Facial? No. A haircut? No. Something had to work. A walk around the block, and I'd push the baby in the stroller? Another no. Finally, I told her in no uncertain terms that I was taking her out whether she liked it or not, so she better go upstairs, get dressed, and be back down in five minutes, or I was coming up after her. I changed Joy, strapped her in her car seat, and got the diaper bag together.

She came down the stairs looking like a moody teenager, but I didn't care. I knew getting her out was exactly what she needed. Or at least a very tiny little part of what she needed. Maybe time to adjust to her new role of motherhood was what she needed. I had never been a mother, but I did know things got better with time, and Joy was only three weeks old. Three weeks was not long enough to adjust to such a life-changing experience. But I decided a little sunshine and some frozen yogurt would make things temporarily better.

We drove to the closest yogurt place. The topic weighing on my mind was not something I was looking forward to discussing with Cali. "Maybe you're depressed," I cautiously suggested. I knew I wasn't necessarily the expert, but Cali seemed depressed.

Her reaction was what I had expected: denial, outrage. "Why would you think that?"

Suggesting to someone that she might be depressed was a little like being stuck in quicksand. If I proceeded slowly and calmly, I was more likely to get through it than if I got all energetic and pushy and sank. Then again, Cali was a lawyer. Maybe I wasn't going to win with my depression case against her.

I leaned casually back in my seat, trying to convey that this conversation was not going to turn into a big deal. "I've been there, done that, and you remind me a lot of me when I was struggling."

She seemed surprised. "You were depressed?"

"I was. I never expected to be nineteen and divorced after four months of marriage."

"So quick. I'm sorry." Her reaction was how I assumed it would be, a mixture of surprise and pity. I could handle the surprise a lot better than I could the pity. I didn't want to be the object of pity.

"It happened last April, and I came back home and pretty much stayed in bed and cried for three months. I did not handle it very well."

"Who handles divorce well?"

"I don't know, but it wasn't me."

"I'm sorry. It sounds awful."

"It was. So that's why I think I kind of get what you're feeling."

Cali bent close and said, "Do you want to know a secret? It's completely irrational, but I feel like Joy reduces me to helplessness. Taking care of her, which from the outside doesn't look or seem so hard, completely overwhelms me, and I just want to cry. Shouldn't I love being a mother?"

I didn't have an answer for her. *Shouldn't* questions never had easy answers.

She continued after a minute of my not saying anything. "I kind of admitted it to your mom; I think that's why you're here. She suggested I needed a helper. But she just kept saying, 'Cheer up. It gets better. Every day it gets better.' It didn't cheer me up; it made me angry."

"I know exactly what you're talking about."

Cali started laughing. Something I had never seen her do. Maybe my ice cream-sunshine-true-confessions outing was working.

"Your mother didn't say anything about you being divorced. She said you were out of school for Christmas."

"My mom thinks if I'm not busy, I am falling back into the depths of depression."

"So what happened with your marriage?"

"Oh, Cali. He was beautiful, and I thought he was perfect. We were young, and it was fast," I said.

One hour and another serving of frozen yogurt later, I had relayed my tale to her. Joy waking up signaled it was time to leave.

"Wow. I'm sorry about your marriage," Cali said as we got in her car.

"I know," I agreed.

We made our way back to her house, where I followed her in with the diaper bag.

"Well, thank you." She set the car seat down on the floor and turned and gave me a hug. "I feel better. You were right—getting out was a good idea."

I looked at her and smirked. "Sometimes I hate to admit that my mother is right. She was constantly telling me last year that I needed to get up and out, and I didn't want to. But I sheepishly admit she was right."

"I'll see you tomorrow?" That hint of desperation and anxiety was still in her voice.

"Yup. I'll be here. See you, Cali. I had fun."

"Me too," she said and shut the door behind me.

I felt good leaving Cali's. I felt energized by the knowledge that maybe in some small way I had helped her feel better. Somewhere along the way of Travis's leaving and my trying to find my way again, I had forgotten how good it felt to think of someone other than myself.

Chapter Twenty-Three
Really?

ON MY LAST DAY OF babysitting, my mom, Cali, and I went shopping. My mom insisted I needed some jeans that didn't hang off me. I also bought a real winter coat so I could stop freezing in Utah. I was willing to go shopping because after being with Cali, I realized maybe it would make my mom feel like she was helping. I had never thought of it that way before, but with my new perspective, we actually had a fun time shopping together. It was nice to have Cali along and to see her a little bit happier.

We had just come home from shopping when Luke called. He was driving back to Provo and was almost to Vegas and wanted to stop in. I was right in guessing my mother's reaction. She completely overreacted when I told her Luke was stopping by.

"Who is he? You've never mentioned any Luke. Do you like him?"

"Gosh, Mom. He's just my home teacher. He's been . . ." How could I describe how Luke had been without giving my mother the wrong impression? Kind? Supportive? My friend? My confidant? "He's been nice to me. He knows I've been going through some stuff."

"And he's coming to visit?" Her voice got higher and higher.

"It's not a big deal. He's driving up from California to Provo and wants to take a break. That's all."

My brother happened in on the conversation while getting a drink. "A guy's stopping by to see you?"

"Yes, Dan. But you don't need to join this conversation." As much as I loved my brother, sometimes he couldn't pass up giving me a hard time. "If it was me and I was going out of my way to visit someone, it would not be because I needed a 'break.'" He made quotation marks in the air when he said *break*.

My mother shook her head knowingly. "See, Dan knows. He's a guy."

I rolled my eyes. I wasn't in the mood for Dan's teasing. "Yes, he's a guy, a guy who never dates. So don't give me grief about what you think Luke's intentions may or may not be."

Dan smirked and raised an eyebrow. "I'm just saying, he's not going to waste his time hopping off the highway for a detour unless it's worth the trip."

"It's twenty minutes up Flamingo Road. It's not like he's driving hours out of his way. He's just taking a break."

Dan sort of snorted. "Whatever, Sophia, but I know there's . . ."

"What do you know, Dan? You're no expert on dating. So don't lecture me on what guys want."

"Sophia," my mother reprimanded. "Don't get upset with Dan. And I have to agree with him." She folded her arms and gave a nod of closure.

"My gosh, Mom." I could feel my cheeks burning. "Why do you even want me dating? He's just my friend. Can't I just have a friend?"

"Calm down, Sophia. I was only hoping . . ."

"Do you want me to get married again? It's not like the first one turned out that great." I was tearing up.

"Oh, honey, don't cry. I only want you to be happy." My mom came over and hugged me.

"I would be if you'd drop the whole boy thing. There are no boys in my life."

Dan snorted again.

"Shut up, Dan," I said.

"I didn't say anything." He hid his smile by taking a drink of milk. I wanted to take an orange from the fruit bowl and chuck it at him, but I'd probably miss and break the kitchen window instead.

I growled and stomped my foot. "You guys are so frustrating."

"Just truthful," Dan muttered under his breath.

I went upstairs and fidgeted with my hair, put my new jeans on, and checked myself out in the mirror. I felt anxious. I convinced myself it was because my mom and Dan were making such a big deal of Luke's visit.

Then the doorbell rang. I couldn't get down the stairs fast enough. I knew my mom would rush to the door, and I had to get there before her. But I didn't want Luke thinking a thundering herd was coming at him from the other side of the door either. Unfortunately, my mother made it first. Dang it.

"Hi, you must be Sophia's friend," she said in greeting.

"I'm Luke." He was shaking my mother's hand when I came up behind her.

My heart was pounding. I blamed it on my rush to get to the door and not that I was nervous. Because I wasn't nervous, was I? *Breathe. Be calm.* I wanted to be cool and collected so my mother and brother didn't think they'd gotten to me. I didn't want to give Luke the impression I was too excited to see him—like I thought he was visiting me in a more than "just friends" way. Why did Mom and Dan have to complicate everything right before he got here? Now I felt like I was under the microscope while he visited.

"Hey, Sophia." He gave a casual wave.

"Hi. Come on in. It's cold out there." I stepped in front of my mother, trying to crowd her out of the way. In fact, I wanted to crowd her right out of the room and keep her away while Luke visited.

She took the hint and retreated to the kitchen. I heard footsteps going upstairs. Hopefully, she was joining my dad in the family room to watch football.

"Can I take your coat?"

I was hanging up his coat when I heard my mother yell up the stairwell, "Brian, come meet Sophia's little friend from BYU."

No. She didn't just call Luke my *little friend*, did she? Oh. My. Gosh. I wanted to die.

"I'm sorry, Luke," I whispered, my face getting warm. "I told them it's not like that, but my mother assumes too much."

"It's okay, Sophia. Parents are supposed to embarrass us."

"I don't want her to embarrass you."

"I'll be fine."

I conceded. "Okay, but you've been warned."

I led him to the kitchen. "Here, have a seat. Are you hungry?" I motioned to the table. "Do you want a drink?"

"Water is fine."

My mother came into the kitchen while I was filling Luke's glass. "I'm Karen, Sophia's mom." She sat next to him.

I handed Luke his glass, and he took a long drink.

Dan came downstairs with my father in tow.

"This is my brother, Dan, and my dad."

"Call me Brian." My dad stuck out his hand. Luke stood up and shook hands with my dad and then with my brother.

Dad and Dan sat down at the table. I hoped Luke didn't feel like a lab rat.

My mom clapped her hands, breaking the silence. "Have you offered Luke anything to eat, Sophia?" She looked at me expectantly.

"I was just getting to that."

"We have sandwich fixings, or I could make tomato soup and grilled-cheese sandwiches." My mother loved playing hostess. It kept her *involved*. By the look of my brother and father planted on their chairs, this was turning into a family affair. Just what I'd feared.

"Um . . ." Luke looked at me with a plea for help.

"Are you even able to stay long, Luke?" I jumped in to rescue him. "Have you already eaten, or do you have time for a quick bite?"

"Yeah." He caught on. "Probably a quick bite. I want to get to Provo by early evening."

"A quick bite it is." Approval rang in my mother's voice. "What shall we have?"

"A sandwich?" I said.

"A sandwich would be great," Luke said.

My mom opened the fridge and started pulling out cold cuts. "Maybe we'll all have a little bite."

I rolled my eyes at Luke as my mother continued with her suggestions. Luke raised an eyebrow.

In the middle of eating, my dad turned and said to Luke, "So what are your intentions with my daughter?"

I choked. Luke coughed a little and took a gulp of water. "I'm sorry?"

"Your intentions," my dad repeated.

There was complete silence. I wanted to die.

"Brian!" my mother whispered fiercely and shook her head. Her eyes were bugging out.

"What?" my dad said loudly as if he had done nothing wrong. As if he hadn't just opened his mouth and stuck his foot in it. "Didn't you say he was Sophia's boyfriend from BYU?"

He must have heard wrong because he was too busy watching his football game. My mind raced to find something I could say to alleviate the situation.

My mom had actually said he was my *little* friend from BYU, but I wasn't going to repeat that. "No, Dad. He's my friend. Not my boyfriend."

"Oh, well . . ." my dad huffed, getting defensive. "It sounded like your mom said something else."

Dan was trying not to laugh. He snorted once or twice, keeping his head down. I could see his shoulders shaking with amusement.

Luke was intently chewing on his sandwich, staring at his plate.

My mom kept smoothing the tablecloth, picking up imaginary crumbs.

I was shielding my eyes, not wanting to look at Luke.

Then Dan busted out into big, huge snorting laughter. He dropped his sandwich on his plate and half stood, backing away from the table. He held his hand out. "I'm sorry," he managed to say to Luke. His eyes were tearing. "I can't believe you just said that, Dad."

I joined in without meaning to. My brother was staggering around his chair, holding his stomach, making a fool of himself.

"Oh my," my mother said. "This is a little bit embarrassing. We don't normally snort at the table."

I don't know if my mother thought before she spoke or if she was just hurrying to lessen the awkwardness. But snorting at the table?

I could feel my face burning. "Mom, I'm sure Luke doesn't think we normally snort at the table."

"No, I would have never suspected that," Luke reassured my mother.

I think that came out wrong too because Dan broke into more laughter, which made my mother laugh. She tried being discreet, but then she snorted too, and we all lost it, including Luke. Excluding my dad, who somehow didn't find it funny.

Luke excused himself to use the bathroom. I was grateful because it gave me a few minutes to regroup.

"Really, you guys? Snorting at the table?" I reprimanded them, dead serious. "You are totally embarrassing me. I knew it'd be like this."

"Relax, Sophia," my brother said, still chuckling. "It's all in good fun. Besides, if he can't take a little joking now, what's it going to be like when he's part of the family?"

I about blew up at Dan. I shot him a warning look, clenching my teeth. "Cut it out," I said threateningly.

"Dan, Dan." My mom patted Dan's hand resting on the table. "Don't give Sophia too hard of a time. Be nice to her little friend."

"Mom, could you stop referring to him as my 'little friend'? Please? It's embarrassing."

"Sorry. I'll try not to embarrass you. I like him. He seems like a very nice boy," she said.

Dad still sat there not saying a word.

Luke returned a few minutes later. "My sister, Leia, has the same Liz Lemon Swindle picture you have in the hall."

"Wait. Wait," Dan said. I could tell by his expression he was up to something. "Your sister's name is Leia? Like Luke and Leia?"

Here we go again. "Dan." I tried sending him a look of death. I could easily guess where the conversation was headed. I wished I had a light saber handy to zap him.

"Your parents named you after Star Wars characters?"

"Yup," Luke said.

"You're named after Stars Wars?" Dan reiterated. "Is your middle name Skywalker?"

"Is yours Solo?" I said.

"You like Star Wars, then?" my mom asked excitedly.

I also knew where this was going. I silently begged Luke not to answer the question. But when mental telepathy failed, I tried catching his eye to warn him. That didn't work either.

"Yeah, as much as the next person. My family used to watch the movies occasionally. My dad was the biggest fan in our family."

"We should have a Star Wars party," my mom said excitedly. "Would you like to stay? We could watch the last three episodes. I could make Darth Vader chips and Princess Leia cinnamon rolls—"

"Mom," I stopped her. She'd have Luke here all night if she had her way. "Luke can't stay that long. He has to get back to Provo. In fact . . ." I suddenly had a great idea. "Maybe I'll hitch a ride with Luke back to Provo." I turned to him. "If that's okay with you."

"Uh, yeah. Sure." Luke looked completely surprised. "No problem."

"Sophia? You mean you'd be leaving today?" My mom sounded a little wounded.

"It'd be easier this way." I justified my rash decision. I looked back at Luke. "Do you mind giving me a few minutes to pack? I don't have much stuff; it shouldn't take long."

"Okay," he said.

"Do you have to leave right now?" my mom asked as I hopped out of my seat and hurried up the stairs. She was right on my heels. "Sophia," she said when we were in my bedroom, "I'm sorry. We were just having fun. You don't have to leave. Luke seems like a very nice bo—person."

"Mom," I said. "It's not about today. It's easier for me to go with him since he's already on his way. And I'm all done at Cali's, so I won't have anything to do. Besides, I could use the extra couple of days to get those boxes out of storage that you are always reminding me about."

"Oh." She was disappointed.

"This saves you a trip." I started packing my pink bag.

"I don't want you to leave because we embarrassed you."

"It's not that." Driving back to school with Luke was much more appealing than driving back with my mother. "I really could use the extra couple days."

"Are you sure?"

"Yes," I reassured her. I threw in my new clothes, some more shirts from my drawer, my ever-reliable yoga pants, all of my new divorce books, my crocheting, and my toiletry bag. I was good to go.

My mom sat on the edge of my bed. "Are you sure, honey? I don't mind driving you."

I sat next to her. "I know. And I appreciate it. But this way is easier."

"If that's what you want to do." She stood.

"Hey, Mom," I said, taking a deep breath. There was more I needed to say.

"Yeah?"

"You were right about helping Cali."

My mom sat back down. "Oh, honey, I knew I could send you. You have a very kind heart."

It brought tears to my eyes. "I'm sorry about how I've been behaving. I didn't realize my divorce was hard on you too."

"I know." She gave me a long hug.

"Thanks for taking care of me."

"I just want you to be happy," she said as she let go of me.

I hugged her again. "I see that now."

I headed back down the stairs to tell Luke I was ready. My mother went into the kitchen to pack us snacks for the trip. I hugged my dad and my brother as Luke stood awkwardly looking on.

"Thanks, Mom." I hugged her when she handed me a bag of food.

Luke and I climbed into the truck and waved good-bye.

"Don't forget to get your stuff out of storage," Mom yelled as we drove off. I half expected her to chase us down the road.

It wasn't until we pulled away from my house with my mother still yelling reminders that I wondered what Luke and I would talk about for the next five and a half hours.

Chapter Twenty-Four
You're Kidding Me, Right?

"YOUR FAMILY SEEMS NICE," LUKE said as we headed east toward I-15 North.

I looked at him in disbelief. "You're kidding me, right?"

"No. I mean nice."

"By 'nice,' you mean weird?"

"No. They are nice."

"I'm sorry they embarrassed you. And me."

"You warned me," he said.

"Yes, I did."

"I wasn't too embarrassed," he said.

"Just a little embarrassed, then."

"Maybe just a little. I'll get over it."

"Is it really okay that I hitched a ride? You don't mind?" I suddenly wasn't sure about my rash decision.

"It's nice to have your company."

"Thanks, Luke. I appreciate it. At the beginning of break, my mom was driving me nutty."

"How was Christmas? You got a new coat." Luke noticed.

"Yes, I did. And my mom gave me five books about divorce for Christmas."

Luke smiled at me. "You had plenty of time to read, then?"

"I didn't open any of them. I taught myself how to crochet instead," I said.

"Very . . . productive," Luke said with approval.

"How was your Christmas? Did you get anything good?"

"Well, nothing as good as five books about divorce, but I did get time with my family, and I liked that. I've learned you can't buy time spent with family members."

I figured he was referring to his dad. "That's very true."

"So what else did you do other than crocheting and *not* reading your books?"

"My mom arranged a babysitting job for me while I was home." I felt like I was thirteen saying it.

"So that gave you something to do?"

"It was actually very cool. I mean, the situation wasn't, because the woman had just had a baby and was struggling with postpartum depression. But I could totally understand what she felt like." I paused. "Not the baby part but the sadness. And I felt like I actually helped her."

"Good for you, Sophia."

"Yeah, it made me feel good. Kind of made me realize my mom wasn't nagging me last summer. She just wanted me to be okay."

"I think it's always easiest to take our emotions out on family members."

"Because they're stuck with us?"

"Something like that." Luke nodded.

It was quiet for a moment. "You know, I didn't even say good-bye to Cali. Do you mind if I make a quick phone call?"

"Yeah, sure, go ahead."

Cali didn't pick up, so I left a message saying how much I enjoyed meeting her and hoped to see her when school was out.

Luke started up the conversation again. "So your brother lives at home?"

"Yeah. He graduated last year, found a job in Vegas, and moved back in with my parents. He's twenty-four," I answered. "I always tease him that he better start dating, or he's going to be one of those menaces to society Brigham Young talked about."

"Uh-oh," Luke said. "I'll be twenty-four in April."

"Yeah, but you're still at school. You at least date, don't you?"

There was an awkward pause. Maybe I was just imagining it. Maybe I shouldn't have said that.

"About as much as you do, Sophia. I'm in the laundry room every Friday night too," he said lightly.

The conversation felt like it was getting weird. Was my brother right? Did Luke like me? Luke must have felt the same weirdness because he changed the subject. "Your brother doesn't look like you."

"No, he doesn't. That's because he comes from a galaxy far, far away."

Luke started laughing. "You're so funny. Do you share your family's passion for Star Wars?"

"It's okay, but I don't get all into it anymore. Unlike my brother, who is a big fan."

"What kind of movies do you like?"

"As of late, it's been tear-jerker romantic dramas. But before a certain man came into my life, I liked thrillers."

"Yeah, I think thrillers are my favorite," Luke said. "What about books? Do you like to read?"

"My roommates think I read all the time. I pretend to read classic novels so I can avoid conversations. Growing up, I always hated reading because my mom made me do it. It's ironic that I hide behind it now. So I don't know if I will ever get around to actually reading those five divorce books I got for Christmas. How about you? Do you like to read?"

"Yeah. John Grisham, Tom Clancy. You know, the intrigue, conspiracy theory type."

There was another pause in the conversation. We hadn't even made it out of Vegas. Did I make a mistake hitching a ride?

"Do you want to be in charge of the radio?" Luke asked.

I hesitated. "Um, I'm not up with what's current."

"It was that bad, huh?" Luke immediately understood what I meant. "Yeah."

"Okay. Who needs the radio? It doesn't tune in most of the way anyway."

"True," I said.

"So," Luke started. "Are you into sports?"

I half laughed. "Remember my jogging incident? I would say the answer is no. A resounding no. Back in high school, I was always chosen first for basketball because I'm tall. Once people figured out the height was no help, I was always chosen last. Dead last. What about you? Did you do sports?"

"Basketball and track. I was never good enough to get scholarships. It was fun to play, but I wasn't planning on making it my life's goal. How about cheerleading? Were you a cheerleader?"

"No. That's worse than basketball to me. Could you imagine?"

"I could imagine. If it was anything like when we spilled our drinks at the store, I understand why you wouldn't."

My cheeks burned at the memory.

"Justin was a cheerleader," he said, then cracked up.

"No. Really? Justin?" I was shocked.

"Yeah, Justin. He said it was a good way to pick up chicks." Luke tried catching his breath.

"Justin would stoop to that level just to get girls to go out with him."

"He quit after a couple of months. He was getting a lot of grief from his friends, and he had dated most of the squad."

"They probably couldn't pick him up for lifts anyway," I added. My eyes were tearing up.

Luke continued with his questions once we were able to catch our breath. "Were you popular in high school?"

"Yeah, you could say that. That used to mean something to me. It made me feel important. But now I don't know. A lot has changed since Travis."

"Who were you before Travis?"

I hesitated. I wasn't sure I could fully explain it. "So, I was popular in high school. Clothes, makeup, shoes, and purses—material stuff was so important then. I thought I needed that stuff to look good and feel good.

"When I came to BYU, it wasn't like high school. It was weird to be just another student in a sea of students. I wasn't sure where I fit in. Then Travis swooped in and swept me off my feet."

Luke didn't interrupt, so I kept going. "Everything became so centered around him, I never took the time to figure out who I was without him."

"Did you have a major the first time you were a freshman?"

"No. After I met Travis, I didn't care about school. I thought I would stay home, have babies, and be a housewife."

"So you want kids?"

"Someday. Not now. Travis wanted to try right after we were married, but I didn't want to. I was too young and too scared, but I didn't want to tell him that."

"Do you like cooking?"

"I like it. I don't do it. I used to cook all the time when I was married. I'm by no means into it like Rhonda is."

Luke smiled. "We all appreciate Rhonda's cooking. It's a refreshing change from our usual Ramen noodles, macaroni and cheese, and hot dogs."

"Those foods can be quite versatile given the right ingredients," I said.

"Sometimes Justin mixes things up by throwing hot dogs in with macaroni and cheese. And Landon adds tuna to everything."

I cringed. "Like his tuna surprise casserole?"

Luke nodded. "Yup. So what do you want to do when you grow up?"

I snickered. Maybe I was a little bitter. "I don't know. I'm not as grown up as I thought I was a year and a half ago." I looked out the window at the barren roadside and was quiet for a couple of minutes.

"Sorry, I don't mean the twenty questions."

"I think you're only up to fifteen. You're allowed five more," I said easily.

"Oh, okay. If that's the case, what's your favorite color?"

"I like pink. What about you?" I didn't mind the banter. Because Luke knew my secret, I didn't have to be so guarded answering his questions.

"I don't think I have a favorite. I wear a lot of blue."

"You look good in blue," I said absently, thinking of his french blue oxford shirt he wore to church. I suddenly hoped he wasn't thinking I noticed how he dressed.

"Do you prefer cats or dogs?"

"Neither. Small animals make me sneeze, and large animals scare me."

"So you probably don't want to live on a farm or be a vet?"

"Yeah, I try to keep away from animals. What about you?"

"I like dogs."

I stopped for a moment and thought about our conversation and what Dan had said earlier. "You're not, like, screening me for marriage potential, are you?" I tried to sound like I was joking.

"We have a six-hour drive," he said good-naturedly. "I was trying to be conversational."

"Kind of like BRT-ing?"

"Well, that wasn't the reason I was doing it. It's nice to talk with you, kind of like Thanksgiving. When you are alone, you're a different Sophia than you let others see."

"That's because you already built a relationship of trust with me," I said softly, not quite sure where I was going with that or what I was expecting would come from that admission. I wasn't sure I wanted to go there yet, but Luke would be a good one to go there with. Whoa, did I just admit to thinking that?

I felt like Luke was asking questions around what he really wanted to ask about—my divorce. My divorce hung in the air like a big, fat, white elephant—felt but unseen. I could easily discuss it, but I wasn't sure I wanted to. To me, that didn't classify as small talk.

I decided to take the elephant by the trunk, or whatever you would do with an elephant, and address the issue. I would navigate the conversation as carefully as I could.

"Can I ask you something?" I asked Luke cautiously.

"Sure."

"Did it freak you out when I told you I was divorced?"

He didn't answer right away. I didn't know if that was a good sign or not. "I was more surprised than freaked out."

"Really?" I wasn't sure I believed him.

"Really," he said. "Now can I ask you something?" Luke looked over at me.

"Okay." I held my breath.

"Tell me about your marriage. What was your ex-husband like?"

I was surprised. "You want to know about him? Why?"

"I'm trying to figure out what kind of guy . . . would leave you."

"A stupid one," I said sarcastically.

"Seriously."

"Okay. Um. Travis and I met in September, were engaged by October, and were married two days after Thanksgiving."

I debated if I wanted to say the next part but went ahead. "I was mesmerized by his good looks. I was his arm candy. Most of the relationship was centered around how attractive we found each other. I excused a lot of his behavior and arrogance because I was so attracted to him.

"It was all very quick, and I didn't know him very well. We disagreed a lot, but I thought that stuff would work itself out."

"I'm still trying to figure out what kind of person he was," Luke said.

"He was very charming and charismatic and *always* seemed to get his way. Very egocentric and possibly commitment challenged, since he changed his major twice in nine months."

"I can't picture you with someone like that."

I rested my head on the headrest. "I was young and naïve, and I thought he could walk on water. Getting married was very attractive and exciting and seemed to be the thing to do. Isn't that stupid? Peer pressure to get married."

"It's true; everybody's doing it."

I continued. "For the short time I knew him, I did love him. Although, I don't know, maybe I was more caught up in getting married than in who I was marrying? Luke, I thought by getting married in the temple, our marriage would be perfect."

Luke looked at me. "Kind of like going on a mission is guaranteed to be a great spiritual experience?"

"Exactly."

"So what happened? I mean, where did it all go wrong?"

"I think married life wasn't what he thought it would be. I'm not sure what he was expecting. I know there were times I was definitely immature and selfish. Maybe I wasn't the perfect homemaking wife. I tried my best, but I wasn't what he wanted. Maybe I wasn't perfect like his mother."

"Ah, yes, the dreaded mother-in-law."

"I did everything for him. I put school on hold, worked full-time, cooked, cleaned, helped him study. At the time, I was willing. He was my husband." I shrugged. "That's what marriage is, supporting each other. I didn't think anything was wrong. We would fight sometimes and disagreed a lot, but I thought we were adjusting to married life, learning to compromise. Then one day he told me I had changed, he felt I resented him, and he didn't want to be married to me anymore. He completely blindsided me. I begged, I pleaded, I tried to bargain with him, make deals. But he had made up his mind. And for someone who can't decide what he wants to do when he grows up, he was very decided about the divorce.

"There were things I could have done better or differently, but in the end, it came down to him. No matter what I did, it was not good enough for him."

"Sophia, he was not good enough for you."

I sighed. Maybe Luke was right. "It's amazing how clear things are in hindsight."

"Yup," Luke said.

"That's enough doom and gloom from my life." It wasn't so much that I was uncomfortable telling him about it. It was more that . . .

"Am I being too nosy?"

I shook my head. "No, it's okay. I don't mind telling you. You're a good friend."

"Are you saying that because you want to clarify things?"

I looked at him for a moment, not knowing what to say. *Was* I trying to clarify things?

Luke kept his eyes on the road. "Don't worry, Sophia, I'm not doing anything because I expect something."

I felt a little panicky. I didn't want Luke thinking I didn't appreciate all that he had done for me. "I guess what I'm trying to say is thank you. You get what I've gone through and . . . it means a lot to me that you're my friend."

Luke looked at me thoughtfully but didn't say anything.

"I appreciate it, Luke."

"Anytime, Sophia."

"Maybe someday when I'm the perfect Molly Mormon, I'll bake you some cookies to show my gratitude." Then I added, "But don't hold your breath. I don't see that happening anytime soon. Will you accept a verbal thank you for now?"

"You don't have to thank me." Luke's voice was soft.

"But I do. You have been . . ." I paused to gather my thoughts. "Very kind to me."

"It's the thought that counts."

And if anyone was counting, I kept thinking about Luke.

Chapter Twenty-Five
A New Year, A New Me

A NEW YEAR, A NEW me. That was my new motto. That was my mantra. I was going to repeat it until I believed it. I was moving beyond Travis and getting on with my new and improved life.

I started by getting my boxes out of storage (with Luke's help) and getting rid of almost everything in them. Most of it no longer meant anything to me. A lot of the clothes didn't fit anymore. I did find my wedding gown wadded up in a ball in one of the boxes. I assumed Travis packed that box. I decided to keep it, not out of sentimentality but because it was a Vera Wang and I couldn't bear to just donate it after what I paid for it. I also found my bright red KitchenAid mixer, a wedding gift from my parents. At that point, I got overwhelmed and put the last two boxes away to sort another time.

Part of my resolution for a new me was that I was going to put forth an effort in my education. I signed up for an English survey class, Introduction to Art History, LDS Temples, Food Prep in the Home, and another bowling class. I didn't want to overdo the enthusiasm, so I took only enough credits to be considered a full-time student. Most of my classes were in the early evening. Again, like last semester, I wanted to give myself a nice buffer zone in case I got overwhelmed or depressed. I never knew if and when I might have a major or minor Travis episode.

I was careful to avoid Preparation for Marriage, Marriage Enhancement, and Forming Marital Relationships. I was steering clear of all marriage stuff.

Well, I thought I was steering clear of the marriage stuff, but Sarah and Ned were practically glued at the hip. She was spending every free minute and waking hour with him. He was eating dinner at our apartment every night and picking her up in the morning to walk her to campus. He was always at our apartment. Frankly, it was a bit annoying. Had I been like this when I was with Travis? Sadly, I think I had. Someday I'd have to apologize to Gretchen.

Rhonda returned with renewed energy and rejuvenated spirits. She was armed with a cheesecake cookbook, some new clothes, and *A Guidebook to Meeting Your Mate*. It made me wonder what her resolutions were.

Claire must have gotten straight A's or an internship for the summer or something because she was *smiling* when came back from the break. "How are you?" she asked us.

"Good. Did you have a good Christmas?" Sarah asked, glancing at me questioningly.

"I did. You guys?"

"It was so nice," Rhonda said, then went on to detail her break. Claire waited until Rhonda was done before she went into the bedroom.

"What's up with her? Did she get some Valium in her stocking?" I whispered. She didn't seem so . . . hardcore. Maybe she had an exceptionally good Christmas or got a massage. Whatever it was, something was different.

Sarah chastised me. "Sophia! Don't be snarky." But then she giggled.

"I'm not being mean," I whispered fiercely. "But you have to admit she's acting . . ."

"Happy," Rhonda filled in.

"See? See. Rhonda thinks so too."

Claire reentered the kitchen awhile later with her empty book bag slung over her shoulder. "Time to buy books," she said as she headed out the door.

So quick she was to return to her old self.

* * *

My first appointment with Dave after Christmas break was deemed a turning point.

"You seem . . . happier," Dave said as I sat down in his office.

"I feel better." I hadn't exactly put my finger on why.

"How was break?"

"Well, Christmas was . . . I don't know. Predictable? Overbearing? Embarrassing? Surprising? I'm not sure how to classify it with one word."

"Okay. Start with the first." He crossed his legs and leaned back. I got the impression he thought he was in for a wild ride.

"It was predictable because my mother was exactly how I expected. She was her typical overenthusiastic self. She gave me a bunch of books about divorce. But I have come to realize this is her way of trying to help, though she kept asking if I wanted to start dating again."

He interrupted. "Do you?"

I squirmed. I hated thinking about this. "I don't know. I don't need to jump into a relationship after I finally got over the last one. And it's not like I have anyone in mind." But I had to admit, Luke had been on my mind a little bit. It was probably because he'd been helping me so much lately.

Dave grinned at my assessment.

I didn't wait for him to say anything before I kept going. "And then I had a few realizations while I was home."

"Such as?"

"Well, for one, my divorce was also hard for my family, not just me."

"Okay, that's good."

"And that I'm ready to try again."

"What does that mean?"

"I'm ready to be a person again instead of a zombie. I'm joining the land of the living and getting on with my life."

"That's good. How are you going to do that?"

"Well, I got the boxes from married life out of storage and donated most of the stuff. I didn't want it anymore. It didn't mean anything to me."

"So you feel you've been able to let go," he said, summing it up. "What else?"

"I'm going to go to my classes."

"Good."

"I've started crocheting."

"Crocheting? Okay." He nodded in approval.

"Yeah, it's becoming a fun little hobby. My roommate gave me a book about it for Christmas, and I've been teaching myself."

"You have?"

"Yes. Instead of dwelling on Travis all day, I crochet little voodoo dolls named Travis and then poke them in the eyes with my crochet needle." Then I burst out laughing. I couldn't help it; I found myself quite amusing.

"Really?" he seemed concerned.

"No."

He cleared his throat. "So you're letting go, moving on, finding new hobbies."

"As soon as I'm good enough, I'll crochet you a tie."

"Thanks." He chuckled.

I left the counseling center feeling strange. There was so much I didn't tell Dave because I had already told Luke and didn't need to rehash it. Did I finally have closure? I felt good enough that I didn't make a return appointment. I could always make an appointment if I felt like I was crawling back into that deep, dark hole. But right now I was okay. Like Luke said after I told him I was divorced, I did want to feel better. Was this what feeling better felt like?

Chapter Twenty-Six

A Disturbance in the Force

BY THE SECOND WEEK OF school, I was ready to tackle the last two boxes in the back of my closet. Surely I didn't need that stuff. I hadn't missed it in almost a year.

In the first box, I found the garment bag for my wedding dress, put my dress in it, and hung it in the farthest edge of my closet so it'd be out of sight. There were a couple of high-end purses I liked enough to keep but dumped out the debris left in them. There was old gum, tissues, melted lip gloss, some hair elastics, and a used packet of birth control pills. Oh yeah, the pill. I didn't need that anymore, so it went into the bathroom trash along with everything else. I shook out similar contents from the other two bags as well.

What I found when I opened the last box was mostly what I'd expected: clothes that no longer fit, class notebooks, photos of someone I no longer was and didn't want to remember, usually with the person I could no longer stomach, and paperwork, like ATM receipts and bank statements. My red blender that matched my red KitchenAid was also in there, but the jury was still out on whether I cared about appliances anymore.

I also discovered something totally unexpected that wasn't mine, nor had I ever seen it before, packed in with my stuff. It was a shoebox of mission letters and loose papers belonging to Travis. I figured since I had been married to him and they were in my box, it gave me the right to look through them. As I read, I learned things I never knew about him, things he had never told me. He had left his mission early. The loose papers were journal entries describing Travis's struggle to live in such a poor country like Bolivia. The letters were from his mom expressing her disapproval about his wanting to come home but also deciding on an explanation to save face. Some of the rawness of my wounds from the divorce seemed to heal when I realized it wasn't just me he betrayed—he betrayed everyone. Maybe his arrogance and callous walking away wasn't something he saved for me personally but was something he could have done and would have done to anyone.

When I finally finished reading every bit of writing, I put it back in the box, put the top on, and set it aside. I wasn't sure what to make of what I had just read and needed time to process it.

If I had known about this before I married Travis, would I have still married him? Would I have had enough wisdom to recognize the insight from these papers and letters was the real deal? I don't know if it would have been enough for me to realize it was better *not* to marry him. But what I did know was I could finally let myself off the hook that it wasn't me; it really *was* him.

* * *

By the time Rhonda got home from classes just after four, any evidence of what I had been doing earlier had been cleaned up. I kept one box for the KitchenAid, the blender, the purses that I didn't want but didn't want to throw away either, and a few other random things. I had put away any clothes that still fit and put the rest into a black trash bag for DI, and the boxes went to the trash. I felt very good about my accomplishment.

While I was deciding what meal to pop in the microwave before I left for class, Rhonda called me from the back.

"Hey, Sophia, come here." She sounded strange.

I found her in the bathroom.

"Look," she said in a rather quiet voice. "Look what I found."

I looked around. What was wrong?

"No, look, down there." She pointed at the trash can beside the toilet.

"What? Is there a mouse or something?" I hoped not. I hated rodents.

She moved away a tissue with a Q-tip to expose the used foil bubble pack as if it was a biohazard. "One of our roommates is on the pill." She sounded shocked. "Can you believe it? Should we call the bishop?"

I stifled my laugh. Seriously? That's what was so shocking? "Rhonda." I kept my voice very even. "People take the pill for more reasons than just preventing pregnancy. You know, to regulate periods, alleviate cramps, help acne. There's lots of reasons someone could be taking the pill."

"But one of them could be having premarital sex."

This time I did laugh. "I highly doubt it's Claire or Sarah." There wasn't time for boys in Claire's schedule, and Sarah wouldn't want to jeopardize the chance of a temple marriage. "Besides, they were mine."

"What? Yours?" Rhonda's mouth dropped open. "You're on the pill?"

"No. They're left over from the person I used to be last year," I said and walked back into the kitchen. I quickly grabbed my dinner, a fork, and my book bag before rushing for the door.

"Wait. Wait, wait." Rhonda caught up to me, stepping in front of the door before I could escape. "You were on the pill?" Rhonda's eyes were huge.

"Um, yeah. But don't worry, I don't take them anymore."

"I can't believe you would . . ."

"Rhonda, don't worry. I was a different person before." Not that the kind of person I was before was necessarily bad.

"How can you act like it is not a big deal?"

"Rhonda, it's not something I want or need to discuss with you. What I need to do is go to class." I stepped around her and walked off, well aware that Rhonda's curiosity was not satisfied. I knew better than to tell her the pills were mine. But Rhonda would not have let it go and would have questioned Claire and Sarah until she ended up back at me. Hopefully, although I highly doubted it, there would be no more discussion about the pill packet.

A couple of days later, a new neighbor moved in and distracted Rhonda from the discarded birth control pills. Her name was Ashlee Lowe and she quickly became Rhonda's new BFF.

Ashlee was a cute, bubbly, petite girl from Texas. She had short hair that looked great on her and a soft voice with a hint of a Southern drawl, and she was a student at the hair academy. She and Rhonda were both on the Relief Society committee and they instantly bonded.

Rhonda had found a bosom buddy who liked boys, baking, and dating as much as she did. Probably worst of all, though, was they had taken to baking a cheesecake every Sunday after church at our apartment. Thus far we had had New York cheesecake, turtle cheesecake, and chocolate truffle cheesecake.

I was already tired of Ashlee and cheesecake. She was at our apartment as much as Ned, who I was also sick of. She was here almost as much as Claire was *not* here. She was even here when Rhonda wasn't. She would simply knock on the door, walk right in, and call out for anyone who might be home. Sometimes I thought about forging one of Claire's yellow sticky notes saying *Ashlee, go home.*

I didn't *dislike* Ashlee; she was nice and sociable, but she talked nonstop. And I also came to discover she seemed to have a small crush on Luke.

"So, Luke James is your home teacher?" she asked casually late Friday afternoon while waiting for Rhonda to get home.

The hair on the back of my neck stood up. Why the interest in Luke? I had to admit I was a little possessive of him. He was my friend, my emotional crutch, my confidant. I didn't want any competition claiming him.

"Yes, he is."

"He's a cutie." I swear Ashlee just about purred.

"I guess." I tried sounding nonchalant. Secretly, I had to agree with her. Secretly, I also had to admit that her liking Luke made my blood pressure rise.

"Is he dating anyone?" she asked with feigned innocence.

"No, I don't think so." I turned my attention to finding something for dinner in the freezer so she wouldn't know I was bothered by the conversation. There was no way I was telling her about the standing Friday night laundry room rendezvous.

"He seems to be over here a lot," she said, still digging for information.

"He's our home teacher. He checks on us because he's very dedicated. Or maybe he just likes cheesecake."

"But he's not dating anyone?" she asked again.

"You should ask him. Why the interest?" I knew it was for her, obviously. I needed to keep my cool, not wanting her to think I had a crush on him. But it's amazing what a little competition did to clarify my feelings.

Oh. My. Gosh. Did I like Luke? Maybe that's why I never felt connected to Bradley. I hadn't given it much consideration because I had always been too wrapped up in my feelings for Travis then. And when Luke visited over Christmas, at the time, I was too embarrassed by my family to stop and analyze if I had feelings for him.

The thought of liking Luke floored me. I sort of slid into a chair. Thankfully, Rhonda arrived at that moment, taking the attention off of me. She and Ashlee immediately started chatting, leaving me to wonder why I had to have this realization right before I was going to do my laundry. I knew Luke was going to be there. He was always there. And now I was all self-conscious. Crud.

Chapter Twenty-Seven
Ruffled

ONE WEEK LATER, A WEDDING dress arrived in the mail for Sarah. It had a fitted bodice with a full skirt and was completely accessorized in ruffles. There were ruffles at the waistline, wrists, and neckline, as well as the whole length of the skirt and the train. It was absolutely hideous.

I invited myself to be in Sarah's bedroom when she opened the box. Apparently, her mother thought it would be a great surprise because Sarah was literally speechless as she held up the dress. I was speechless as well, not sure whether I should make a crack about all the ruffles or just keep my mouth shut. Maybe she absolutely loved the dress, and I didn't want to offend her.

"Oh my gosh," she muttered. She held the dress out as if to get a better look at it. "What was my mother thinking?"

I still couldn't tell what Sarah thought. I think she was leaning toward ugly.

"Do you like it?" I asked brightly.

"Do *you* like it?" she threw back, not looking at me. I took that as a definite lean to the ugly side.

"Well," I said. I didn't want to hurt her feelings. "It's unique."

"It's awful." Sarah wailed and flopped on her bed. "I'm going to look like a marshmallow. What am I going to do?"

"Why did your mother send you a wedding dress? Is that the one she made for you, or did she buy it?" It didn't look new because the fabric was slightly discolored. Perhaps her mom bought a used dress? Or vintage? But why would anyone want such a hideous dress?

"It was my mother's," Sarah said, muffled by her pillow. "I told my mom I didn't want her to make me a dress, and she suggested hers." She rolled over on her side. "I used to dress up in it all the time when I was little. We moved when I was six, and the dress got packed away, and I never saw it again." She paused for a breath. "I didn't think my mother would find it."

"Apparently she did." I didn't know what else to say.

Sarah scowled. "She must have ripped through the whole house looking for this." Then Sarah started crying. "Ugly thing."

I picked up the dress to examine it. It was definitely old; the tag looked like it was from the seventies. "Look. Look." I got excited. Maybe there was a way out. "It's a size four. Will it fit?"

"No," Sarah said, sounding even more depressed. "I'll never get into that dress."

"Isn't that a good thing?" I asked, confused. "Do you want to wear it?"

Sarah flopped over again, burying her face in the pillow. "No!" she said, crying in frustration, then lifted her head, her hair staticky. "I don't want to wear that, but my mother will be so disappointed."

I had an idea, but I didn't know if it was a good idea. I had a dress. Maybe Sarah could wear it. Was that even a possibility? Would it make Sarah feel better? Would I be able to come up with a good explanation for why I had a wedding gown in my closet for no apparent reason? Hmmm.

"What if you told your mom it doesn't fit and you traded it for another dress?"

"I don't know."

"Because . . ." I motioned for her to follow me to my bedroom. I made a split-second, game-changing decision.

"O-kay?" she said slowly, not understanding what was going on.

I pulled my gown out of the garment bag and showed it to her. Even crumpled, it was beautiful.

"So I was thinking," I said cautiously, "that you should wear this instead."

"Wow," she breathed. "It's gorgeous. Is it yours?"

I nodded.

She stood and admired it, stroking the silky fabric and touching the delicate beadwork.

"But . . . why do you have a wedding dress? Were you going to get married?"

I took a deep breath. *Here we go.* "I did get married."

"You're married?" She shook her head and blinked. "But where is your husband? Is he in the military? And the pills."

"No, he's not in the military. He . . . left after four months."

"You don't know where he is?" Sarah's eyes grew wide.

"No. We're divorced."

"Oh, no, Sophia. I'm so sorry."

"Thus the reason for my profundity about the marriage being more important than the wedding. And my behavior. Which I'm sorry about. There were several times I thought about telling you, but then I just couldn't."

"Sophia, what happened?"

I shook my head. "It was fast; we didn't know each other very well. He was unhappy."

She came over and hugged me. "Were you completely devastated?"

"Yeah, that's one way to put it. But I'm doing better," I said, then redirected the conversation. "So you're welcome to the dress."

"Can I try it on?"

"Yeah, definitely. I hope it will work."

She looked at the tag and squealed. "It's Vera Wang. You'd trust me?"

"Of course. Go try it on. I want to see what it looks like."

She came back in, and I helped her with the zipper. The bodice was a little snug. "You might need to have this altered, but other than that, it looks great."

She twirled in the mirror and admired her reflection. She looked over at me, grinning from ear to ear. "You'd really let me borrow it?"

"No, but I'd give it to you. I don't have any use for it, and I don't want to donate it. If you want it, it's all yours."

"You'd just give me your Vera Wang?"

"Yes."

She stared at the gown. "No strings attached? You don't want anything for it?"

"I want to trade it for your wedding gown. That is, if your mother is okay with that."

"I'll call and ask her. I'll tell her it is way too small."

"And I need to ask a favor," I said cautiously.

"Sure, anything."

"Would you mind keeping the whole marriage thing a secret? I'll tell the others when I'm ready. The dress too. I'm sorry; I know I'm asking a lot."

"Of course. I totally understand." She hugged me. "I just acquired a great secondhand dress—enough said."

She twirled around and looked in the mirror. "I'll definitely have to get some alterations; it's too long, and I can barely breathe, but it is so beautiful."

The front door shut, and before we could see who it was, Claire walked in and stopped momentarily to look at Sarah. "Nice dress," she said, then went into our bedroom.

Sarah and I looked at each other, surprised. It was unusual for Claire to be home so early and for her to be complimentary.

She walked back out and held up her calculator. "Forgot this. See you later," she said and then was off.

"What was . . ." I started whispering, then heard her say from the kitchen, "Ready?"

"Is someone out there?" Sarah asked in a low whisper.

"She's probably on her phone," I said.

"Do you think so?"

"Who knows?"

"I want to see." Sarah rushed by with the wedding dress dragging on the floor. Because the back wasn't totally zipped, Sarah opted to look out the window instead of go outside. "I can't tell. You go look."

"And say what when she looks up, is totally on her cell phone, and wants to know why I'm following her?"

"Yeah, good point." Sarah gathered up the dress and went back to the bathroom mirror. I followed behind her. After looking at herself from every angle, she turned to me. "Are you sure you want to give this to me?"

"Yes," I said, happy that she was so happy.

I had her dress stuffed in a trash bag to donate it before she even got off the phone with her mother. Come to find out, her mother only kept it because she thought Sarah wanted it. She had no sentimental attachment to it, so off to DI it would go.

* * *

Letting go of my wedding dress inspired me to make an attempt at some closure with Travis.

I texted Travis, and after several attempts, I was able to make arrangements to meet him. He agreed only after I told him I had some of his belongings. We planned to meet on Friday at the Cougareat after my last class.

Travis was waiting when I walked in.

There he sat in all his faded glory, looking as gorgeous as ever, but my heart didn't skip a beat for him the way it used to. It was pounding, in fact, because even though I wanted to do this, I was scared to face him and hoped I had the courage to say what I had to say.

As expected, things were awkward, and he didn't make it any easier for me.

"So. What's the reason for all the texting? Are you here to beg me to take you back again?"

"That girl, the one who came to your apartment crying and begging you to take her back? That's not me anymore. I don't want you back."

A smug look crossed his face. "But you're here, Fi."

"Sophia," I corrected him automatically. "I came to bring you this." I set the box on the table.

"What's that?" Travis asked.

"It's letters. It's the real you that I never saw."

Travis's expression was both quizzical and apprehensive. "Yeah, so?"

"I took the liberty of reading them."

Travis turned a little bit pale. "Are you trying to blackmail me?"

That was actually pretty funny. "No, I hadn't thought about that. But that's good." I entertained the thought for a moment but gave it no further consideration. "No, nothing like that. Give me a little credit."

He sat there stonily, waiting.

"They're mission letters from your mother. You never told me you came home early from your mission and only because you wanted to."

And just to be dramatic, I lifted the lid and pulled out a packet of letters from inside that I had carefully grouped together and secured with an elastic band. I dropped them on the table.

I stared at him. He held my gaze for a moment but said nothing. Was he too arrogant to be ashamed?

"Or," I pulled out more letters, "that your mother disapproved. Or that despite being totally against the idea, she came up with an explanation so you both could save face from the shame and embarrassment."

Travis's eyes narrowed, but he still said nothing.

"You told me you were a great missionary. That it was the best two years of your life and you'd go back in a heartbeat." I paused again for effect. "So basically, everything you said was a lie. You are a liar and a quitter."

"Are you done? You always did talk too much." I don't think Travis was embarrassed. I think it was more that he was angry he got caught, that he had been exposed.

"Oh, yes. I am done. Finally, I am done."

"You think you know everything, Sophia, but you don't." His voice had an edge to it.

I stood. "I know one thing, Travis. I know you did me a favor." And then I walked away.

Growing up, I used to hear my mother quip, "A winner never quits, a quitter never wins." At the time, it drove me nuts. I heard it so often its message fell on deaf ears. But now I could understand the wisdom behind those simple words. That was the difference between Travis and me—he quit when the going got tough, and I didn't.

I hadn't realized until now that I was at a point where I could stand on my own two feet and not be swayed by him. It felt good. When I walked away from him, I was finally able to let go of the guy I thought was everything but ended up being nothing.

Chapter Twenty-Eight
The Spirit of Contention

I was so excited to tell Luke about what just happened. Then I had the strange realization that Luke was the first person I thought of telling.

Needing a ride to donate Sarah's wedding dress gave me a great excuse to stop by his apartment.

"Hey." He was surprised as he opened the door.

"Hi." I suddenly felt self-conscious. Had I been too impulsive? Would he even care about what I wanted to tell him?

"Do you want to come in?" He moved aside so I could come in.

I looked around. "Is anyone else home?"

He looked around too, puzzled. "No, why?"

I chickened out. "Just wondering. I was, uh, hoping you might be able to give me a ride later. To DI and the mall."

Not surprisingly, he was willing to help me out. "I can go right now if you want. Are you getting rid of more married stuff?"

He got his keys and put on some sneakers.

"Sarah's wedding dress." I nodded toward the apartment. "I need to grab it. How about I meet you down at your truck."

He looked confused again. "Okay, sure."

Once we were driving, Luke asked, "You're donating her wedding dress? Does she know about this?"

"Yeah, she said I could."

"Why would she get rid of her wedding dress?"

"It was hideous. So I gave her mine."

"You gave her your wedding dress?"

"I didn't want to donate it; it's Vera Wang. I'm not planning on wearing it again, so why not give it to Sarah so she can have a pretty dress instead of an ugly one?"

"What's Vera Wang?"

"You know, Vera Wang. She's a designer, and her dresses are gorgeous. I paid way too much money to just donate it. It felt good to give it to Sarah. She seemed to totally appreciate it."

"So your dress was pretty expensive?"

"It was. But I thought it was worth it. At the time, I had the 'you only get married once' mentality." I snickered. "I had no idea things would turn out like they did."

"No one gets married to get divorced, Sophia," Luke said kindly.

"If I only knew then what I know now."

"But you didn't, so give yourself a break."

I took a deep breath. "Guess what I did today?" I said.

"Other than donate your roommate's wedding dress?"

"I saw Travis."

Luke seemed to pause. "Is that supposed to be a good thing?"

"It was a good thing. See, I found his mission letters in one of my boxes. Come to find out, he left his mission early because it was too hard."

"He left his mission? And you never knew it until now?"

"I know, crazy, huh? I met him today to give him back his letters and give myself permission to finally be over him."

"How'd that go?"

"It was great for me, probably not so great for him. Finding those letters made me realize he gave up on our marriage like he gave up on his mission."

"So you're done with Travis?" Luke looked at me with raised eyebrows.

"Yes, I am."

"We should go celebrate. This is a huge milestone in your life."

"Way better than a millstone," I joked.

"Okay, where to? Your choice, my treat."

We went to a cupcake bakery by the mall. After that, we went to the mall to buy Rhonda an apron from Flirty Aprons. Her birthday was coming up, and a new apron would be perfect. I was not an apron person, but their aprons did justice to the idea of having to wear one. They were cute and ruffly and right up Rhonda's homemaking alley.

We dropped Sarah's dress off at DI, then went to campus to the bookstore. Luke needed to buy a book for one of his classes that had been accidentally omitted from the syllabus. I needed Oreos since it was laundry night. He headed upstairs to the textbook section, and I went in search of the cookies.

While paying for my Oreos, I heard someone call my name. Only it wasn't my name anymore because it was my married name.

"Sophia Duckk?"

I turned around to see my old neighbor Megan Peacock. We had become fast friends the year before while commiserating over our fowl names.

"How are you?" she said loudly, giving me a hug.

"Good. I'm good."

She took a step back to look at me.

"So you're doing better? You look great."

I didn't remember talking to her after *that day*, but maybe she had been one of the friends who had called.

"Yeah."

"You were gone so fast. I feel bad I never visited or called or checked up on you. I was so worried."

Wait a minute. She said she didn't call. What exactly was she talking about?

"What do you mean?" I felt apprehensive.

She was hesitant. "You know, your . . . breakdown?"

"Breakdown?" I said much too loudly. Nearby shoppers turned to look at me.

"That's what Travis told me—that you had had a breakdown."

"He actually said that? Are you kidding me?" I couldn't help but yell.

Megan suddenly seemed self-conscious and took a step back. "Well, yeah. That's what he said. Then he moved right after that, and I never heard anything more."

"I didn't have a breakdown! What a jerk. He *seriously* told you I had a breakdown?"

"Yeah." She bit her lip.

"What happened was he wanted a divorce."

Megan was stunned; her eyes darted to my left hand. "You're divorced?"

"Yeah, we're divorced."

"What happened? Was something else going on?"

"No, he completely blindsided me."

"Wow." She shook her head.

"I know."

She gave me a hug. "I'm so sorry, Sophia. I just thought you were going through some stuff. I didn't mean to lose touch, but . . ."

"Oh, Megan, it's fine. I've moved on."

"So you're okay, then?"

"It depends on the day, but things are much better."

"It sounds plain awful. I still can't believe it." She checked her phone. "I'm meeting David soon. But it was great seeing you. Maybe we can get together at the Cougareat sometime."

"That'd be fun, Megan. Let me get your number." We exchanged phone numbers, then said our good-byes.

"See you later, Sophia." She gave me another hug. "Again, I'm sorry to hear about your marriage."

"It's okay. I'm glad I ran into you."

I went looking for Luke. I had calmed down a little from my initial reaction to Megan's revelation, but thinking back on it made my temper flare a bit. I was still in disbelief at the gall of Travis. I stomped up the stairs and almost banged right into Luke.

"Hey," he said, smiling. "You get what you needed?"

"Yeah, and a little bit more," I said dryly. Luke missed my heavy sarcasm. "I see you got Oreos. I hope you're planning on sharing those tonight."

A little shiver of excitement distracted me momentarily from my rage. He was going to do his laundry tonight too.

"Yeah, I'll bring them. I kind of owe you for today."

"You don't owe me. But I'll accept a donation of Oreos. Hey, speaking of cookies, look what I found." Luke was obviously proud of himself. I could hear it in his voice. "*The Star Wars Cookbook*." He held it up. "It has recipes for Wookie Cookies and Yoda Soda and other Galactic recipes." He read from the cover of the book. "Isn't that a riot? I bought it for you. You know, you could give it to your parents or something. Or we could have our own Star Wars party and eat Wookie Cookies."

Any other time, I would have found Luke hilarious. Not so at the moment. "So can we go now?" I was anxious to leave the bookstore and be alone with him so I could unload my burning information. I sounded more abrupt than I'd intended.

"Did I miss something, Sophia? Are you mad at me? I mean, you weren't mad ten minutes ago." Luke furrowed his brow.

"No, I just have something I need to tell you." I walked away, hoping to speed up our departure.

Luke caught up to me. "What's going on, Sophia?"

"So get this," I said as we headed for his truck. "I ran into a neighbor from when I was married, and she was under the impression I had had a nervous breakdown. That was Travis's explanation for why I was gone. He said I had a breakdown."

"A breakdown?"

"I can't believe him. He wouldn't want anyone to think badly of him, so he made up a complete lie about me."

"At least you know it's not true," Luke said mildly as we got into the truck and he started it up.

"*I* know it's not true, but everyone else thinks I lost it." I slammed the truck door a little too passionately.

"But that's done with; remember your talk today?" He looked at me calmly, then pulled out of the parking space.

"Yeah, but that was before I knew he was telling lies about me. I don't want everyone thinking there's something wrong with me."

"Would it matter?"

"Whose side are you on, Luke? Of course it matters."

"Sophia, you know I'm on your side, but what's done is done. He's the jerk, he's the liar, he has the problem."

We stopped at a red light.

"But it's infuriating."

"What can you do about it? Publish something in the *Daily Universe* declaring that you are not crazy, just divorced? That it was him, not you? The way I see it, there's not much you can do."

I couldn't believe him. "How can you be so calm about this?" I was outraged at the injustice done to me, and he was playing the devil's advocate. "I feel wronged."

He shrugged his shoulders. "It's in the past. Let it go, and get on with it."

"You think I need to get over it? Thanks!" I said angrily.

"I didn't say get *over* it. I said get *on* with it. You know, move forward."

I was not ready to let it go. "But he spread that vicious lie. It's so hurtful and untrue."

"Sophia, that was a year ago. You can't do anything about it now." He spoke the last sentence slowly.

"Yes, I can. I can go over to his apartment and confront him. I can yell and scream at him." At least, I thought that would make me feel better. The yelling and screaming part might confirm to Travis that I was crazy.

Luke's tone surprised me. He was angry. "For what? So he can apologize to you? So he can tell you how very deeply sorry he is for lying about you?

Do you think he will? You tried that once, remember? Do you really think he's the least bit concerned about the stuff he's made up about you?"

"Well, he should be."

"Just let it be. He has the problem, not you. You know that. Be the bigger person, and walk away. What's done is done; leave it alone."

"You of all people should understand why I'm so upset. He wanted the divorce. He has no right making up lies about me. That's my point." My eyes filled with tears.

"And what do you want? For him to care? Because he obviously doesn't. Why do you keep wasting so much energy on him? He's not worth it. All he does is make you feel bad. I don't get it. Two hours ago, you said you were finished with him."

Travis may not have been worth it, but I still wanted to let loose my rage and fury on him. I started crying, completely frustrated. "Why aren't you on my side, Luke?"

"I already told you I am on your side, but it kills me that you keep letting him hurt you over and over. You're not even married to him anymore. It's like this shadow always following you, and you just allow it." By now we had reached the apartments' parking lot. He pulled into a space and shut the engine off.

I didn't know what Luke's problem was. I thought he would have agreed with me, no questions asked. Why did it feel like I did something wrong? "That's not fair, Luke. You haven't been through what I've been through."

"What?" Luke demanded loudly as he turned to face me. "You think you're the only one to lose someone you loved? You think you're the only one who feels like you failed? Open your eyes. We're all dealing with loss and failure and disappointment. But nothing's going to change if you don't move on. Did you forget about earlier?"

I was taken aback by his anger. "Why are you mad at me?"

"Because I am so sick of seeing you be yanked around by your emotions for Travis. I thought you said you were done with him. Why do you give him so much power over you?"

"I don't."

"Yes, you do," he yelled, then tossed his keys at me. They landed in my lap. "If you want to confront him, go ahead. Here. Take my truck."

I had never seen Luke so mad. Unfortunately, I sort of knew he was right but wasn't ready to admit it.

"Never mind, Luke." I threw his keys back at him. But because of my bad aim, they landed by his foot. "Forget I even told you."

I opened the passenger door, and the Oreos fell to the ground. I stepped on them, not being coordinated enough to avoid them. I picked up the package and dropped them on the seat. "I'm sorry I bothered you with my problems." I slammed the door and rushed up the stairs to my apartment.

Chapter Twenty-Nine
Laundry Room Rendezvous

I DIDN'T WANT TO DO laundry later that night. I was still stewing about the fight with Luke. Truth be told, I didn't want to face him because he was right. But it was almost eight o'clock, and there was nothing else to do. I knew there'd be nothing on TV, and Sarah would be out with Ned. Claire was on campus studying. Who knew what Rhonda would be doing, but guaranteed it would be with Ashlee, or they'd have people over to do something "fun." So what else was there for me to do on a Friday night other than laundry?

Ashlee ended up being the deciding factor. She came over, and she and Rhonda began discussing their plans for a group date coming up soon. What I gathered from their conversation was it would be a girls' choice.

Ashlee was her usual bubbly self, providing a continuous stream of random conversation. I was sitting in the kitchen picking at my Lean Cuisine when she planted herself in the chair next to me. Rhonda went to the back to change.

That's when the bubbliness became serious. "I don't think Luke likes me," she said.

Yeah, I didn't think Luke liked me very much at the moment either. "Oh, no? Why not?" I was not interested in her whining because I was doing a great job with my own whining in my head.

"I asked him out for the date we are planning, and he said no."

"He said no?" I knew she had a crush on him but didn't know she had gone so far as to ask him out. That was bold. Jealousy was starting to rear its ugly head, and with the fight I'd just had with Luke, it fueled my fire of fury. I was mad at Luke, and I was mad at Ashlee, and I didn't want her moving in on my man, even though, technically, he wasn't my man. In fact, he probably had no idea how I felt because I always talked about Travis when I was with him. Why was I wasting the precious time I spent with Luke?

"Yeah, he said no. Do you think there is someone else?" Was she hinting or wondering?

I could only hope there was someone else and that that someone else was me. "He hasn't said anything to me, so I wouldn't know."

"Hmmm," she said thoughtfully. "I was hoping you knew because he seems to hang out with you. A lot."

Again, I wasn't quite sure of the answer she was looking for or where she was going with this. I didn't have an answer. Yes, he did hang out here a lot, but I also tended to be emotionally needy. As for him liking one of us, specifically me, I could only hope.

But I might have to hope pretty hard, because after this afternoon, he would probably never want to talk to me again. All right, I was being dramatic. But I felt bad about the fight, and I needed to apologize.

"I don't know what to tell you, Ashlee. I don't have any info for you."

"Dang it. I wish I knew."

Me too.

Lucky for me, Rhonda rescued me from the Texas Inquisition, which had put me in an even worse mood than I was already in. I was so irritated about my fight with Luke and the lies Travis had told about me. I shouldn't have cared, but I did. I was mad about Ashlee's interest in Luke, my crushed Oreos, and being out of clean clothes. I had to do laundry tonight. If I waited until tomorrow, the laundry room would be at its busiest all week. Nothing was going right.

I figured the grown-up thing to do was apologize to Luke and get it over with. Then I could at least get my laundry done. Sometimes I hated being an adult, especially since, technically, I was *not* an adult.

There was a knock at the door, which Rhonda promptly lunged for. When she did stuff like that, she reminded me of my mother.

It was Luke. Ashlee perked up. I wilted farther toward the table. I was planning on apologizing, but I thought it would be on my own initiative, without an audience. I wasn't expecting him to come over.

"Hey, Rhonda. Ashlee."

"Hi, Luke," Ashlee said lightly.

He turned his attention to me and handed me a brown paper bag. "These are for you."

"What is it?" I wondered out loud, puzzled.

"Yeah, what is it?" Rhonda chimed in, enthusiastically clapping her hands in quick succession.

"Open it. Open it," Ashlee said encouragingly.

Suddenly, I was self-conscious. I didn't want to open Luke's offering in front of them.

I peeked inside. Oreos. Like the ones I left in his truck, only unbroken.

"Thank you," I said, taking them out of the bag, feeling even worse.

"You're welcome," he said. "They're not Wookie Cookies, but I figured they'd do."

"Oreos?" Rhonda wondered. "Wookie Cookies? Huh?"

"Oh. Cookies," Ashlee said as if she was disappointed.

What did they think was in the bag?

Suddenly, Rhonda brightened up, apparently struck by a good idea. "Ooh, Oreo cheesecake. That'd be good." She looked at Ashlee. "We should try that."

Ashlee heartily agreed with her. "Yeah. Yummy."

I was going to have to develop lactose intolerance to escape being subjected to yet another taste test of a new type of cheesecake.

"What do you think, Luke?" Ashlee questioned him.

"About what?"

"Oreo cheesecake?" Ashlee watched his reaction closely.

"Yeah, uh, good luck with that," he said, then looked straight at me. "Now, if you'll excuse me, I have to go do my laundry." He winked and backed out the door.

Did he really just wink at me? The butterflies in my stomach performed backflips. How crazy. I had butterflies about doing laundry.

"Why did he give you Oreos?" Ashlee asked, sounding a little dismayed. Did she think she was going to lure him to stay with the promise of Oreo cheesecake?

"My last package got crushed. I guess he wanted to replace them."

"Oh." She nodded as if she understood, but she looked confused. "And what's that all about with the Wookie Cookies?"

I waved my hand dismissively. "Ah, it's just a Star Wars thing. It's nothing."

"I love Star Wars. I want to try Wookie Cookies," Rhonda said.

Ashlee wrinkled her eyebrow in confusion. "Huh?" I couldn't tell if she was suspicious of something more going on.

I wasn't sure if there *was* more going on.

I pretended to be very interested in eating while Rhonda and Ashlee made plans for the evening, but instead, I was eavesdropping on them. I had to figure out how to get to the laundry room with my laundry but not let on to where I was going. Fat chance of that. I finally decided to just go sans laundry if need be. But then Rhonda and Ashlee decided to go to Smith's to buy the ingredients to make an Oreo cheesecake and rent a movie.

As soon as they were jetting out of the parking lot, I grabbed my laundry basket, Oreos, and two bottles of water, and hurried to the laundry room. Luke was already there loading a machine.

I selected two machines opposite from the one he was using.

After starting my laundry loads, I turned to face him. He was sitting on a table at the end of a row of machines. He was watching me, and I was struck by how good-looking he was. How had I missed that before? Could I have been so wrapped up in Travis that I hadn't seen what was right in front of me? Coming to this realization today made it that much more difficult to eat my humble pie. But Luke was right, and I was wrong, and I had to apologize. I wanted things to be back to normal between us.

But I chickened out. "Bleach?" I offered him the bottle I'd taken from my basket after adding some to my own whites. I held out the empty measuring cup with it.

"No, thanks. I hate the way it tastes." He shook his hands in refusal.

I rolled my eyes. "For your laundry?" I put the bottle close to him on the table, setting the measuring cup on top of it.

"I'm good, thanks," he said playfully, pushing it far enough away to make room for me to sit.

I still needed to apologize but, again, didn't. "Oreo?" I pulled the package out of my laundry basket and peeled open the top seal.

"Sure. Thanks." He grabbed two.

"Water?" I held the bottle out without waiting for an answer. I already knew he would take it.

I took a couple of cookies, opened my water, then boosted myself up on the table next to him.

"Luke," I said. "I'm sorry about earlier. I didn't mean to tear into you like that. I know you're only trying to help."

"I'm sorry too. You know I'm on your side, right? I just hate seeing how unhappy he makes you."

"I'm moving on though." Maybe if I kept saying it, I'd finally do it someday.

"That's right. Just keep on keeping on," he said.

"Talking about keeping on—Ashlee has not let up about you. She's driving me crazy. She is pining over you bad. You do realize she likes you, right?"

"Yeah, I sort of got that idea."

"What was it? The cookies, the bread, the dinners, the cheesecake slices she keeps bringing over? Or maybe the invite for a date? I'd almost ask you as my friend to go out with her to put her out of her misery."

He looked at me all serious suddenly. "You're the reason I didn't go out with her."

Whoa. Didn't see that coming. "What?" Hope started climbing up my stomach and into my throat.

"Yeah, um, I don't want to date Ashlee."

"You don't?" My heart pounded a little faster.

"No, I don't."

"Good, because I don't want you to date Ashlee either."

"You don't?"

"No, I don't." I was starting to feel an adrenaline rush prick at my skin. Was this going where I hoped it would go?

Luke looked a little uncomfortable. He looked down at the floor.

I was struck by how funny we sounded. "Are we getting anywhere with this conversation?" I knew where I wanted it to go, but I wasn't sure where Luke wanted it to go.

He looked up at me again, then back down at the floor. Then back up at me. "I guess what I'm getting at is . . . you."

"Me?" I was confused but tingling with excitement.

"Yes, you. It's all about you."

"Me?" I asked again stupidly, as if I needed it reiterated. Then I shook my head quickly, trying to clear out all the crazy, hopeful thoughts running through my head. "Okay, wait. I think I know what you're talking about, but I'm not sure what you're talking about." And if I let my imagination have its way, it was me he liked.

"You, Sophia. It's all about you. It's not Ashlee I'm interested in; it's you. I like being with you but don't want to ruin our friendship. I just haven't figured out how to tell you."

"You like being with me?" It took a minute to register because I hadn't been the best company since I met Luke.

"Haven't you noticed? I've never been such an attentive home teacher before. Ever." He smiled as if enjoying a private joke.

"You haven't?" I liked where this was going.

"No, I haven't."

"That's good for me, right?" I realized I was holding my breath.

"Yeah, that's good for you," he said.

"Oh, good." I let out a sigh of relief.

"You are clever and funny and beautiful. And kind—look at how you gave Sarah your wedding dress. It amazes me that someone would be stupid enough to let you go."

"It does?" I found myself leaning toward him. I wanted him to keep talking. I liked what he was saying.

"It does." He put his hand on the back of my neck and pulled me toward him. Then he kissed me.

He kissed me! I knew it was cheesy to be making out in the laundry room, but technically, we weren't making out. It was just one kiss.

Well, two kisses. Okay, three kisses. I scooted over closer to him and bumped into something but didn't bother to see what it was. I was too busy kissing Luke. I felt a warmth spreading through my body. Wait, it wasn't warmth; it was water. Water was seeping into my pants.

Then I caught a whiff. It wasn't water—it was bleach. I had accidentally knocked over the bottle of bleach in my kissing fervor, and it was leaking all over the table and dripping on the floor.

"Oh," I said as Luke and I both hopped up at the same time, almost tipping the table over. More bleach splashed on the floor. "Whoops."

Luke set the bottle of bleach upright, but it had already done its damage. The color was leaching out of my jeans.

"All of my towels are in the wash," Luke said helplessly.

"Great." I acted mad, but given the current situation, it wasn't all that bad. Other than the bleach burning my nose and my pants sticking to my legs.

"I think your pants are ruined."

"It's okay. I'll go change." I tried to duck out as gracefully as I could.

Despite the uncomfortable cling, I ran up the three flights of stairs toward my apartment, all the while singing to myself, "Hee, hee, hee, Luke kissed me! Hee, hee—he-llo."

My singing and rejoicing came to an abrupt end when I opened the front door to find Rhonda and Ashlee. Crud. They were back already? How was I going to explain the giddiness despite the bleach-soaked pants?

"Uh, hi?" Rhonda looked at me weird, then sniffed. "Is that bleach?"

"What happened to your pants?" Ashlee leaned back to view my backside.

"Yeah, um . . ." I couldn't think. "I was doing laundry and accidentally spilled bleach all over myself." Okay, maybe it didn't make complete sense, but it was the best I could come up with on short notice . . . and with bleach fumes killing my brain cells.

Chapter Thirty
Quagmire

I WAS IN A BIT of a quagmire. Kissing Luke changed things, and I had to approach the Luke and Ashlee situation with care. Yesterday I was claiming to not know Luke's love interest, and today I was Luke's love interest. Okay, maybe not *love*, maybe just his *like* interest.

Last night it took me a long time to fall asleep. I felt all tingly with nerves and excitement. I hadn't felt like that in a long time. Not since— well, Travis. It was weird feeling this way again. It was good feeling this way again. It was surprising to feel this way again after resigning myself to a loveless life.

I woke up buzzing. This must be what it feels like to drink four cups of Starbucks coffee. Not that I've ever had coffee before.

Now what?

Should I call him?

Maybe text him?

Would he call me?

Even though we had kissed, I couldn't say we had defined the relationship; I couldn't even say it was a relationship. We were in a weird state of "like." We liked each other, but what next?

And as much as Ashlee could be slightly annoying, I couldn't be hurtful and openly flaunt the fledgling relationship I suddenly had with Luke. It wasn't fair to her, and I wouldn't want it done to me. So what to do?

I lay in bed contemplating, replaying the events of last night and reveling in my memories of my laundry room rendezvous. Gosh, I had it bad. Look at me. One kiss, well, three kisses, and I was going all giddy.

I had to act normal. I couldn't let on that something was going on. But what was normal for me? I almost didn't know anymore. I wasn't as mopey as last semester. But I couldn't be happy and giddy either. Rhonda would pick up on that in a second, and I wasn't ready to share my new secret.

My main priority was figuring out if Luke and I were going to see each other today. I tried to come up with some sort of excuse to call him or stop by to see him or some way to innocently run into him.

I couldn't believe what my thoughts were reverting to. I actually started thinking I could make some cookies or something and drop them by. Wookie Cookies could be the perfect excuse. Oh. My. Gosh. Look at me. I got kissed, and I turned into a typical girl trying to bake my way into a guy's life. All the times I secretly mocked Rhonda and her baking escapades and here I was, doing the same obnoxious thing. Whoa. What was wrong with me?

I decided to ask him for a ride somewhere. Maybe to the grocery store? I could always use more frozen dinners. And bleach. Or jeans.

Rhonda joined me at the vanity while I was drying my hair. I had to dust off my hair dryer, it had been that long since I had used it.

"Where are you off to all fancied out?" Rhonda asked while doing her leg lifts and putting her hair in hot rollers. I should have asked her the same.

"What?" I looked in the mirror and saw her staring at me. Oh yeah, I had put on makeup.

Again, unintentionally, I was giving away that something was out of the ordinary, and she didn't know what. It was amazing that I had kept my divorce a secret for so long.

"I just felt like it," I said, knowing I was probably not all that convincing.

"For no reason at all?" she asked, clearly unconvinced.

"My mother keeps telling me it will make me feel better. I have to admit, maybe she's right."

"You should've tried that months ago," Rhonda said. I think she was trying to be encouraging.

She poured herself a bowl of Cheerios and followed me to the table. I had my usual Diet Coke and Pop-Tart.

Rhonda changed the subject, chatting about the group date she was planning with Ashlee and Sarah in two weeks. Valentine's Day fell on a Friday, which conveniently coincided perfectly with the day of their big date. I knew Ashlee didn't have a date as of last night because Luke had declined. I wasn't sure if Rhonda even had a date yet; maybe I needed to start paying attention to what she was telling me. But I was having a hard time listening when I was trying to figure out how to see Luke.

Luke solved my problem because right then he knocked on the door. Rhonda jumped up to answer it.

"Oh, hey, Luke," she said brightly, letting him in.

"Hi, Rhonda. Hi, Sophia."

"Hi." I had to control the overwhelming . . . happiness I felt when he walked in the door. I felt my face getting warm. "Want a Pop-Tart?" I asked awkwardly, trying to take attention away from my blushing.

"Sure." He sat next to me, and I handed him a foil packet.

Rhonda rejoined us at the table. "So what's up, Luke?" she said, trying to start up a conversation.

"Not much." He looked at me. "I wanted to buy you some jeans to replace the ones you ruined on account of me."

"Oh." I didn't know what to say.

"You were there?" Rhonda asked quickly.

"It's sort of my fault she spilled the bleach," Luke said.

I almost choked on my soda.

She looked from him to me and then back again. "Huh." Rhonda looked intrigued.

"How'd the cheesecake turn out?" Luke asked, quickly changing the subject.

"Great. You want to try some?" Rhonda was already on her feet.

"No, thanks. It's too early in the morning for something so rich. Maybe later."

"Sophia, how about you?"

"No, thanks. I worry if I eat too much of it, my thighs will look like cheesecake."

She scowled at me momentarily, then turned to Luke. "We could drop some by later." Rhonda's reference to "we" certainly included Ashlee.

"I'm sure Justin would love it."

Rhonda cocked her head and again looked back and forth between Luke and me, but she said nothing.

"So how about it, Sophia?" Luke asked.

Rhonda was still studying me.

My heart jumped at the chance to spend time with Luke. But was Rhonda catching on?

"So, Ashlee's sort of sad you turned her down for the group date," Rhonda suddenly cut in before I had a chance to answer him.

"Yeah, I appreciate her asking, but I have something else going on."

I got both meanings of what he said. I took a sip of soda to hide my smile.

"That's too bad," Rhonda said dully. "It's going to be fun." Then without warning, she announced, "What about you, Sophia? I kind of assumed you knew, but maybe you didn't realize you're invited too."

I was sinking further into my quagmire. "Oh. Thanks, Rhonda. I don't know yet."

"Well, get thinking. It's coming up quick, and we need to work out the details. Maybe we can get Claire to come along. Remind me next time I see her to invite her."

Good luck with that. Claire was even more nonexistent this semester than last. I was so glad I didn't have her major. I guess in reality, though, I didn't have any major. Hmmm. I'd have to figure that out someday.

Rhonda finished her cereal, stood, and announced that she was going to Ashlee's.

"You look nice," Luke said once Rhonda was out the door.

I started to blush. "You don't have to take me to buy new jeans, you know. I consider what happened last night with the bleach an occupational hazard." I blushed even more.

"I'm willing to. We could get lunch too."

"Yeah, I'd like that." Obviously I didn't need much convincing.

"You got Pop-Tart filling on your chin." He reached over and wiped it with his thumb, then stopped, thumb still lingering on my face.

"Great. Now you know I snort at the table and dribble food all over my chin. You probably think I chew with my mouth open," I said. I had to break the intensity of the moment.

"You're a funny girl, you know that?"

"You know what, Luke? I'm happy right now," I said, then I burst into tears.

Luke leaned toward me and took my hand. "You have a weird way of showing it," he said lightly.

"All this time I've worried I'd never feel happy again. But I do. And it feels so good. I didn't know how I'd tell someone I was divorced . . . and . . ." And I let out a huge hiccup. Nothing like an embarrassing hiccup to ruin the moment, or save the day or whatever the situation could be considered that I was presently in. "Oh, excuse me."

As if one was not enough, the loud, obnoxious hiccups kept coming.

Luke grinned. "You snort, you dribble, and you hiccup. Anything else I should know?"

I started laughing too, regularly interrupted by my hiccups. "I think you know all my secrets now. Do you still want me?"

"Absolutely," he said and kissed me. Which was interrupted by a hiccup.

* * *

As the night of the big date approached, Rhonda and Ashlee could hardly contain their anticipation. Sarah, on the other hand, was not so exuberant. The closer her wedding came, the bluer she seemed to get. Not the normal emotion for someone getting married. Then there was the bizarre behavior I happened to walk in on.

"What are you doing?" I asked Sarah, who was sitting at the kitchen table staring at a spoonful of brown powder.

"Trying to convince myself that I should eat this," she said without looking up.

"What is it?"

"Cinnamon," she said dully.

"Cinnamon? Why would you eat cinnamon?" It sounded nasty to me.

"I read somewhere it helps you lose weight."

"Really?"

She frowned. "Supposedly."

"So why try it now?"

"For the wedding."

"For the wedding? But you already have the dress fitted, and it looks great."

"Ned said something."

Without even knowing what he said, I was already feeling defensive for Sarah. "What did he say?"

"Just an off-hand comment that I obviously wasn't starving."

"That doesn't sound off-hand to me."

"He didn't mean anything by it." Sarah defended him, but her eyes were tearing up.

"If he didn't mean anything by it, why would he say it? And if he didn't mean anything by it, why are you staring down a tablespoon of cinnamon?"

"Because he's right. I could lose some weight." A tear ran down her cheek.

"Sarah, he fell in love with you, not your weight. If he had a problem with your weight, he shouldn't have kept dating you. He is marrying a wonderful person. It shouldn't matter what you weigh."

"But he *is* right. And I don't want him to be disappointed on our wedding night." A sob escaped.

"Is this about your weight or the wedding night? Because it's understandable to be nervous."

"It's everything, Sophia," she cried.

"Sarah, what's going on?"

She wiped her tear-streaked face with her hand. "I'm sorry," she apologized. "I'm just a little emotional. I'll be all right." She sniffled, then turned her attention back to the cinnamon. "So what do you think? Am I crazy?"

"Well, I think it needs some sugar with it. You know, to improve the flavor and texture. Isn't cinnamon extremely bitter?"

"I don't know. I've never tried it by itself."

I grabbed a spoon and helped myself to her little tin of cinnamon.

Sarah was surprised. "What are you doing?"

"Well, misery loves company, and I can't let you do this by yourself, so . . . bottoms up?"

We looked at each other, took a deep breath, and shoved the whole tablespoon in our mouths at the same time.

Bad didn't begin to describe it. Bitter—it was beyond. Sarah was desperately trying to swallow. I was barely able to keep it in my mouth. I tried to swallow but started coughing instead. Sarah was either not as determined as I was or just couldn't stop herself because she burst out laughing. A big brown cloud puffed out of her mouth *and* her nose. I lost it. I started laughing, creating my own cloud of cinnamon, coughing and choking, tears running down my face. I tried not to, but I coughed my mouthful of cinnamon all over her. Sarah ended up with a dusting of brown powder covering her face.

"That is awful," I said as I spit the cinnamon into the trash. "It's not even edible. If you're worried about your weight, how about we go buy some fat-free frozen yogurt? At least that tastes good."

"Your idea is way better than this," Sarah said, dropping the tin of cinnamon in the trash as we headed for the door.

Chapter Thirty-One
Surprise

To FURTHER COMPLICATE MY QUAGMIRE, Rhonda threw herself a surprise birthday party. Luke and I would be there, not officially together yet, and Ashlee would be there, not knowing Luke and I were not officially together yet. It was slightly complicated.

Yes, Rhonda being Rhonda and wanting everything to be "just so," she planned and implemented her own surprise birthday party. She called it a "surprise" so she could invite as many guys as she wanted without them knowing she invited them.

She took care of all the details, from the guest list to the menu to the invitations. She planned an impressive spread of cheese and crackers, Ramen noodle and cabbage salad, brownies, cookies, and, of course, cheesecake. I think she spent all the birthday money her parents sent her throwing herself the birthday party.

Dan called to tell me he was driving up the same day as Rhonda's party for a job interview in Orem that afternoon. He planned to stop by to say hello in the early evening. Chances were he'd be here for at least some of Rhonda's party. And chances were he'd reference Luke's Christmas visit sometime in passing conversation, which was one of many details I had neglected to tell my roommates. Rhonda would be sharp enough to notice that Dan and Luke had somehow met before. After all, her radar seemed to be on Luke lookout overload lately, for Ashlee's sake, of course.

My brother showed up earlier than expected the next day. I didn't know what to do with him. I was on my way to the grocery store with Luke because I'd offered to take care of the chips and dip for the party. It was just an excuse to have some time alone with Luke before we were plunged into an evening of socializing with Ashlee crushing on Luke.

I was surprised when I heard the knock on the door. It was too early for Luke and much too early for my brother. But my brother it was.

"Dan, you're early."

"Hey, sis." He stepped into the apartment and gave me a hug.

"Hi." I ushered him into the kitchen. Rhonda was in a whirlwind of panic trying to get everything done before leaving the apartment so she could return and act surprised about the party.

"Uh, this is my roommate Rhonda," I said. "Rhonda, this is my brother, Dan."

"Your brother?" Rhonda turned from the vegetables she was chopping. She looked at Dan in passing, then stopped and took another look. "Dan, hi." She gave him a huge smile.

Dan took Rhonda's hand and shook it. "I think sometimes Sophia pretends I don't exist."

He smiled back at her, still shaking her hand.

I raised my eyebrows at the two of them smiling like fools at each other, still shaking hands. "That's because you can be so annoying at times." I playfully punched his arm.

Dan didn't even look at me. "I love you too, Sophia." He took a seat at the kitchen table. He picked up a book sitting on the table and turned it over. "Hey, Mom gave me this for Christmas." It was Rhonda's copy of *How to Meet Your Mate*. What were the chances?

"Are you planning on staying for the party?" Rhonda asked him nicely, maybe even coyly.

"Party? What party?" Dan was falling for it hook, line, and sinker.

"I'm having my birthday party tonight."

"I'm up for a party."

"Hey, Dan, since you're going to be hanging out, we're going to put you to work." I plunked down a cutting board in front of him, placed a knife next to it, and set down a bag of carrots. "You're in charge of chopping those for a veggie plate."

"All right," he said and went to work.

I snorted at his willingness to help. "Oh, I forgot how domestic you are." I sat down in the chair across the table from him, enjoying the show he was putting on. It had to be for Rhonda's sake because he certainly wasn't trying to impress me.

I doubted my brother had ever chopped carrots in his whole life because he was completely unsuccessful and eventually sliced his finger open.

Rhonda was quite happy to play nurse and had barely finished taping his finger when Luke knocked on the door.

"Hey, Luke," I said after I opened the door. Then I turned to my brother. "Dan, this is Luke. Luke, this is my brother, Dan."

Dan gave me a look like *No kidding, I know that.* What he didn't know was I was making introductions solely for Rhonda's benefit.

"How's it going?" Luke said easily. I was worried it might come off as too familiar.

Dan stood. "Great." He went to shake Luke's hand but realized his bandaged finger was still a bit bloody.

"What'd you do to your finger?" Luke asked.

"Dan tried to chop it off while cutting carrots. Yummy," I said.

"Ha. Ha. Very funny, Sophia," Dan said.

I was afraid if Dan and Luke were in the same room together for too long, something was sure to come up about the Christmas visit. "Hey, Rhonda, do you mind babysitting Dan for a little bit? Luke was going to drive me to the store to get some stuff for your party."

"Oh, yeah, of course. No problem."

Rhonda was probably secretly gloating. A chance to be alone with a boy.

"Don't let him near anymore knives." I smirked at him, then added, "Make sure you behave yourself, big brother."

"You should talk, Sophia," Dan shot back.

I could have smacked him on the back of the head for that comment. Rhonda stopped what she was doing and gave me an inquisitive look.

Rhonda's party didn't end up being as big as she'd hoped, even after her grand reentrance. Only her immediate roommates (minus Claire), Ashlee, Luke's apartment, and Reed, who was from Rhonda's New Testament class, showed up. Oh, and I couldn't forget the unexpected, suddenly-turned-guest-of-honor Dan.

We all hung around the kitchen, munching on appetizers, waiting for others to arrive. After an hour, it was obvious but unspoken that no one else was coming.

Reed was supposed to provide the entertainment, but what he provided was just plain embarrassing. He came armed with his acoustic guitar but not with the knowledge that he had no singing ability. Whatsoever. He played the same two songs over and over again. I felt kind of bad for him.

It all came to a crashing halt when Claire unexpectedly burst through the front door. She was home early. What was the occasion? Maybe for Rhonda's birthday party? But Claire never joined roommate get-togethers.

She looked around the room, stopping momentarily to listen to the musical entertainment, then took in the others before facing Rhonda.

"You're having a party?" You could hear the annoyance in her voice.

Nope, she wasn't here for the party. But why she was so perturbed?

"It's my birthday party. You were invited."

"Nobody asked if it was okay with me." Claire had her hand on her hip.

It was getting uncomfortable in the room. "Maybe we should go to the living room," I said. "We could . . ." I wasn't sure what we could do, but anything was better than standing there watching Claire argue with Rhonda.

"Good idea," Luke said, leading the way. I followed behind him, not wanting to get into a fight with Claire. The others followed behind me.

"I have a very important test tomorrow. I'm not going to get any sleep with you carrying on in here and that guy butchering songs on his guitar." We all cringed at her honest assessment of the entertainment. The poor guy sank back against the wall.

Sarah went in to try to help diffuse the situation. "Claire, we can keep it quiet—"

"That's not good enough," Claire snapped.

"Claire, it's completely unreasonable to expect us all to be quiet because you decide to come home and go to bed at seven thirty at night. You're not the only one who lives here." I could hear the hitch in Rhonda's voice. She was close to tears.

Justin voiced the thought that was probably going through everybody's head. "Is Claire always like this?" he asked in a low voice.

"Sadly, yes," I answered softly. Then I had an idea. "Hey, Dan"—I leaned over to him—"maybe you could treat Rhonda to dinner. She's going to be crushed that her birthday party was not a success."

Dan and I may have been good at giving each other a hard time, but Dan was still a good guy. "Sure." He nodded, getting the whole picture.

In the other room, the disagreement raged on. "That's unreasonable," Sarah argued.

"No, it's not," Claire said. "It's disrespectful to me."

"What about me, Claire?" Rhonda asked. "Don't you think you're being disrespectful to me? You can't just barge in here and demand that everyone go home because you have arrived."

"What should we do?" Ashlee whispered, looking right at Luke.

He shrugged.

"Claire's ruining everything," Ashlee whispered, pleading, looking to Luke and then me.

My jumping into the fight was not going to help things.

"Let's go get something to eat," Dan said, standing up. He went to the kitchen, stuck his head around the corner. "Hey, Rhonda, let's go out for your birthday." Then he added, "And you're not invited." It took me a moment to realize he was talking to Claire. There was a huff, and then a door slammed.

The kitchen was silent. Rhonda sniffled and said, "Okay."

Dan walked back into the living room. "Anyone up for going out to dinner?"

Rhonda slowly walked into the living room, wiping her eyes, Sarah's arm around Rhonda's shoulder.

Everyone stood. Christopher, Landon, and Entertainment Boy excused themselves. The rest of us piled into two cars and headed to Los Hermanos.

Rhonda ended up in the front seat of Dan's car, with Sarah and Ned in the backseat.

Ashlee claimed shotgun as Luke unlocked his truck, jumping in with lightning speed and leaving me to sit in the backseat with Justin. Luke rolled his eyes at me as he looked over his shoulder to back out.

Again, at the restaurant, Ashlee plopped herself down next to Luke as we slid into our spots on the bench. Rhonda, Dan, Sarah, and Ned sat in the chairs on one side of the table. Ashlee, Luke, Justin, and I sat on the bench against the wall. It was uncomfortable and awkward because Ashlee kept scooting closer to Luke, who kept scooting closer to me. If I scooted over any more, I'd be sitting on Justin's lap, and there was no need to give him any ideas.

Once everyone ordered, Dan addressed the obvious topic of conversation. "So what's up with your roommate?" He asked me but then looked at Rhonda.

"Who knows? But something was *definitely* up with her tonight," I said.

"Claire's a bit abrasive," Sarah said gently.

"I was thinking more like psycho." Dan laughed at his assessment.

"She's not usually home. I don't know why she showed up so early tonight," I said. Rhonda was still visibly upset by the incident. And she had every right to be upset.

"That's one way to ruin a birthday party," Justin said, then winked at Rhonda. "But don't you worry, we'll make sure you have a happy birthday."

Count on Justin to brighten the situation. Maybe that's why he had been a cheerleader. Cheer came naturally to him.

The food arrived soon after and the discussion moved on to other things. I noticed Rhonda calming down as the evening progressed. She sat next to my brother, beaming. They chatted happily, Sarah and Ned joining in. The conversation seemed to come easily and flow freely.

Our side of the table was a very different story. Ashlee kept trying to engage Luke in conversation. He politely answered her questions but did not encourage the conversation by asking her questions back. Justin joined the conversations on either side of the table when he had something to add. Meanwhile, I was wishing Luke and I could be alone. I think he felt the same way because every once in a while he would rub my knee under the table.

Then he gave up on my knee and decided to try something else. He grabbed my hand and held it where no one could see, intertwining his fingers in mine. If everyone could have disappeared at that moment, it could have been so romantic. But instead, we were surrounded by Ashlee putting the squeeze on Luke, Rhonda and Dan engrossed in each other, and Sarah and Ned openly affectionate and having a subdued, private conversation. And then there was Justin, just sort of hanging out at the end of the table, waiting for opportunities to ad lib.

Still secretly holding hands under the table with me, Luke continued deflecting Ashlee's attempts at conversation. I sat there half listening to Ashlee's chatter, watching my brother and Rhonda hitting it off, and rubbing Luke's thumb. Justin wasn't saying much, and I could have started some small talk with him, but I was too busy wishing I could change the seating arrangement. If only Ashlee could be on the other side of Justin, working her charms on him instead of Luke.

I thought nothing of it when Justin knocked his silverware wrapped in his napkin off the table while trying to make room for the food. I thought nothing of it when he leaned close to my ear to say something. It was loud in the restaurant, and it was hard to make yourself heard. I thought he was going to want his water glass refilled.

"So, you and Luke, huh?" he whispered. I could hear the teasing in his voice. I'm sure the surprise was evident on my face. I instantly let go of Luke's hand.

I could see out of the corner of my eye that Luke looked at me as I turned to look at Justin.

"What?" I was hoping I heard him wrong. But I think my smile gave me away.

Justin had a look of supreme satisfaction. "I thought so."

"What?" I did my best to sound incredulous.

Justin looked over my shoulder as if looking at Luke and Ashlee. "I saw you guys holding hands under the table," he said in my ear in a low voice.

I slowly shook my head at him and said through clenched teeth, "You can't say anything."

"Now I get doing the laundry all the time." Justin was enjoying himself now that he was in the know.

"Shh," I whispered harshly.

"What are you two whispering about over there?" Ashlee asked brightly, causing everyone's attention to turn to Justin and me. I couldn't stop blushing.

"Sophia was just telling me how she and Luke . . ." He trailed off momentarily, looking at me, his eyes full of teasing.

"Know Justin was a cheerleader in high school. But we could never decide if Justin wore spandex shorts or polyester." I smirked at Justin. "Care to clarify?"

"Is that true, Justin?" Ashlee asked in a pitch so high I was surprised all the glasses in the immediate vicinity didn't shatter.

"What's going on?" Luke whispered discreetly, leaning into me.

Meanwhile, Justin nodded his head, all smug. "You better believe I was a cheerleader. Great way to pick up chicks."

"Justin saw us holding hands," I whispered to Luke, bringing my water glass up to take a drink.

"Oh," Luke said, understanding.

"But what kind of shorts did you wear?" Rhonda giggled.

"It was a pair of lovely polyester," Justin said without hesitation. I swear the boy was shameless. "A skirt would have been cooler, but administration wouldn't go for it."

"Can you do backflips and everything?" Ashlee asked, clearly fascinated.

"Someday I'll show you my moves." Justin grinned.

"You know, I was a cheerleader in high school." Ashlee kept on with the cheerleading thing, but she was directing her comments to Luke, not Justin. Ashlee was probably a great cheerleader because she was so bubbly.

Justin took the opportunity to dig a little deeper.

"How long have you two, you know, been together?"

"Not long," I whispered fiercely, giving him an annoyed look. "That's why we're keeping it quiet." Then I nodded my head, motioning toward Ashlee. "Plus, there's her."

"Love triangle. Love it."

"Justin. Seriously." I hoped the tone of my voice was enough for him to realize it wasn't as funny as he seemed to think it was. "Anyway, it's none of your business."

"And I understand his insistence about home teaching."

I blushed some more. Thank goodness the restaurant wasn't well lit.

Ashlee interrupted our powwow. "Are you two still whispering? Is something going on with you guys?" she said teasingly. If she only knew how much I'd rather be talking to Luke instead of Justin.

I choked on my drink.

"Nope, nothing going on here," I managed between coughs, trying to clear my throat. Then I added, "Justin was thinking that for entertainment tonight he would show us how he slides down the rail of the RB stairs."

"You can do that?" Ashlee was amazed.

Justin winked. "I got the scars to prove it."

Ashlee's eyes were wide. "Wow."

There was a lull in the conversation. Justin looked like he was deciding his next move.

"You seem to know all my secrets. How long has this been going on?" Justin was genuinely curious; he had one eyebrow raised and a perplexed look on his face.

"Does that make you nervous, Justin?" I said. I had never seen Justin uncomfortable before.

He stroked his chin. "More like curious."

I patted his shoulder. "Don't you worry your pretty little head over it. Your secrets are mostly safe with me."

"That's what I'm worried about. What exactly did Luke tell you?"

I felt I had some containment on the situation. "How about we make a deal? You keep our secret a little bit longer, and I won't share any more of your secrets tonight."

Justin considered it for a moment. "Deal."

The waitress returned and asked if we wanted any dessert.

"No, thank you," Rhonda said. "We have dessert at home."

"We'll just take the check," my brother said.

"Do you think Claire will be up when we get back?" Ashlee asked.

"I hope not," Sarah said. "One confrontation tonight is enough."

"It's past her bedtime anyway," I said, checking my phone for the time.

Once we got the bill, everyone paid their part. Dan sweetly told Rhonda he would pay for her meal. After all, it was her birthday. From the smile on her face, it looked like Rhonda had all but forgotten the confrontation back at the apartment.

"Let's go have dessert, then," Justin suggested, standing up. Everyone else followed suit.

The rest of the evening played out uneventfully, for me anyway. Luke was able to direct Ashlee to the backseat for the ride home. And I was able to avoid any more inquiries from Justin.

Back at the apartment, true to her word, Claire was asleep. She had left us one of her famous yellow sticky notes: *Keep it down.* With that kind warning, we took the festivities to Ashlee's apartment.

When Ashlee brought the cake out with the candles lit, Luke leaned over and whispered, "Is that your chocolate, chocolate chip cake?"

I shook my head no.

"Dang it," he said under his breath.

"I'm pretty sure it's a double-layer-cheesecake something or other."

Luke seemed dismayed. "More cheesecake?"

I shared his sentiment. "Yeah."

While everyone sang happy birthday to Rhonda, Luke added to his opinion. "I'm a little cheesecaked out."

I grinned at him. "Me too."

Rhonda loved the Flirty Apron I gave her. It was pink with large black flowers, and the pocket fabric was the opposite color scheme. What was not to love? Sarah gave her some crocheted hot pads. I wondered if Sarah had gotten the same crochet book for herself that she had given me. Ashlee gave her a fondue cookbook. Luke and I glanced at each other in fear. I hoped that didn't mean everything she made from now on was going to be ripped up into bite size pieces with some sort of dipping sauce and skewers for utensils.

By the time the party ended, it was almost eleven thirty. Too late for my brother to head home.

"You're welcome to stay with us, Dan," Justin said generously. "You'll only get a couch, but it's better than the floor."

"And we could all have breakfast together." Rhonda bubbled with happiness at the possibility.

"Yes. *Let's*," I added with a bit of sarcasm. "We could make C-3PO pancakes. Dan *loves Star Wars*."

Rhonda lit up with excitement. "*You* love Star Wars? *Me* too."

Oh no, what have I done? Should I be encouraging them?

"Are you going to make Princess Leia cinnamon rolls, Sophia?" Dan asked me.

"Sophia?" Rhonda was genuinely surprised. "She doesn't know how to cook."

Dan scoffed. "Since when?"

"Since I've known her." Rhonda looked back and forth between Dan and me in disbelief.

"Then you don't know my sister."

I interjected before the conversation got any deeper about what Rhonda didn't know about me. "Hey, I'm going to bed. I'll see you in the morning, Dan. Make sure you call Mom and tell her you're staying. I don't want her calling me tonight wondering where you are." I hugged him and headed out the door.

"Yeah, I'm gonna say my good nights too." Luke got up.

Ashlee flashed Luke a smile. "It was fun, Luke. Maybe we can do it again sometime."

Luke had a weak, bewildered look but said nothing to her. "Hey, Rhonda, if you want to show him to our apartment when you're done, we'll leave the door unlocked." Luke had picked up on the interest between Rhonda and Dan.

Rhonda was more than happy to comply, though I felt like she was making mental notes as Luke left the party following on my footsteps. Like Rhonda should even be paying so much attention to me when she and Dan were so drawn to each other, like two light sabers sparking in the night . . .

Chapter Thirty-Two
PDA

Twitterpation was a very enjoyable state of being, and love could do wonders. Luke and I hadn't said the *L* word yet, but things were going very well. That, in turn, seemed to make everything in life go very well. I even considered baking a batch of Wookie Cookies and dropping them by Dave's office to let him know I was feeling a whole lot better. It was amazing how everything seemed better. Even Claire seemed happier and more affable. It was almost as if she was getting vicarious benefits from my happiness. She even surprised us all one Sunday by making brownies and leaving some on a plate for us.

Despite my state of happiness, I had two things weighing on my mind. First, Rhonda had asked for my brother's phone number. She wanted to invite him to be her date for the big date. It was a little too weird having Rhonda asking my brother out, but regrettably, he couldn't make it.

The other thing on my mind was the Ashlee and Luke situation. Luke and I had managed to keep our relationship low-key, even with Justin being in the know, by meeting up on campus, in the laundry room, and at other occasional run-ins.

Rhonda had been pressuring me to get a date for the big date on Valentine's Day, which was this Friday night. Rhonda's date was a guy named Ken from her biology lab. Ashlee asked Justin. I wondered if it was a ploy to get access to information about Luke or if she was truly interested in him.

Apparently I wasn't the only one Rhonda was pressuring because I woke up at 6:30 a.m. to Rhonda following Claire into our room. They must have made up since the birthday confrontation.

"Think about it. It would be fun," Rhonda said.

Claire hesitated. "I don't know. I am slammed with assignments. And the TA I work with is sick, so I need to grade double the papers."

"Just try. It would be so fun to have it be a real apartment date."

Claire packed her book bag. "Count me as a maybe. But I don't think I can swing it."

Rhonda jumped up and down and clapped her hands in succession. "Yay! It's gonna be so fun."

I considered staying in bed until she left for school so I wouldn't have to go through what Claire went through.

It was already Wednesday, and if I didn't have Luke, I didn't know where Rhonda expected me to whip up a date. But I couldn't just show up with Luke. I worried Ashlee would be crushed.

Luke and I decided I should just tell Ashlee, and if it didn't go well, we wouldn't join the group date. Not that I would *mind* the alone time with Luke. Unfortunately, though, I couldn't delay informing Ashlee any longer.

Lucky for me (and that was a very sarcastic *lucky*), Ashlee was at my apartment when I returned home from class. Rhonda was there, Sarah was off with Ned, and Claire was, of course, studying.

"So, Ashlee," I said, sitting across from her at the kitchen table. "I . . . um . . . have something I wanted to talk to you about."

"Okay, but before you do, we *have* to tell you something." Ashlee seemed oddly excited.

Rhonda sat down next to her.

"We figured out what's going on with Luke. You know, why he said no to Ashlee about the date," Rhonda said hurriedly. Then she did her quick clapping thing again.

"What?" I was dumbfounded. Did I hear her correctly? What did they think? Or better yet, what did they know? Had someone seen us together on campus? Or in the laundry room?

"Yeah," Ashlee said. "We think we know who he likes."

"Who he likes?" I caught myself holding my breath, waiting for the worst.

"Yup." Rhonda was obviously very proud of herself. "You."

"Me?" Crud. They knew. I swallowed hard. "Why do you think that?"

"I'm surprised you haven't figured it out, Sophia," Ashlee burst out. "Gosh. It has been so obvious. How come we didn't see it sooner?"

Why would she be happy about this? "See what?"

"Luke," Rhonda said. "You know, liking you."

I gave her a questioning look.

"He knows Oreos are your favorite cookie, he borrows your bleach, he stops by all the time, he said no to me for the date. He likes you."

"Because he borrows my bleach?" I said weakly. I was a little confused. Didn't Ashlee like Luke? Why would she be happy about this?

"The clues have been there; we just never put them together until now," Rhonda said.

"But I thought you liked him, Ashlee." I made a feeble attempt to get a feel for what I was up against before I addressed their not-so-outlandish accusations.

"Well, I do. I mean, I did. But he seems to like you, so there isn't much I can do about it."

Hmmm. I didn't expect her to concur so easily. Was she being 100 percent honest? Like I should talk. I wasn't exactly being forthcoming with all that I knew either. It was better for me to keep quiet and let them do all the talking.

"So? What do you think?" Rhonda practically demanded.

"Um . . ." I didn't know what to think. What was the best way to handle this? "Um . . . maybe I should go ask Luke myself."

"You are so brave," Rhonda said with almost worshipping awe.

I was not brave. I already knew the answer. If I didn't, I would never do something like that in a million years. Without even knowing it, they saved me from confessing to Ashlee that Luke liked me, not her. This was turning out better than I hoped.

"You should do it. I'm *dying* to know if we're right," Ashlee said.

"Yeah, go, go. We'll watch from the window." Rhonda was just as encouraging as Ashlee.

"Okay, but don't be disappointed if you're wrong," I added, having a little fun.

"Go, go," Ashlee and Rhonda said together, practically pushing me out the door.

I paced myself walking over there, knowing they were watching. I kept my face as expressionless as possible. I didn't want to be caught with a Cheshire grin when I was supposedly apprehensive.

I knocked on Luke's front door, then peeked back at my apartment. Sure enough, they were watching, trying to hide behind the curtains and not be completely obvious. They gave me two thumbs-up.

Much to what would be their satisfaction, Luke answered. He smiled at me.

"Don't smile too much; we have an audience," I said quietly.

"What?" He was confused.

"Can I come in? You'd never guess what Rhonda and Ashlee just told me. But they're watching from the window, so act like nothing is up."

"Okay, sure." He stepped back and let me in. I ducked back out the door quickly and gave a thumbs-up, all for their benefit, of course.

"Hi," I said brightly, closing the door behind me. I looked around. "Are you alone?"

"Justin's taking a shower, why?" He was puzzled with my bizarre behavior.

"Can we sit?" Our only choices of seats were the kitchen table, which was in front of a window, or the living room couch, which was also in front of a window.

He gave me another strange look. "Yeah," he said slowly, heading toward the living room.

"I started trying to tell Ashlee what was going on with us, you know?"

"Right."

"And before I even got into it, she and Rhonda launched into this whole thing about how they've figured out that you like me and that's why you said no to Ashlee for the date, and—"

"They know?"

"Yeah, but they think I didn't know until they told me."

"So it's not like anyone saw us? They came up with that on their own?"

"Yes. I said I'd come ask you about it. That's why they are over there in my kitchen gawking at us," I said. "I'm tempted to just start making out to make their staring worthwhile."

"Well, then, come here." He put his hand on the back of my neck.

"I don't know. That might be too much for one night. Maybe it's better if I go back and tell them you accepted my invitation to the Valentine's Day date. That way we're breaking it to them gently."

He pursed his lips. "I'd definitely rather kiss you, but I think you're right."

I could hear drawers opening in the back. "Sounds like Justin is out of the shower."

"It does."

"I should go. Justin would love to give me grief about us. Besides, I'm sure Rhonda will have the news spread everywhere by tomorrow," I said.

"You ready to face . . . them and their twenty questions?"

I took a deep breath. "I'll let you know how it goes."

"So, thanks, I guess, for the invitation, of course," he said.

"Sure," I said.

"I'd kiss you good-bye, but with the audience and all . . ."

"How about a hug? That's not too graphic for the viewing audience."

Luke stood up and pulled me into a hug but froze.

"What?" I asked.

Luke turned me slightly to see what he was looking at. There, at Luke's sliding glass door, with faces pressed against the glass, were Rhonda and Ashlee.

"Guess the cat's out of the bag," I said.

"You have a good time answering those questions." He had an amused look on his face.

"Thanks. I'm sure it will be fun." I rolled my eyes for effect.

I took a deep breath and went to face Rhonda and Ashlee and their questions.

Chapter Thirty-Three
Gobsmacked

THE NIGHT OF THE BIG date arrived. Rhonda's excitement was enough for all of us. It reminded me of the night of the ward opening social so long ago. Rhonda was certain something big was going to come of this evening. After all, it was Valentine's Day.

I think Rhonda was secretly hoping for a fairy tale, that this date would be the first date with her future husband.

I was excited because it was Luke's and my first official date. The initial fervor about Luke and me had died down, as had the many questions. I was thankful it was out in the open and Ashlee was left without hurt feelings.

The plan for the evening was dinner at our apartment, bowling at the Wilk, and dessert at Ashlee's. They had planned out the menu meticulously and worked out all the details for the night's activities, including who would be baking what and in which oven.

The menu consisted of colorful food. I was surprised it wasn't all red or pink to go with the holiday. Maybe they realized that might be a little overboard for a first date. We were having green salad, green Jell-O, white rolls (homemade, of course), chicken cordon bleu, green bean amandine, and roasted baby red potatoes. And last but not least, red velvet cheesecake. Despite my mocking of the colorful menu, the chicken smelled dang good.

I was not involved with the planning, preparation of the food, or execution of the evening. All I had to do was show up, which I was very happy about.

I had a weird sense of freedom. Free of responsibility. Free to display my new affection for Luke. And most importantly, free from Travis for the first time in months. It was quite liberating.

The biggest surprise of the evening, which I heard thirdhand, was Claire's announcement that she would be joining us this evening *and* bringing a date. Rhonda was even more excited because, finally, for the first time all year, all of the roommates (plus Ashlee, our unofficial roommate) would be on a group date together. Throw that together with Ashlee's roommates joining us with their dates and we had a pretty big crowd. I was more excited to eat some of the chicken cordon bleu.

The biggest disaster of the evening was that Sarah, who was in charge of the green Jell-O, forgot the Cool Whip to top it. Luke and I volunteered to run to Smith's to pick some up.

"Could you imagine if I had agreed to this group-dating thing at the beginning of the school year?" I said as we were returning with the Cool Whip. "Yikes. She'd have me doing this kind of date like once a week," I said.

"I'm glad you didn't. I might have lost out on my chance," Luke said, putting his arm around my shoulder and pulling me into him.

"That is one thing we can thank Travis for. I didn't want to date after him."

"Aagh. Travis," he said with distaste. "Let's not think about him tonight."

As we walked up the apartment stairs, I caught sight of a white BMW in the parking lot. It reminded me of Travis's. But I was not going to think of Travis for the rest of the night.

Luke casually took my hand as we made it to the top of the stairs. It was nice to be able to openly do that. Then screaming suddenly interrupted my thoughts. Not bloody murder screaming but happy, obnoxious, girly screaming. I was pretty sure it was coming from our apartment, and it sounded like Rhonda. And Ashlee. Possibly Sarah? Had Rhonda burned the chicken? No, it was the wrong kind of screams for that. Maybe they taste-tested the chicken and it was *that* good. I could picture the three of them in a circle, holding hands, jumping up and down, screaming about their recipe success. Could they really be screaming in happiness about chicken?

"*Oh my gosh!*" I heard distinctly as we were almost to the front door. "*I can't believe it. Oh my gosh! Aaahhh!*"

When we entered the apartment, there was a small mass of people converged in the middle of our kitchen. The girls stood tightly in the center, the dates awkwardly around them. The screaming on the girls' part was so loud no one heard us come in.

Ashlee happened to look back at us and screamed, "Claire's engaged! Can you believe it?"

Claire? Engaged? No, I couldn't believe it. That had to be wrong. Claire didn't even have a boyfriend—a necessary component to an engagement.

Claire didn't even date. How could she be engaged? And who would want to marry her? She was so uptight and unpleasant. Who would want that?

I couldn't see Claire in the throng of group-date participants. I couldn't even see who the lucky (or unlucky) guy was. This was crazy. Surely it had to be a mistake? Maybe an early April Fool's Day joke?

Rhonda caught my eye. "Come see," she said and reached out to pull me closer. I took a step in, only to stop. I realized it wasn't an early April Fool's joke. And when I saw Claire, I realized it wasn't even funny.

Because I also saw Travis. My Travis. I mean, my old Travis. My ex-Travis. Travis was standing with Claire, his arm proudly around her shoulder, making up the other half of the happy couple. My hand closed tighter around Luke's. He squeezed back, taking it for an act of affection. He didn't realize it was because my blood pressure was shooting sky high.

This had to be a sick joke. This wasn't truly possible, was it? Was this some sort of revenge on Travis's part? Maybe for the letters? But how would he know who my roommates were? Why would he care? He initiated the divorce. Why should he feel spiteful? If anyone should, it would be me. Reality seemed to have slowed down, and I was in a surreal world.

"Travis?" I said in disbelief, almost to myself. My expression probably gave away my disgust. "Travis?" I said even louder.

"Travis?" Luke looked at me, confused.

"Yes, this is Travis." Claire stood up, smiling proudly, pulling him with her. Suddenly, she stopped. "How did you know?"

I stared at Travis, my mouth gaping, my heart pounding, my blood racing. I suddenly processed all that was being said and realized what was going on. "You and Claire?" I was shocked. "Are you kidding me?"

Travis was clearly dumfounded. "Why are you . . . ?" He started talking at the same time as Claire.

"Travis?" Claire turned to him, confused.

"Travis. Oh." Understanding dawned on Luke as I suddenly lurched toward Travis. I yanked Luke with me a little before I let go of his hand and went at Travis with full force. I shoved him as hard as I could.

He stumbled back, losing his balance and taking Claire with him.

"Hey!" he snapped.

"Sophia! What are you doing? Don't push him. What is your problem?" Claire barked at me.

My eyes narrowed in hatred, and I got right in his face. "You're marrying Claire?" I spat at him as I pointed at her. "You're marrying *Claire*? I can't believe you! It hasn't even been a year!"

Travis put his arms out, trying to make me back off, and Luke caught hold of my arm and pulled me away.

"Travis? What is going on?" Claire demanded in a no-nonsense voice.

"Claire—" Travis started.

"You mean he didn't tell you about me?" I didn't give him a chance to finish before I cut him off.

"Sophia? What are you talking about? What's going on? You know each other?"

"Know each other?" I said sarcastically, "Oh yeah, we know each other, and in the biblical sense of the word too!"

"Maybe this isn't the place to discuss this," Luke said.

"What?" Claire was clearly confused.

"Claire—" Travis started again.

There was a crash from behind us, pausing the drama momentarily. Rhonda was by the fridge, the bowl of green Jell-O broken at her feet. Her eyes were wide. "You slept with Claire's boyfriend?"

There was a unison intake of breath.

"Whoa," Justin said to no one in particular.

"No," I said, giving her a mean look. "I did not sleep with Claire's boyfriend. I slept with my husband," I spat out.

"Husband?" Rhonda's voice was high, sounding strangled. She turned to Sarah. "Did you know about this?"

Sarah hunched her shoulders. "Maybe a little bit." She started chewing on her thumbnail.

"Husband?" Claire repeated, staring at Travis. "You mean . . . *Sophia*?" I could see the pieces starting to click.

I felt like I had the trump card. I felt powerful. "Did he forget to mention he was married to me? Ooops!"

Claire looked back and forth between Travis and me. Suddenly, strangely calm, she said, "She's Fifi?" Disbelief shrouded her face.

"Yeah." Travis looked bewildered.

"Fifi?" I snorted in disgust. "You're still calling me Fifi? I'm surprised you didn't drop that pet name as soon as you dropped me." Maybe this was my chance to not only stick the dagger in but give it a good twist.

"I don't get what's going on," Rhonda interrupted. She looked at me and then at Travis. "You were married?"

"Yeah, Rhonda." I scowled at her. "You know, the pills?" I waited expectantly for her to understand. "Yes. I was married." I held my hands out, adding a silent "Duh."

"Wow," Justin whispered.

"Really? Married?" Rhonda burst out. "Oh. My. Gosh!"

Why was she still here?

"Guys, do you think you give us a minute?" I'd have thought the others would have scattered by now. Talk about awkward. They obliged and went to the living room. Not that it gave us much privacy, but it was better than having them in here witnessing the whole thing.

"Claire . . ." Travis almost snapped at her. "You know I'm divorced. I didn't know you *knew* her, let alone lived with her."

"You didn't tell me . . ." She paused. "But you said . . ."

"There's a lot of things he won't tell you," I said. "Like that white BMW out there he says is his. It's not. It's eye candy. It's to lure you in. As soon as you get married, his parents will take it away." I felt like I was finally getting back at Travis.

"Shut up, Sophia!" Travis gritted his teeth, seemingly regaining his footing.

I continued on my mean, spiteful roll. "And his career. Are you ready to put your degree on hold for him to become a lawyer?"

"An accountant," Claire corrected proudly.

Suddenly, it all clicked. He had changed his major—again. *He* was the divorced one in Claire's study group. Travis was the source of Claire's humming. Her happiness after Christmas surely came from spending time with him over the break. Salt Lake to Logan was just a short drive.

"An accountant?" I laughed and looked at Travis, smirking. "That's what it is now?" I turned to Claire. "When I met him he was premed. The next semester, it was law. Now accounting? He changes majors as much as he changes wives." I could feel Luke's arm on mine, gently trying to pull me back.

"That's not true," Travis said at the same time Claire spoke.

"It won't be like that," Claire declared defensively.

"Oh, no? He hasn't convinced you he should finish school first? You know, you take a break, work, put him through school, and then you can finish your degree? It's the you-support-me-then-I'll-support-you story. Do you by chance like multilevel pyramid jobs?"

"Enough!" Travis exploded.

"I never took you as the doting type, Claire." Enlightenment suddenly struck. I turned to Travis. "That's it. It was the doting, wasn't it?"

Travis looked confused. "The doting? What are you talking about?"

"When we dated, I chased you hard, constantly paying attention to you. Once we were married, it sort of settled down, since I didn't need to impress you anymore. Is that why you thought I changed? I wasn't giving you my constant time and attention?"

"That's stupid," Travis objected.

"It's the truth. Get ready to cater to him, Claire."

Claire cocked her head. "It will be a partnership."

"You go on believing that. It's going to be tough though, both of you trying to wear the pants in the family."

"It's none of your business, Sophia!" Travis practically spat acid at me. "Butt out!"

"Don't talk to her like that." Luke stepped up.

"I'll talk to her anyway I like," Travis growled.

"She's not your wife anymore," Luke declared simply.

"Yeah, well, hopefully she won't be yours either. She's not exactly top-notch material, if you know what I mean."

"From what she's told me and from what I've seen, you're the one who's not the top-notch material," Luke shot back.

"Why are you even in this conversation, dude? You have no idea what you're talking about."

It took a lot to provoke Luke, but Travis was doing a good job. Luke opened his mouth to say something, but I stopped him. "Don't waste your time."

Arguing with Travis suddenly didn't matter anymore. I wasn't going to prove anything to him, and neither was Luke. Yet Travis had proved to me many times over that he lacked commitment. He was a guy who said all the right things but never did the right thing. He loved himself more than he loved me. He wasn't willing to fight for his marriage when it got too hard. That's what I had wanted: I had wanted him to love me enough to fight for me, and he didn't. It was true, and it hurt, but I knew he would never take responsibility for his behavior. I wanted someone who loved me enough to fight for me. I wanted someone who did the right thing more than said the right thing. And that person would never be Travis.

"No, I want to hear what your boyfriend has to say." Travis was chomping at the bit.

"C'mon, Luke." I tried to step in front of him and push him away from Travis.

Luke didn't move. "Sophia told me what happened."

"She only told you her side of the story," Travis defended himself.

"Is there *any* other side?" Luke stared at Travis.

"Yeah, mine."

"Hey, you wanted the divorce. You didn't want to work it out. You didn't want her back. You made up lies about her. It sounds like you have the problem."

"Right now, you're my only problem." Travis moved to within inches of Luke's face.

"Trav." Claire pulled at his elbow, but he shook her off.

This was when we needed Rhonda to go tearing out of the apartment yelling, "We need priesthood!"

I didn't want it to get out of hand. Travis had a temper. "Luke, come on, don't." I pulled on his arm because now I *really* wanted to leave. "Let's just go." I motioned toward the door, weary.

"That's right, Sophia, walk out," Travis taunted.

"Just stop it, Travis!" I snapped, turning to face him. "I am so glad I am over you because you are so not worth it. You never have been."

"I told you she resented me," he said to Claire, smug.

"No, Travis. I don't resent you. I feel sorry for you because you don't realize it doesn't matter how many times you get married. *You* will *never* be happy. You just haven't figured out yet it has nothing to do with the girl," I said.

I took Luke's hand and walked to the door, then stopped. I turned and looked back at Claire. "I know we're not exactly best friends, but I wouldn't be much of a friend at all if I didn't tell you to run. There's still time." I grabbed my coat and left.

Coming down from the adrenaline rush was hard. I started shaking and crying. I walked toward the stairs but had nowhere in particular to go. Luke caught up to me and grabbed my arm. I shook him off and kept walking.

"Sophia, stop." He reached for me again.

"No, don't." I wiggled out of his hold.

He stepped in front of me and took both of my arms and held them by my side, forcing me to stop walking. We were at the top of the stairs.

"Sophia, calm down. Calm down." He carefully let go of my arms as if he was afraid I was going to take off running.

"I can't believe he's getting married. I can't believe it. It hasn't even been a year."

"What's upsetting you more? Seeing Travis or that Travis is marrying Claire?"

"It's not so much Claire. How can he move on so soon?"

"But you've moved on too."

"I know I have. It's not like I want him back, but he just makes me so mad."

"Soph, you can't change him. You can only change how you react to him."

"I can't go back in there. I can't. I don't want to see him again. I don't want to be around them . . ."

Luke pulled me into a hug. "Let's go for a drive, and we'll figure things out. C'mon."

I sat in his truck and rested my head against the headrest, totally and utterly gobsmacked.

Chapter Thirty-Four
DTR

"WHERE DO YOU WANT TO go?" Luke asked as we drove away.

"I don't care. Anywhere but here."

"How about Park City?"

"Great."

We drove in silence as we left Provo and headed into the canyon. My phone vibrated in my pocket. I shut it off, not bothering to see who was calling. Most likely it was Rhonda or Sarah, and I didn't want to talk to either of them right now.

"Do you feel like skiing?" Luke asked.

I took a deep breath. "Not unless you feel like going to the emergency room. I'd end up breaking a leg . . . or two."

Luke smiled. "So we'll get something to eat and then figure out what to do?"

I wasn't sure what to say. I felt like Luke was trying to act normal and pretend all the drama that happened a few minutes ago hadn't happened at all. I knew I was.

"I'm sorry," I said quietly.

"You don't have to be sorry. You did nothing wrong."

"I haven't always had such a penchant for drama. Not until I met Travis."

"I know. If you did, tonight's blow up would have happened a long time ago," he said kindly.

We chose a quaint restaurant on Main Street. We were seated at a small table in a corner next to the front window, and the way the candlelight flickered and the street lights reflected off the snow was almost magical. It was peaceful and quiet. It felt like we were a world away from Provo and all the craziness.

"I don't want to go back. It is so beautiful and still here."

"I don't blame you. It is nice."

The conversation paused while we looked at the menu.

"I still can't believe it," I said as I perused the menu.

"So that's Travis, huh?"

"Yeah. That's Travis. I'm embarrassed to admit I was married to him."

"Live and learn, I guess," Luke replied mildly.

"I don't want to have to learn something that hard again. I couldn't survive another blow like that."

"You're a strong girl, Soph."

"I don't feel strong."

"Did you ever hear the story about the guy who is out in his yard pushing a huge boulder? Day after day, he tries to move it, but it never budges. Then one day he decides to give up because he realizes he will never move it. He doesn't feel like he's accomplished anything until someone points out how strong he has become. So although he didn't ever move the boulder, his effort wasn't in vain because of the strength he gained."

"So I should go bang my head on that boulder for being so stupid?"

"Honey, you don't need to keep beating yourself up about it. You said it yourself—he's a jerk."

I was distracted from what he was saying because he had just called me honey. I kind of liked that.

Luke stopped short, suddenly self-conscious. "What?"

I reached across the table for his hand. "Nothing . . . it's just something you said."

"How could he ever let you go? He really is stupid." Luke winked at me.

"I wonder if he and Claire will make it." I thought a moment, then said, "But Travis and Claire? How did that ever happen? Maybe it's because she's bossy like his mother? Maybe he has an Oedipus complex."

Luke made a look of distaste. "Let's hope he's not in love with his mother."

I giggled. "Maybe that's not the right complex."

"But . . ." Luke paused for effect. "I can thank Travis for getting you alone tonight. I was wondering how I could steal you away from the group. My plan was a little less dramatic, but at least we get to spend our first Valentine's Day together alone."

Thank goodness for dim lighting because I was blushing. "I'd much rather be alone with you too."

He put a package on the table. It was a heart-shaped box of chocolates. He set a card next to it.

"I don't have anything for you," I said, trying to explain why I couldn't be a part of the exchange.

I wasn't sure how to express what I felt for Luke. How could I show him how much I cared for him? How could I show him I appreciated him, his thoughtfulness, his caring, and everything he had done for me these last few months? Our relationship was still at the beginning, and though it was going well, we were not at the point of saying we loved each other. At least, I wasn't at that point, and I was scared to death thinking about ever getting to that point.

Luke pushed the gift toward me, interrupting my thoughts. "Go ahead, open it," he said. "It's not very original, but . . ."

The box had caramel-filled chocolates. My favorite. I wasn't sure why he wanted me to open it. When I lifted the top off, all the chocolates had googly eyes on them and a smile drawn in decorating gel. In the lid, he had written, "I'm so happy you're mine."

He was smiling when I looked up at him. "I love it. How cute is that?"

"My sister told me how to do it."

"How did you get the eyes to stick?"

He laughed. "Corn syrup. And it took forever. I kept dropping the eyes. So please savor every one of them."

Picturing Luke gluing all the tiny googly eyes to the chocolates made me smile. And who said only Mormon women were crafty?

I opened the card. It wasn't the preprinted sentiment that melted my heart but what Luke had written: "I fall asleep thinking about you and wake up still thinking of you."

"Thank you." I leaned across the table to kiss him but almost caught my hair on fire in the candle. "Whoops." I quickly moved back.

"If you're determined to go to the hospital tonight, at least let me take you skiing," Luke joked.

"No way. But thank you for all of this." I leaned around the candle this time to kiss him. "I appreciate it."

Dinner didn't last long enough, especially since ending the date meant going back to the apartment. I was nowhere near ready to do that.

"What do you want to do now?" Luke asked.

"Anything but go home. Rhonda's sure to have twenty questions, if not a hundred and twenty questions, Sarah's going to offer sympathy, and

Claire—who knows what Claire's going to do. Probably shoot laser beams from her eyes to try to kill me." I laughed at my own humor. "I'm afraid to face the aftermath."

"Okay, then, let's do something else."

I got a little nervous when he pulled up to a ski resort. "I told you skiing is very dangerous for me."

He looked mischievously at me. "I was thinking maybe they'd let us ride the ski lift."

"*Ride* the ski lift?"

"You know, like at an amusement park, only a real lift? Where else could you get a better view?"

"That doesn't sound like amusement to me. If I fall off, I'm blaming you," I said jokingly but was secretly very afraid of falling off the ski lift.

I didn't know people could ride the ski lift. The ski lift operator was a little hesitant. I think it was when I offered him one of my googly eyed chocolates that we won him over to the idea. He muttered something about not telling his boss as we started up the mountainside. It got a little precarious when we approached the drop-off point at the top. After the first round, I relaxed a little.

"I don't want to go back." I rested my head on Luke's shoulder. It was so peaceful. Being up in the sky on a starry night with everything so calm and quiet embodied what it was like being with Luke. Calming. "I wish I could stay here forever and keep going around and around. The view is beautiful, I'm warm even though it's cold out, I'm with someone I—" Whoa. Did I almost say love? I didn't mean to. I wasn't planning to. It just sort of slipped out. I stopped short.

Luke was looking at me sideways, eyebrows raised, an amused expression on his face. "You were saying?"

"I love being with you."

"I feel the same way," Luke said without hesitation.

I snuggled closer. "I'm so happy. This is one of the most perfect moments of my life."

"Is that all?" He was still smiling. He knew what I had almost said, but it wasn't something I wanted to say until I was absolutely sure. I did love being with him, especially right now. I didn't feel like he was pressuring me; I think he just enjoyed hearing me *almost* say how I felt about him.

"Can I ask you something?" I asked cautiously. It was something I had wondered since *we* began.

"Sure." Luke was stroking my hair.

"What made you . . ." I wanted to say take a chance on me. But for fear of having him break out in the ABBA song, I paused to rephrase my question. "Interested in me?"

He looked at me for almost a minute before he said anything. It was one of those times again when I felt transparent—as if he could see all my thoughts, all my emotions, all my sorrow.

"Your sadness. It struck a chord with me."

"But I was so depressed. Why would that be attractive?"

"It wasn't that you were depressed, Soph; it was the profound sadness that made you look so vulnerable. When we were over for dinner the first fast Sunday, I saw you tear up when I read that quote. I wondered what could be so wrong that you would have such a strong reaction. Then I started watching you at church or FHE or while we were home teaching. It was like catching glimpses of myself after my dad died. You were very protective of showing your emotions, and you kept to yourself, and I remember being the same way. In some ways, I could identify with you.

"If I wasn't your home teacher, I don't know if I would have ever talked to you. Justin does for me what Rhonda does for you. He's my social alter ego. Last year he used to set me up on dates all the time, but I never met anyone who intrigued me. Until you.

"The times I was alone with you, you were a different person. You made me laugh when you tried to army crawl away from me at Thanksgiving, I enjoyed burning the turkey with you, you make an awesome chocolate cake." He paused momentarily. "You were refreshing—"

"Refreshing? I was a mess." I didn't mean to interrupt because I liked what he was saying.

He shook his head. "You were refreshing because you didn't try to pretend to be something you weren't. You weren't trying to impress anyone. You weren't trying to display your homemaking skills or make yourself seem like you were a good candidate for marriage. So many girls parade around like peacocks, showing off their feathers to attract a mate, and you were the opposite. You were this beautiful girl doing everything you could to hide yourself. You were funny, you'd say it like it was, you could laugh at yourself, you were thoughtful. How could I not be attracted to you?"

Wow. Who knew my profound sadness would have been such an asset? "I'm glad you were patient and persistent."

"Sophia, I would have waited forever if that's how long it took."

"Thanks," I said, dropping my head, suddenly shy from our unabashed confessions about our feelings for each other.

He put his hand under my chin and lifted my face to look at him. "Anytime."

I could have stayed there with him forever.

Chapter Thirty-Five
Aftermath

AND WE ALL LIVED HAPPILY ever after.

Wouldn't that have been nice? But so not true.

I awoke Saturday morning thinking I might need to go back to therapy. Seriously, what were the chances my ex-husband would end up engaged to my roommate? I considered this while I lay in bed, surreptitiously checking the other side of the room for Claire. Luckily, her bed was empty and already neatly made. I was also bracing myself for the bombardment of questions that would come when I saw Rhonda.

"You were married?" Rhonda burst out the moment I stepped foot in the kitchen. I wondered if she'd ever learn a little restraint? Or tact?

"Surprise!" I threw up my hands with feigned festivity.

"Oh my gosh. That's what you've been hiding all these months? Why didn't you say anything?"

"What do you want me to say, Rhonda? Travis swept me off my feet and then walked away after being married barely four months. He simply told me over breakfast one morning that he wanted a divorce. I was so depressed I didn't get out of bed for months. It's not an 'oh, by the way' conversation."

Rhonda's mouth was literally hanging open.

I backed off a little. "Sorry, Rhonda, I don't mean to be harsh. It was devastating, and now I just want to get on with my life."

"It's so crazy," Rhonda said.

I rolled my eyes. "What's crazy is Claire being engaged to my ex-husband. That's awkward. I don't even know what to do the next time I see her."

"Maybe you guys should sit down and talk about it," Sarah said.

"Yeah," Rhonda agreed. "Just because she's engaged to your ex-husband doesn't mean you have to be enemies."

"It doesn't?" I asked, but by the looks on their faces, I could tell they missed my joke. Sometimes I would like to live in Rhonda's world because in my world, I did not see us getting along.

Seeking out Claire to talk about it was not anything I wanted to do, so I took the easy way out and avoided it. I spent the whole day with Luke, hiding out at his apartment, and I called Rhonda to make sure the coast was clear before I returned home.

I slept in the living room that night. But the next day was Sunday, and we were all home and trying to get ready for church at the same time. It was hard to avoid running into each other. It only took passing Claire once to realize we were going to have to deal with the situation.

I went into the bedroom with trepidation. "Claire, we should talk."

She didn't even look at me. "There's nothing to talk about."

"But this is awkward for everybody." Especially me.

"That isn't my problem." She chose an outfit from her closet.

"Maybe we could work something out. Some sort of schedule, so we don't have to . . ."

Claire finally looked at me, anger flashing across her face. "I have every right to be here."

"I'm not saying don't come home. I just thought"—I paused—"out of respect for me, you could not bring Travis here."

"Out of respect for you? When have you ever respected me?"

I thought about the sticky notes she randomly left around the apartment about the fridge needing to be cleaned and the heat being too high and on and on. I changed tactics. How could I nicely say we should avoid each other? "We have eight weeks of school left. I was hoping we could get through them uneventfully. Then we never have to see each other again." There. I said it.

"You just don't like me now because Travis is mine."

Was she under the impression we were great friends before? Because we weren't. And did she think I was jealous? Scorned was more like it. "You can have him. I'm just saying for now, you and I still need to live with each other."

"I would rather not live with you," Claire said and walked past me to the vanity area.

I followed her. "We can't ignore this, so let's just deal with it now." I was exasperated. This wasn't fun for me either, but I wanted to get it over with.

Claire didn't say anything. In fact, I think she was trying to ignore me. She brushed her hair and then went into the kitchen. Rhonda and Sarah were already eating breakfast. I followed her, stopping in the doorway. "Claire, seriously. We need to—"

"What do we need to do?" Claire spun around. "I don't need to do anything for you. You're moody, lazy, and unstable, and I like you even less now that I know how terribly you treated Travis."

Rhonda stopped eating her Cheerios, and Sarah stared at her toast.

Obviously, Travis told Claire the same lies he told our former neighbors. "I'm unstable?" I repeated, my fury growing. Unfortunately, I knew my behavior since Claire had known me did nothing but support Travis's misrepresentation of the truth. I had been depressed. I'd had days I moped around, didn't get dressed, and acted antisocial. But still.

"Maybe you guys should take a time out?" Sarah suggested.

Ashlee chose that moment to knock on the door and walk in. "My flat iron broke. Do you think . . .Whoa, what's going on here?" She stopped and took in the situation.

Was there even a way to explain what was going on here? No one said anything for a minute.

It was Sarah who broke the silence. "It's uncomfortable for Sophia and Claire to be living together."

Ashlee didn't miss a beat. "What if Claire and I switched? She could move into my bedroom."

Suddenly, I felt bad for my lack of tolerance toward Ashlee. Her offer was incredibly gracious and a huge gesture. Life could be survivable until the end of the semester, and everyone could be happy with that arrangement. It was only a question of whether Claire would go for it. I held my breath as I waited for her decision.

She folded her arms across her chest and glared at me. "I would love to be as far away from her as possible."

I was surprised Claire jumped at the offer, but I wasn't going to look a gift horse in the mouth. In fact, I was willing to help her pack if that would speed it up. All right, maybe I wouldn't help her pack, but I would be helpful by not standing in the way.

Chapter Thirty-Six
Maybe It's Just a Bad Case of Spring Fever?

LIFE IMPROVED IMMEDIATELY WHEN CLAIRE moved out. The mood in our apartment was way less tense. And best of all, Rhonda and Ashlee got to be roommates. I wasn't sure if it was Ashlee living with us or the arrival of spring that was making Rhonda behave happier than normal. She seemed to have spring fever or some sort of fever that had her smiling and humming all the time. I guess I was so wrapped up in my newly official relationship that I missed some key clues in the case of Rhonda. It wasn't until my brother called that I put the pieces together.

"Hey, sis."

"Dan, why are you calling?" He never called in the middle of the week. Usually, it was on Sunday, right before or immediately after my mother called. Maybe he was coming back to Utah for another job interview.

"I can't seem to get a hold of Rhonda," he said.

"Rhonda? Why would you want to get a hold of her?"

"Because I want to invite her to something."

Oh. Of course. I'd had a sneaking suspicion they'd been in touch. Thus, the real source of Rhonda's happiness. More so than her usual exuberant self.

"I'll tell her you called when I see her," I said before hanging up.

Not too long after that, as I was leaving for class, I heard Rhonda on the phone. When I returned from class *and* a trip to the bookstore, she was *still* on the phone. I couldn't compare notes or opinions with Sarah because she was in a bit of a funk, so I was on my own with my theory.

Curiosity got the better of me, so I grabbed my phone and dialed my brother's number. It rang and rang and rang and finally went to voice mail. I immediately redialed, and this time it went right to voice mail. And because I was being obnoxious, I called right back, and this time he answered.

"Sophia, what?" he demanded.

"How are you?" I asked brightly.

"Fine. What do you want?"

"I just wanted to call to see how you were doing."

"That's it? That's why you're calling?" Dan sounded exasperated.

"Yeah, you know, I haven't talked with you yet this week. How's my favorite brother?"

Dan huffed. "There's no emergency?"

"No. Why?" I tried to sound innocent.

"No one's dead? Bleeding? Maimed? You're not going into anaphylactic shock from eating shrimp?"

"No," I scoffed. "Why would you think that?"

"Because you just called me three times in the last minute. I'm on the phone and need to go."

"You're on the phone?" I asked with feigned innocence. "Oh, with who?" I tried to sound casual.

"With Rhonda. Now if you don't mind, I need to get back to her."

I was right. "I knew it! You *are* talking to Rhonda! How long have you guys been on the phone? At least two hours, right?"

"So what, Sophia? Who are you, the phone police?" Dan said and hung up on me.

I was right. I decided to call Dan back later and apologize for being so obnoxious and annoying. I supposed I could have just asked.

* * *

Sarah, on the other hand, seemed to be getting more and more depressed. Not the normal emotion for someone getting married in six weeks.

And I was not too unobservant to notice that she had been crying. I recognized the all-too-familiar signs: glassy red eyes, tip of the nose red, and sniffles.

"Sarah, what's wrong?"

She sank down into the couch. "I'm going to call off the wedding."

I felt a sickening twist in my stomach. "Why?"

Sarah nervously played with her engagement ring on her finger. "I don't feel right about it."

"If it's not right, you should go with your feelings."

She started crying. "But I'm letting so many people down."

"Like who?"

"Like Ned."

"Okay, yes, but who else?"

"My parents. They've already spent so much money."

"But no matter how much they've spent, it doesn't matter if it's not right."

"The invitations are ordered. And my dress . . . It's so pretty."

"Sarah, a dress is not a reason to get married. The dress is yours. I don't want it back."

"I don't know what to do."

"I think it's better to have a little heartache now than to do something you don't feel right about."

"But Ned is going to be heartbroken."

"But if it's not right, it's not right."

"What about you?" Sarah sniffled. "Did you feel like something wasn't right when you married Travis?"

I thought it through for a moment. "I don't have a definite answer for that. It was all so quick, and we didn't know each other very well. Once we got engaged, all my focus was on the wedding. I don't know, it might have worked out, but we would've had to work hard at it. There were a lot of problems that I realized only after the fact. I don't know if I would have admitted to them or acknowledged them if we hadn't gotten divorced."

"I don't know what to do."

"How do you feel when you pray about it?"

"Like I'm not supposed to get married."

"Then go with that. There's got to be a reason."

"But what if this is my only chance? What if I never meet anyone else or never get married? What then?" She looked so sad.

"Sarah, I am by no means the marriage expert. I mean, look at my marriage. It lasted four months. But don't do it if you feel it's not right."

"But why? Why is it not right?" Sarah was almost begging through her tears.

"I don't know, Sarah. I don't know. I don't know why my marriage didn't work out, but I truly believe that someday I'll understand. Someday it'll all make sense. I probably just need to be patient, which is definitely a challenge for me." I smiled and shrugged. "I guess I have something to look forward to. And maybe something different is meant for you."

"Calling it off is not something I want to do. It makes me sick just thinking about it."

"Yeah, sometimes I hate being an adult too. But it's not like you can ignore it and it will go away." I gave her a hug. "Besides, you'll feel better once you get it off your chest."

Sarah looked at me weird.

"What?"

"For someone who hates being told by your mother to look on the bright side, you've learned well from her."

I *did* sound a little like my mother. Scary.

* * *

Somehow, other people were under the impression that I was full of good advice. Or at least marriage advice. Several people asked for my opinion, including one of Ashlee's friends from two doors down. I think her name was Sabrina.

"Hi," I said when I opened the door. "Ashlee's not here."

"I wasn't looking for Ashlee, actually." She chewed on her fingernail.

"Oh, well, Rhonda's not here either."

"I was hoping I could talk to you. I only need a few minutes."

"Me?" I wondered why.

"Yeah. Rhonda and Ashlee suggested it."

This ought to be good. "Really?"

"My boyfriend and I are talking about getting married."

Oh dear. Another person thinking I was the marriage advice counselor because I had been married. But if I got divorced, did that qualify me as a person to go to for marriage advice? I was worried I would sound more like someone named Dear Crabby than Dear Abby. "Okay. Do you want to come in?"

She shuffled in and plopped down on the couch. I hadn't even sat down on the other couch or recalled her name before she said, "He's a great guy, and we get along great, but . . ."

I stopped her. "It's the *but's* you have to live with."

She looked surprised. "What?"

I think she thought she misunderstood me.

"Whatever you're going to fill in the blank with is what you're going to have to live with."

"I was going to say that he totally lacks ambition."

"So what you're saying is everything is great with your relationship, *but* it bothers you that he's lazy?"

She nodded. "Yeah, I guess so."

"Okay, so you have to decide if that is a quality in him that you can live with. Because chances are, what you see is what you get. Any red flags waving now are still going to be around after you get married. It may even get worse or become a source of resentment."

"But I think if I can just push him to be better, he will be."

"You can't change people. It's better to be honest with yourself about whatever you fill in the blank with after you say 'He's great . . . but' than think it's going to change."

"Do you think so?"

"I do. There's a reason they say love is blind. I'm sorry. It's not fun to hear, but I truly believe it."

"Oh." She thanked me sullenly and slunk away.

It was probably hard for her to hear because she was in love and believed love could conquer all. Or at least that was what I had believed until I'd actually gotten married and found out love conquered nothing.

Chapter Thirty-Seven
The Four Dreaded Words—"We Need to Talk"

LUKE AND I NEEDED TO talk, and I was sort of dreading it. We had already DTR-ed and established that we were in a relationship, but the end of the semester was coming, and because of said relationship, I felt like we needed to know what each other's plans were for the summer. Because all of a sudden, my plans and his plans became *our* plans. What scared me about sharing and deciding plans was that it showed commitment. Because where were we going with this relationship?

I figured the best time to address the subject was Friday night in the laundry room. The laundry room provided a quiet, private, albeit ugly atmosphere where listening ears and inquiring minds were not around to casually eavesdrop.

"So," I said as I peeled open a new package of Oreos and offered them to Luke. I wasn't sure about the best way to approach this, and I was definitely nervous. I had tried many scenarios in my head, but none of them seemed quite right. I needed a girlfriend to help me out. Rhonda was out of the question, Sarah was preoccupied, and Ashlee was not that kind of friend. My mom was not an option because, like Rhonda, she would jump to conclusions. She was better with pep talks, not love—I mean *like*—advice. Why did Gretchen Clark have to be in New Zealand at a time like this?

Luke cocked his head sideways. "What's up? You seem worried."

"I, uh, have just been wondering what our plans are." My heart was pounding. I scolded myself for being so worked up about this.

"Our plans? For what?"

I tried acting casual but didn't succeed. I was feeling too self-conscious to pull it off. "You know, like the summertime. Am I going to see you next fall, if you're renewing your contract to live here . . . You know . . . plans? Are you staying in Provo to work at Especially for Youth?"

He sat on the table and pulled me into him so he could wrap his arms around me. He kissed me lightly on the forehead and whispered, "Sophia."

The way he said my name made me melt.

I was almost 100 percent positive there was more he wanted to add but didn't. For which I was grateful. Not that I didn't have feelings for him; it was just that he had been feeling them a lot longer than I had. It came down to my being pretty sure he wanted to tell me he loved me but didn't because he didn't want to pressure me. I didn't even have to say anything; he just instinctively knew. My hesitation spoke volumes.

"I want to see you as much as I can over the summer. I have that study abroad thing I applied to, but after that . . ."

That study abroad thing? What study abroad thing? Had he mentioned it and I had missed it? Or had we been so caught up in my drama that he'd never had a chance to mention it?

"Study abroad?"

"Yeah, I applied last semester. It's a tour of Europe, visiting famous architectural buildings and sites."

My face must have shown my disappointment as he slowly trailed off. "You don't remember?"

I shook my head no. "I didn't realize you weren't going to be around."

"It's only for spring term. Six weeks and I'll be back."

"Oh." Six weeks sounded like such a long time.

"I applied for it before anything was happening with us. It's an opportunity I don't want to pass up. But I am sure going to miss you."

My eyes started to tear up. I didn't realize I would get so emotional. Actions speak louder than words, and my actions were screaming just how involved with Luke I really was. More than I wanted to admit to myself. More than I was ready to admit to him.

I swallowed, trying to sound normal. "So then what? Are you taking the summer off from school?"

"I was going to look for some short-term work at home or maybe just hang out and hope you'll visit me," he said. "And call it laziness, but Justin and I were going to renew our contracts here. It's easier than trying to find a new place to live. Plus, there's this girl I like who lives here, and I was hoping she'd be around next fall."

I had to smile. How could I not love him—I mean, *like* him?

I gulped and cleared my throat. "So that's the plan?"

"If you're all for it, then so am I."

Phew. That was easier than I'd thought. But the study abroad thing—that didn't make my heart real happy.

* * *

Apparently Luke and I were not the only ones who needed to talk. After my laundry was done, I opened the door to my apartment and saw Sarah sitting at the kitchen table, her head in her hands. I immediately knew something was wrong.

"Sarah?" I asked cautiously. "What's going on?" When she lifted a tear-streaked face and looked at me, it confirmed my suspicions.

"She broke up with me. Called off the wedding," Ned said from behind me in the living room. I didn't even know he was in there.

"You're not getting married?" I asked.

"No," Ned yelled. "She doesn't *feel* like we're supposed to get married." He sounded more bitter than angry.

Sarah's head sank back into her hands, and she started sobbing.

I put my hand on her shoulder. "Do you want me to go talk to him?" I whispered, not wanting Ned to hear and yell objections. Not that I could do anything. In fact, I didn't even know what I would say to him. But I had to do something. I wished Rhonda were here to go running out the door yelling for priesthood. Where was she anyway? I could use a little help here.

Sarah nodded.

I was a little apprehensive walking into the living room. Ned was sitting on the end of the couch, staring out the sliding glass door.

"Ned," I said, slowly sitting down next to him. I felt like I was trying to diffuse a bomb.

He shot me an angry glare, then went back to staring out the window.

"Ned, I know you must be upset right now."

"What do you know?"

I sighed. "More than you think I know."

"Why? Just because you're divorced, you're the expert on breakups?"

Even though I knew he was angry, I was surprised that he was angry at me. But then again, anger, hate, bitterness, and resentment aren't exactly distinguishing. You take it out on whoever is available.

"I think I'm qualified to discuss feelings about breaking up. So, yes."

"Mind your own business, Sophia."

"Sarah is my business. And from someone who's been heartbroken, take it from me, Ned, it's better to have some pain now than more pain later."

He glared at me again. "And that's supposed to make me feel better?"

I felt defensive because of Ned's cutting words. If only he'd listen. Maybe all my suffering wasn't in vain. "It might not make you feel better, but it should at least make you be a little bit understanding. This was not an easy decision for Sarah to come to. But she shouldn't do something she doesn't feel is right. If it's wrong, isn't it better to end it now then to get married and then get divorced?"

I sounded like Travis. Was this how he felt? I didn't believe he agonized over the decision like Sarah did. I lived with her and saw visible signs of her pain. I was married to Travis and saw nothing of the sort. I don't think he even shed a tear. If I had had a choice, I'm not sure what I would have chosen: having him leave me before the wedding or after.

"If you think you're making me feel better, you're not. So mind your own business and stay out of it." He stood and stomped out, slamming the door behind him.

Sarah let out a loud sob. I went in to face her. Yes, I had wisdom and counsel and experience, but I could feel her pain only too well. I never wanted to feel that brand of heartbreak ever again.

I didn't even know what to do for Sarah other than stay with her until she was tired of talking about it and called it a night.

* * *

Dan and Rhonda's arrival midmorning on Saturday only provided further evidence for my theory of their blooming relationship. Kind of scary, if I admitted the truth. I mentally calculated the drive and the time change to figure out when he got up this morning to get here when he did. If my calculations were correct, he had been up before the sun. Either he was very excited to come or was a little deeper into the relationship than I realized.

I assumed Dan's visit was more of a spontaneous trip, since I hadn't heard about the plans from Rhonda. Or Dan, for that matter. Even more confirmation that they were in a crazy state of infatuation.

"Hey," Rhonda said. "Maybe we could go to Los Hermanos. You and Luke, Sarah and Ned, Justin and Ashlee."

I looked at Rhonda, confused. "Sarah and Ned broke up. You did know that, didn't you?" Had she been *that* wrapped up in Dan that she'd missed the whole drama? Or maybe Sarah was able to hide it well. After all, I had managed to hide mine for almost six months.

Rhonda clearly had no idea. "No. When did that happen?"

"Last night, Rhonda. Where have you been?"

"Um." She looked over at Dan and then back at me. "Nowhere."

Now I felt like I was the one not in the know. "Am I missing something?"

Rhonda didn't answer my question. Instead, she went back to her original question. "So how about tonight? Are we all up for going out tonight?"

Our group was quickly diminishing into a double date. "I think we'll pass."

"Come on. It'll be fun," Rhonda said in the true spirit of Rhonda.

"That's what you said about the group date on Valentine's Day. That was a colossal disaster."

"How many times do you think you're going to have a roommate show up engaged to your ex-husband? You only have one ex-husband, right? It was purely an anomaly."

"I would sure hope so." Dan vocalized my exact thoughts.

"Besides, Ashlee wants to ask Justin," Rhonda said, not to be dissuaded.

I didn't think Justin was that interested in Ashlee.

And I knew *I* was not interested in going out with Rhonda and Dan and witnessing all the gory details of their love connection. The idea of them dating was a little too weird for me.

* * *

Later that evening, instead of doing the group thing, Rhonda and Dan went off on their own, and Luke and I settled in to watch a movie at Luke's apartment. Justin joined us a few minutes later. This was not the first time he had crashed one of our stay-at-home dates.

"Justin, this isn't like you to stay in on a Saturday night. I'm starting to notice a pattern," I said. "You need to get yourself a girlfriend."

"I haven't met any girls lately that I'm interested in."

"Ashlee's interested in you. In fact, I think she might be home alone right now." I couldn't help but bring up Ashlee's little crush.

He grimaced. "I'll pass."

"You sound like you're looking for a wife." Luke joined in my ribbing.

"You should talk," Justin shot back.

All of a sudden, I was ready to stop the teasing. I hated getting into the marriage thing.

"You just need to find the right girl." I genuinely meant it.

"Well, it's not Ashlee. She'd talk my ear off. Or feed me cheesecake until I burst."

I switched back to a safer topic. "I think you secretly just like hanging out with us so much you'd rather do that than date."

Justin grinned. "Hey, what's not to love about spending quality time with the laundry room lovebirds?"

"You know, Justin, it's all in the timing. You'll know when you meet her." I should speak for myself. Did I *know* when I met or started dating Luke? But the advice was sincere. I hoped it would work out for him.

"Yeah, I know. Like that wolf imprinting idea. That would be cool. I see her and—bam—I know she's the one."

"But that would take all the fun out of it for you." I knew how much he usually liked to date.

"Dating gets old sometimes. Imprinting would be instant, no more guesswork."

Suddenly, I thought imprinting was the way to go too.

* * *

Sunday afternoon, after church and lunch with our apartment plus Luke, Dan was ready to head back home. I walked down with him to his car so he could put his bag in before he came up to say his good-byes to Rhonda.

"You got a good guy in Luke. You realize that, don't you?" Dan said.

"Yeah."

"I can tell by the way he talks about you that he cares for you."

"I know," I said, then added, "Are you going to tell me not to screw it up?"

"Why would I say that?"

"'Cause of my . . ."

"Baggage?" Dan filled in.

I was actually going to say *reluctance*.

"I don't have to tell you he's way different from Travis. Luke cares about you. Travis cared about Travis."

"So enough about me. How was your date with Rhonda?"

"I like her," Dan admitted, a smile creeping across his face.

"What was up on Friday night? Were you guys out together then?"

"What do you mean?"

"When I told Rhonda about Sarah and Ned breaking up, she acted like she had a secret."

Dan was silent for a moment, then looked sheepish. "She introduced me to her parents."

No. Way. "What? You met her parents? It's that serious?"

This was surreal. My brother dating my roommate. My ex-roommate engaged to my ex-husband. The theory of six degrees of separation in life was proving a little too true for me. I was averaging maybe one degree of separation. A little too weird for my liking, and a little too close for comfort.

"Why do you like her so much?" I knew there was an attraction; I just wasn't sure what exactly it was for my brother.

"She's so vivacious."

She was *very* vivacious.

"She's a lot like Mom."

"That's a good thing?" I blurted out before thinking.

He nodded. "I know Mom drives us nuts with her PMA, but Rhonda's upbeat and happy and enthusiastic about things. I like that."

I guess that *could* be a good thing. I had never thought of it that way. Not something I wanted in my relationship, but maybe it was good for him.

"And she's pretty," he added. He almost said it . . . dreamily.

Oh no. I sensed a bad case of twitterpation. Bad. I kind of wanted to tease him but didn't. He'd been wanting to meet someone for a while now, even before I met Travis. If Rhonda was who he wanted to date and she made him happy, so be it.

Chapter Thirty-Eight
The Brighams

I WAS LOOKING FORWARD TO the end of the semester with bittersweet emotions. There were certain things I just wanted to be over and done with, like finals, apartment cleanup and check out, and dealing with the Claire and Travis situation. But then Luke would leave for Europe. I had made it through the school year, but I would miss this strange collection of people who had become my friends. Most of all, I would miss Luke.

I made one last appointment with Dave. I told myself it was because I finally crocheted him a tie and wanted to drop it off. But really, I wanted to say good-bye.

He settled into his chair. "How are things?"

I always got the impression he thought he was in for a wild ride. I guess he kind of was.

"Travis got engaged to my roommate Claire."

"What?" Dave sat up straight.

"Crazy, I know. Travis changed his major again, and she was his TA."

"How do you feel about *that*?" He was clearly astonished.

I threw my hands in the air. "I don't see it working, but good luck to them."

"You've come a long way, Sophia. Back in September, you would have been devastated."

"It's still hurtful that he could just walk away, but I know now that it's his problem, not mine."

"Impressive." His eyes were wide. "I believe you have a new perspective."

I rolled my eyes. "Don't be too impressed; I have plenty of days where I backslide."

"You know you're welcome back anytime."

"No offense, but I sure hope I'm never back."

I felt like I had graduated as I left his office. It was a little scary too, because Dave was sort of a safety net. It was nice to know I could go to Dave anytime I wanted to analyze the heck out of anything and everything.

* * *

The closing ward social was the last week of March to give us all plenty of time to study for our finals. It was sure to be a momentous occasion with Rhonda in charge. Her motto of "if it's worth doing, it's worth overdoing" guaranteed an over-the-top evening complete with dinner, entertainment, brownies, and a slide show.

Luke convinced me we should go, with it being the last ward social of the semester and all. We wouldn't be seeing these people till next year or maybe ever again. Last semester, that would've sounded fine to me. This semester, I was willing to be a little more socially active, given my marital status was no longer a secret and having Luke as my boyfriend warded off any interested or formerly interested males. All I knew was it couldn't be as bad as the opening social, and things were way different now, so we skipped the laundry that night and went to the closing ward social.

There was a chili cook-off, a safer bet for a closing activity than an opening social—chili breath could easily be considered an automatic turnoff—and a promise of something more substantial than the standard BYU Food Services brownies usually resulted in a better turnout. Although rumor had it we were having brownie sundaes for dessert. What would a ward activity be without BYU brownies? The entertainment was some repeat performances from the ward talent show, the night Luke and I had our first fateful meeting in the laundry room. Who knew that night would be the start of something great?

Then the real entertainment for the evening started: the Brigham Awards, or the Brighams, our ward's version of the Oscars, which awarded deserving individuals within the ward titles for their achievements this year. I shuddered to think what I might possibly deserve. Most surprising recovery from a divorce? Worst jogger? Wearing yoga pants for a record number of days in a row?

Categories consisted of most likely to be a general authority, most likely to have ten kids, most likely to be famous, most likely to be the next Stephen Covey, most likely to be a bishop, most likely to be the next Martha Stewart, most likely to go on another mission, funniest, most enigmatic, most athletic, biggest flirt, cutest couple. Knowing Rhonda was on the committee that came up with these categories made so much more sense for why such categories were suggested. They had actually passed out a poll two weeks before and tallied up the votes on the returned ballots.

Some of the winners didn't come as much of a surprise: Justin was the biggest flirt, Rhonda won the Martha Stewart category and the ten-kid category, and I won most enigmatic (I wasn't sure if I should take that as a compliment, but I suddenly understood why Rhonda had asked me for help to come up with a word for mysterious). Cutest couple went to Luke and me. The winners were called up to collect their tinfoil awards shaped like *Y*s.

"Your girlfriend is enigmatic," I whispered to Luke as sat I down with my two Y statues.

"That is exactly what attracted me to you—your enigma."

"You mean I was an enigma. We need to make proper use of the word. Because if my mother ever heard us misuse it . . ." I said jokingly.

"Oh, yes, of course. I was thinking it was more like your everything that attracted me to you."

"Yes, because depression is so attractive."

Justin joined the conversation. "Why are you so smiley, Sophia? Is it because you walked away with two awards?"

"Yes," I said, stroking the tinfoil atrocity. "I've always wanted one of these . . . but two? The décor possibilities of these things are . . ." I tried to think of the right description, since I was planning on throwing them away as soon as I got home. Discreetly, of course, since Rhonda was my roommate.

"Limited," Luke said.

"Exactly." I chuckled. "Are you disappointed you only won one?"

Justin pretended to pout. "Well, yeah. Why did you get so many?"

"Enigma," Luke said again.

"Yes, my enigma won me these prized tinfoil *Y*s."

"I don't even know what enigma is," Justin said.

I started laughing. "Justin, I am going to miss you this summer."

He leaned across the table. "So what exactly is enigma?"

"Mystery, something that's puzzling."

"Aha." Justin nodded.

"Like it is an enigma why Justin took the job that he did for the summer," Luke said playfully.

"What are you doing this summer?" I was almost hesitant to ask.

"I'm working in Alaska in the fisheries."

"Sounds smelly. You'll have to let me know how that goes."

"I'll tell you next semester." He paused and thought for a moment. "But will you be back here next fall?"

"Of course. Why wouldn't I be?"

Justin looked over at Luke but said nothing. "Just curious," he said after a few seconds.

There was an awkward pause, so I started babbling. I didn't want to read too much into Justin's insinuation. "I still can't believe you're going to Alaska. What possessed you to do that?"

"There's a shortage of available men there. That translates into a lot of women wanting to date. New fish in a whole new sea. It's time for a fresh school to choose from."

I smiled. "First of all, Justin, if you hadn't already dated half the ward, you'd still have fish in this sea. Second, if you're referring to girls you want to date as 'fish,' then I'm worried what your standards are."

Luke burst out laughing. "She's got a point."

After the awards ceremony, we watched the slide show of pictures of our ward throughout the year. The person in charge of the slide show did an amazing job.

My picture from the ward directory flashed across the screen, bringing me back to the beginning of school. I knew it wasn't obvious to other people in the room looking at that picture, but my pain and sadness was so obvious to me. I had a sudden urge to cry, realizing how different my life was now, how far I had come and how much I had gotten through. Nine months ago, I was lost. Now I was found. In nine months, my life had become totally different. I almost didn't recognize it.

The show went on as I looked around me, not paying attention to the screen anymore. I had Luke, I had Rhonda and Sarah and Justin and, yes, even Ashlee. I had joy. I had happiness. Most of all, I had hope. And it felt so much better than the despair I'd felt when school started. When that picture was taken, I had no idea how different and *happy* my life would be by the end of school. I never would have thought of my return to BYU as a blessing, but it was. I was surrounded by good people, in a good place, where good things had happened.

About the Author

UNLIKE SOPHIA, SALLY JOHNSON IS not tall, blonde, or divorced. Sally grew up in Massachusetts and received her bachelor's degree in English from Brigham Young University. She and her husband, Steve, have four children and currently live in Las Vegas (but not in a hotel). She has always had an overactive imagination and has finally found a way to put it to good use.

Visit her blog at www.Sallyjohnsonwrites.blogspot.com, or e-mail her at Sallyjohnsonwrites@gmail.com.